LIFE AND OTHER DREAMS

RICHARD DEE

ALSO BY RICHARD DEE

For all those battling unseen illness,
for everyone that puts on a brave face.
I salute your courage.

CHAPTER ONE

ECIAS

"VANESSA, what are you trying to do? Slow down. What's the rush?"

The words were torn out of my mouth as we raced over the bumpy road, the open top of the buggy meant that you had to shout to make yourself heard; you had to shout louder when Vanessa was driving. She approached driving like she approached everything else, flat out and head on, daring it to get in her way or spoil her fun.

I gripped the armrests firmly and felt the harness dig into my shoulders every time we bounced. The suspension was doing its best, but at this speed it was fighting a losing battle with the rough surface. The road had been cut through the forest by a squad of army engineers; the uneven sections were filled in and levelled with a hard-packed mixture of earth and stones. It was all held in place by a lattice of tree trunks and metal piling. It swerved around the bigger trees, in places it clung to the hillside over deep valleys and cliffs. If you weren't concentrating on staying alive, there were some amazing views over the land and the ocean, it was the sort of journey that you could easily sell to adventure-seeking tourists.

You were supposed to sound your horn and slow down on the

corners, in case there was someone coming the other way. Vanessa, predictably, didn't bother. She kept the speed on and we shot around the corners, never knowing what would be in front of us. "You can see if anything's coming," she had explained to me, "if you keep your eyes open and look in the right place." Maybe that was right, I had to hope that it was.

If I had leant out of the buggy I could have touched the trees on my side. The strong, equatorial sunlight shining between them cast shadows over the road, exposing us to patches of light and dark as we headed into town. The air was warm and still, at least it would have been if we hadn't been moving so fast that it felt like a full gale in our faces. Ecias was a paradise, with amazing scenery and beautiful wildlife. It was how Earth had probably been before we humans had got our despoiling hands on it. The trees had large flowers as well as their leaves; they were a magnet for bees, butterflies and multicoloured birds that looked like Earth's hummingbirds. If you were quiet and slow you could get right up close to them. Like all the wildlife on Ecias, they had not yet learned to fear man or see what he could do to a planet.

We raced towards a large warning sign. Fixed to a tree that was at least ten metres across, it informed us in large red letters that five hundred metres ahead there was a sharper than usual curve. An arrow underneath the letters emphasised the point. The good news was that after we had got around it, the road straightened out and we could start our descent down the side of the hill into Richavon.

Despite the speed, we weren't in any particular hurry. While it was true that the supply ship was due, it would be here for at least a day. It wouldn't be leaving again without the report that we carried. Vanessa just liked the exhilaration that speed and danger produced.

We had been alone in the forest, just us and our prefabricated trailer, for nearly a month, since the last supply ship had left. Not that I minded that; being alone with my wife, doing what we loved as a team was the best bit about my life.

We were content in each other's company but the journey into town from wherever we had been in the last month was always anticipated. It was the chance to stock up on supplies, get a meal cooked by someone else and catch up on news from home. As we flashed past the sign we were approaching the scariest bit of the journey.

The sign had been put up on the orders of the company's local manager, our boss. He was fed up with scraping wrecked vehicles and people from the riverbed at the bottom of the hill. Mainly, it was those who hadn't been here that long and hadn't got used to the road. Speed was just as much a killer here as it was on any other planet. Sometimes, I cynically wondered if the real reason for the sign wasn't that while newcomers paid their own way to get here, their vehicles were expensive to replace.

The outside of the curve, at the edge of a sheer drop, had been fenced with a wall of tree trunks. I had helped to fell the trees and stack them between two lines of metal piles which we had screwed deep into the rocky ground. The logs were painted with black and white chevrons indicating that a turn to the right would be a good idea. We bounced over another dip in the surface and I saw them ahead.

"Slow down, Vanessa," I pleaded again. She was a good driver, but the road was wet from recent rain; despite the heavy-duty tyres we had already skidded a couple of times in some of the muddier sections. Not that Vanessa would ever have admitted to having lost control, it would have been a perfectly executed slide as far as she was concerned.

She turned to me, brown eyes sparkling and the wind frothing her long hair. "What's the matter, Dan?" she asked holding both my gaze and her speed. "Don't you trust me?"

There were one hundred metres to go, then eighty, still she

held my gaze. I didn't want to, but I started to shrink back into the seat. She laughed, a full-on explosion of mirth.

"If you're with me, you must have the whole package," she said as she hauled on the wheel, dabbing at the brake pedal with a plimsolled foot.

Her left hand went to the traction control lever and she flicked it casually. Instantly the revs dropped and the engine's note changed from a whine to a growl. We started to turn, then slide. The buggy leant over as gravity and momentum fought the wheels for control and I saw the logs at about forty metres away. I closed my eyes; perhaps that would make things better. If I couldn't see them, then we were safe. It didn't work.

Vanessa must have noticed. She took one hand from the wheel and nudged me. "Pay attention," she shouted. The logs were now only twenty metres away. Stones flew from under the wheels as the heavy tread started to grip. She thrust her right foot down on the pedal, flicked the switch again and the engine roared.

We were broadside on to the logs and our sideways motion was slowing as we started to move forward. As she spun the wheel, I saw that we were lined up for the next section of the road; she had timed it to perfection. The logs were less than a metre away as we flashed past them. She changed gear and we took off like a rocket.

Two minutes later we arrived at the crest of the hill. I realised that I had been holding my breath and exhaled gratefully as Vanessa pulled over into a clearing and stopped. We disturbed a flock of large birds. The biologists called them *Anseres Harabus*, after the first settler to describe them, Denise Harabus. I just thought of them as geese. They were large and multicoloured, abundant in the forests and good eating.

We both got out of the buggy, stood side by side. Vanessa was as tall as me, thinner but as strong. Arm in arm we gazed out over the deep indigo sea. Far below us, nestling in the curve of the coast, was Richavon. Looking past the town and the farm compound, we could see that the ship had arrived, or at least was in the atmosphere. There was a red-plumed dot just above the horizon, in front of Claudius, the largest of this planet's moons. The ship would land just outside of town before we got there.

Like I said, it was a regular link with home. It had been late last month; the beer had run out and the atmosphere in town had been miserable. When you had been away from your home planet for over a year, things like that were important.

"I told you not to worry," she said, her eyes sparkling. "You should learn to trust me."

"That was... interesting," I tried to sound casual. My heart was racing, it would never do to show Vanessa fear though, that would only encourage her to do it again.

"You almost lost it," she remarked. Moving to stand behind me, she put her arms around my waist, pulling me close. "I knew what I was doing. Anyway, if you were that worried, you could always have reached over and turned the auto on."

"And that would have made me popular," I said, more in relief than anything else. I had let her drive, I had chosen to trust her ability. In auto, the buggy could have done the trip on its own. Maybe not at that speed but...

She laughed again. "It's so easy to get you going," she said between chuckles. "Isn't that why you love me?"

In answer, I tried to grab her and we ended up wrestling on the damp grass. She threw me easily and landed on top. Once we were both horizontal, one thing led to another. Vanessa was good at that as well.

I loved my life out here; Ecias was the nearest thing to heaven that I'd found so far. With Vanessa by my side, it was just about perfect.

CHAPTER TWO

EARTH

"RICK," Cath's voice in my ear woke me. "Rick, what are you doing?"

I struggled into wakefulness and looked around me; the bedroom was lit by a low energy lamp on Cath's bedside table. It was about as bright as the scrap of daylight trying to creep around the blind on that October morning. Even in its meagre offering, I could see that the quilt and several pillows were in a heap on the floor. Cath raised herself up on one elbow and looked at me; the blue eyes were filled with worry under the mop of short, dark hair which was sticking out at crazy angles.

"You were thrashing about and muttering in your sleep. Are you alright, love?"

I looked at her, trying to focus. I hadn't been sleeping well for weeks now and last night I had taken the first of the new tablets that I had been prescribed. My insomnia was a recent thing; its treatment complicated by the fact that I could go to sleep normally. I just couldn't stay asleep for more than three or four hours at a time.

At first, Cath had put me off going to see the doctor, she reckoned that they would only tell me to try and improve what she called my 'sleep hygiene'. As a nurse, she had her own view of doctors, based on her experience of working with them. It was better to go along with her ideas when she was in nurse mode, so I had tried what she suggested. No computer screens after eight pm, a hot drink, quiet routine, a sleep diary and all the rest. When they hadn't worked, we moved onto meditation and herbal tablets. The tablets left me feeling drugged and hungover and I couldn't get the hang of meditation, no matter how hard I tried.

The thought that I was wasting time on things that didn't work only added to my wakefulness. I was at my wit's end. I was falling asleep in meetings, nodding off while driving or even when I was just sitting at home and listening to Cath. At first, she had got wild with me, used it as a way to blame my lifestyle, the lunchtime drinks and late-night business dinners. I reckoned that her sleep hygiene idea was just a way of getting me to come home early and sober. But, after I had changed my habits without any improvement, she accepted that I had a real problem. So I went to see my doctor.

He was all for CBT and counselling, Cath took over and told him that I had already tried them, without success. I let her do most of the talking, she was insistent, hearing her argue my case I could see how she ran a busy ward. His thoughts were obvious; he was thinking, 'save me from nurses'.

In the end, he said he would arrange for me to see a specialist, but that I would have to try the things I didn't want to do if he said so. I think he really meant the things that Cath didn't want me to do, I was ready to try anything. Cath told me that it was a result. I had the feeling that I was being fobbed off as an 'awkward' patient with a pushy wife.

"I have something that might help you," the consultant had said. To my surprise the appointment had come through quickly. He had listened sympathetically to my tale, then he told me that it was no wonder that what I had tried wasn't working. Beside me I felt Cath stiffen, please don't argue with him, I thought, you're not at work now.

He had obviously worked out how to deal with opinionated nurses. "You're right to try those things, Mrs Wilson," he said, which relaxed her. "However, those things only really work if you can't actually get to sleep. You need to stay asleep, so you need something that works on your brain once you've fallen asleep to help keep you there."

He held up a dark brown bottle, I could see white tablets inside it. "You should only need three or four days of these to break the cycle and get you back into a proper rhythm. They're an experimental drug, not licensed yet but on final trials before general release. The initial findings are excellent for a problem like yours."

I looked nervously at Cath, the idea of a drug trial hadn't entered my mind.

"Is this an official clinical trial?" she asked.

He nodded. "Your GP won't be able to get you any more of these. As I said, in tests they've been very promising, with no reported side effects. If you're happy to sign a release you can have a course."

We had left his office with what looked like at least two weeks' supply of the tablets and instructions. I had to take one before going to bed; even if I slept better immediately, I still had to take them all. I should take no other medication at the same time. That had been so important that he'd said it several times. The good news was that I could still have a couple of beers in the evening. "Just not too many, and not every night," he had said.

"He's not taking anything else," Cath had insisted. "And I make sure he doesn't drink much." She was still in full nurse mode. He nodded, looked at me with a knowing grin.

He told me that I was expected to keep notes, for the drug company research. He made an appointment for me in six weeks to review. It felt like progress, at last.

Now I was waking in a bed that looked like it had been hit by a hurricane.

"Yeah, Cath, I'm fine. It was probably just another of my dreams," I said, kissing her before I got up. "I don't remember waking up in the middle of the night. I'm having a shower."

"OK," she said, avoiding the subject of my 'dreams'. "If they've started to work straight away, it's a good sign. I'll go get the kettle on."

"Bacon sandwich," I shouted as I went into the bathroom.

An hour later I was ready to go. I left Cath; she had the day off and a nightshift to look forward to, hence the bacon sandwiches. As I opened the front door, cold rain blew in from a sky filled with low, fast-moving clouds. I ducked my head and ran across the road to my car. My job was in an office on the other side of town. Like every day I faced the rush hour traffic with dread. Even though I had only run twenty yards, I was soaked when I pulled the car door shut behind me.

As I started my car I realised that I felt a lot more awake this morning, more alive than I had felt for a long time. I had definitely slept better; the tablet must have done something. As I had said to Cath, I didn't remember waking in the night and I didn't have the feeling that the other tablets had given me. Even though they were made from natural ingredients, the herbal remedies had still left me feeling sort of hungover and lethargic.

What was strange was that I couldn't remember anything much about my dreams; I had been retaining good memories of what I had done in the short bits of sleep that I had managed recently. Today there was nothing, just the vague feeling that whatever I had dreamt, it had been interesting.

Strangely, my dreams had been about the usual random things that everyone has, until the insomnia had started. Since then, they had all been about the same subject. I thought of it as an ongoing soap opera. It was like I had an alternative life in another place, with other people. And they had become so vivid that I could almost believe that they were real.

When I first told Cath, she had teased me about them. "Is your alternative life better than this one?" she would ask. I always said, "No, it was just as boring," even though it wasn't.

In my dreams, I explored a virgin planet, surveying for minerals and natural resources. It made my life here, driving to work, advertising cat food and foreign holidays seem boring. Not that I needed dreams for that, my life was boring. I longed for the adventure that I had in my dreams to be real, a psychiatrist would probably tell me that was why I had them.

When I had started having the connected dreams, I had offered to give Cath a summary of what I had been up to. To begin with, she had wanted to know, lately she had grown less interested. The nurse in her probably saw them as hallucinations resulting from sleep deprivation. I suspected that her hope was that they would stop when I started sleeping properly again. Then again, perhaps she was just as bored with her life as I was, maybe she just hated the idea of my having fun without her.

Even when she had been interested, I didn't tell her all of it, especially some of the more intimate details about what I had got up to. Vanessa was never, ever mentioned. Perhaps I was embarrassed by my antics. Then again, I knew that Cath might not be happy to hear about her. She had a quick temper and a habit of impulsive action. The trouble was, it was far too late for me to change that and introduce her now.

I left our estate and joined the stream of cars, all heading in towards town. As usual, we ground to a halt, right where we usually did. They were widening the by-pass to accommodate the extra traffic from all the new housing, on some days it was quicker to go through town. Whichever way I took, I always wondered if the other one would have been better. Today I had stuck with the roadworks. I had plenty of time; Hughie, my boss, understood.

"When I come in, I leave home early, before the rush starts," he always said when I apologised for my late arrival. "But then, I'm the boss and I don't have any reason to stay at home any longer. Take it easy on the road; I'd rather you got here late than not at all."

His wife had died in a car crash on this road about a year ago; her car had skidded off the wet surface into a tree, on a day when he wasn't with her. He was actually away at a corporate party, which she hadn't wanted to attend. While he was getting drunk, while we were trying to find him to tell him, she was fighting for her life. He hadn't known that she was gone until he had sobered up.

He always blamed himself. "If only I had been there, it could have been so different if I had been driving." He repeated it for ages, to anyone who'd listen. After that he had thrown himself into work, some days I doubted if he even went home at all. He had converted part of our offices into an en suite bedroom and a small kitchen. I had the feeling that he stayed there a lot.

We crawled through the roadworks, bright flashing lights on traffic cones randomly illuminated the inside of the car; there was a line of yellow-clad workers moving damp earth. My car bounced over a rough patch of tarmac and suddenly the road cleared. We all increased speed, the traffic thinned out. The rain was still hammering down, the wipers struggled to cope and even though the heater was on, it felt cold.

Parts of my dream were coming back to me. I remembered a journey, but not like this, it had been sunny and happy, full of excitement for some reason, not the daily slog of going to a job that I didn't really care much about but had to do. Then I remembered the geese and the view from the top of the hill, what Vanessa and I had been doing just before Cath had woken me up. I might have smiled at the memory.

Bright lights in my mirror brought me back to reality; a huge lorry was overtaking me. It had a white cab with lots of foreign writing on it and a row of headlights. These were on full as it shot by me, the slipstream made my car rock as it disappeared out of sight.

Stupid driver, I thought, they're going much too fast for the conditions, at least they're in front of me now, out of my way.

CHAPTER THREE

I CAME over a slight rise in the road just in time to see the lorry's brake lights flash, a hundred yards ahead of me. It changed direction violently and the back of the trailer started to swing out of line with the cab. As it slewed sideways across the road, the cars around it tried to take avoiding action, the trailer hit a couple of them; pushing them into the verge.

It tipped over and the cab detached, bouncing over the central reservation it ended up on the other carriageway. Horns blared and there was the sound of impacts. I saw pieces of metal spiralling through the air.

I had started to brake automatically and brought the car to a halt about thirty yards away from the trailer, which was now on its side and blocking our carriageway. The cab had ended up stopping the traffic coming the other way. As I stopped, I glanced in my mirror. The driver of the car behind me had reacted late and was approaching at speed. I had nowhere to go. I watched as it got closer and breathed a sigh of relief when it managed to stop about an inch behind me. I saw the driver get out. In less than a minute, the road had turned into a car park; we would be here for a while, that much was obvious.

He tapped on my window and I wound it down. "Sorry if I

scared you," he said. He was shaking. "I wasn't paying attention." A young lad, he looked almost too young to be driving. The rain had plastered his hair to his skull in the short time he been outside, his clothes were darkening as water soaked into them.

"It's fine," I answered. "Don't worry, you stopped. Get back in the dry."

A few minutes later, a fleet of police cars, ambulances and a fire engine shot up the deserted carriageway to our right, turning the scene of the accident into a hive of activity. They started to try and get the driver out of the cab. Others climbed over the barrier and looked at the trailer. More vehicles arrived behind the trailer and started tending to the cars that had been hit on our side. I thought of Cath, at least she wasn't at work, getting ready for an influx of casualties. I tried to call home, and Cath's mobile; there was no answer to either. I left messages to say that I was fine, in case she had heard about it.

When we hadn't moved after twenty minutes I called Hughie. "I'm going to be late," I told him.

"So you're caught up in that lot," he said. "I've been watching it on the news. Don't worry, just as long as you're safe, have you called Cath?"

I told him that I had left messages. He said he would tell her if she called the office. There was nothing else to do. I sat with the rain bouncing off the roof and listened to the local news on the radio. They said that there had been some serious injuries, the road had been closed in both directions and that the emergency services were working on a plan to get the traffic moving. Ambulances started departing with the injured, lights flashing brightly in the gloom.

While I sat there, I wondered about writing my dreams down as part of the notes for my follow-up appointment. I had considered it before; it might help me to deal with them. I would have to keep the bits about Vanessa separate, in case Cath found them. That was a complication that made me wonder if it was worth it.

They were only dreams after all. The consultant wouldn't be interested in them, only in whether I had slept or woken.

I had wondered where Vanessa came from, what part of my mind had invented her. I had no idea, knew no-one like her. I'd been married to Cath for nine years, we were happy together and I had no intention of straying. Why would I? Cath was everything I wanted, apart from a job somewhere warm and sunny. And a few more pounds in the bank. In that respect, we were just a normal couple. Not only that, skinny women with long hair just weren't my type.

It was a good job Cath wasn't with me now, she would have wanted to get out and take over the medical side of the incident, her 'nursiness' as I thought of it, it was the only thing about her, apart from her tendency to rush into things, that I found irritating.

I could see behind the trailer that a large crane was being manoeuvred into position, it would soon drag the wreckage clear of the road, then we would be on our way. The question was, which piece would they clear first? From the way the workmen moved, it looked like they were preparing to move the cab before the trailer. Typical!

The rain stopped, a few people got out and went to watch the workmen. I joined them as webbing slings were pushed under the cab. These were attached to the hook at the end of the crane's wire. The air was thick with the smell of damp earth, burnt rubber and oil; we were halted ten metres away from the trailer by a row of plastic barriers, manned by a policeman, bulky in his yellow waterproofs.

"No closer please," he said. The crane revved its engine, the noise changing to a low growl as the lifting wire tightened. The lorry's cab rocked; there was a metallic screech that went right through me as it started to move.

"What's the plan now?" a man on my left shouted as the cab was lifted clear of the other carriageway. It swung in the air, there was a lane open now and cars accelerated into the space.

Unwilling to wait for permission they sped away, weaving around the wreckage left by the cab's impact. The cab was dropped onto a trailer beside the crane, the slings were removed.

"We're going to shift the trailer next," the policeman said. "It's too heavy for the crane, we can't pick it up like the cab," he explained. "We're just going to pivot it around one end, enough to open up a lane. The road's closed behind you at the last junction. Once the traffic's clear and the road's empty both ways we can sort things out properly. Now stand well back."

It sounded logical, except that it didn't quite work out. We all retreated as the crane manoeuvred itself into a new position and the hook was lowered from the jib. Once again, the webbing slings were deployed, this time around one end of the trailer. The operator started to pick up the slack. I watched as the end of the trailer stirred, lifted about a metre and then the lifting wire snapped with a loud crack. The hook fell onto the trailer and the end of the wire flailed around, whistling as it moved.

It hit the policeman we had been talking to, knocking him flying in a sudden burst of red. Someone screamed. The trailer thumped back to the ground and burst open, scattering boxes across the now red-slicked roadway. We were stunned by the taking of a life, the casual erasure of sentience by mindless machinery.

"Oh great," said the man stood next to me. "Now they'll have to sort all that out, we're going to be stuck here all day. I've got a meeting to get to."

I mumbled something, trying to resist the sudden surge of anger. I understood what he meant but the attitude annoyed me. Someone had just died; a bit of respect wouldn't have hurt. As Hughie had found, not far from where I was standing, nothing was more important than life, certainly not a business meeting.

Ambulances disgorged green-suited paramedics; they had nothing to do except collect the body, a task they performed with quiet dignity.

The remaining policemen had a discussion; they removed a section of the central barrier and set up a line of arrows, pointing to the right. There was no traffic in the other direction, cars were directed into the gap and soon they were driving up the other carriageway, heading towards the inevitable gridlock we had come from. When it was my turn I joined them. In the end, I got to the office just in time for a very late lunch. Which I would have to miss to catch up on the work I hadn't done. While Hughie might be understanding, clients were generally not.

Hughie ran an advertising agency called Creative Concepts; I was one of his copywriters. I thought up the ideas for advertisements and he pitched them. It wasn't exactly the most exciting job in the world, I was always thinking about leaving, but if all I was going to do was swap from working for Hughie to working for someone else there didn't seem to be much point. The wages were OK, he was a good boss and together with what Cath earned from her nursing shifts we did a lot better than some.

My main problem was envy. I did a lot of holiday promotions; my head was always filled with thoughts of the places that I could never afford to take Cath to. I used to sit and long to go to the places that I was paid to persuade others to visit, with their white beaches, pristine forests and spectacular views. Maybe that was where Ecias came from.

Thinking about Cath, what I wanted for her, made me suddenly realise that all my sleep problems had started when she had changed her working pattern. She had been working long days and we had both got used to her late finishes, the extra hours she had worked past the end of her shift for nothing. "We all do it," she said, with an air of resignation. "We care, the management knows it, they all go home at five and play on our compassion."

Then she was offered a switch to permanent night shifts, the money was no different but the night staff tended to finish on time more often than not. So she said that she would try them. To my surprise, and hers, she found that she really loved them. She said that the lack of bosses hanging around waving targets at her had let her do what she was trained for, looking after the sick. While she was on a run of shifts, we had got used to passing twice a day, one in and one out.

Weekends were a drag, if she had worked Friday or Saturday night I had to either go out or be very quiet in the daytime while she was sleeping. And that was where I had got out of the habit of getting a proper sleep myself. I used to wake up several times in the night, unused to being alone in the bed and wondering what she was doing. Perhaps I should mention that to the consultant in my follow-up, it was so obvious I wondered why we hadn't thought of it before.

The afternoon passed quickly. I tried to catch up, by six I was almost where I should have been. Cath would be leaving for work shortly, I might as well carry on. I was in no rush to go home to an empty house.

"Clear off," Hughie said to the three of us. "There's nothing here that won't wait until tomorrow."

"Are you going home, Hughie?" asked Molly, she was a couple of years older than him and a bit of a mother hen. Since Hughie's wife had died she had taken responsibility for his wellbeing; she would bring him food and offer to do his laundry. He politely fended her off, in all respects except the food, which he admitted was superb.

"I might," he said. "I haven't decided yet."

"I'm gone," said Deanne, the other copywriter. She was a lot younger than Molly and me. Straight out of college, she was new to the job but very clever. She had been Claire, Hughie's wife's, project. Claire used to work here with us; she had spotted Deanne at a trade fair and offered her an apprenticeship. She was a lovely kid, except for her big mouth with no filters on what came out of it. If you wanted a secret kept, she was definitely not your go-to.

Hughie used this flaw to his advantage. "Don't tell anyone, Deanne," he would say to her, "but..." whenever he wanted to put a competitor off or spread a little confusion. She hadn't worked it out yet, there was potential for fireworks when she did.

The two women went off arm in arm, chattering like a couple of sparrows. "Well," said Hughie, "aren't you heading home?"

"No rush," I answered. "Cath's on nights, she'll be gone by the time I get there."

"Yeah well," he said with a grin, "I want to lock up, I'm off out tonight."

"Hot date?" I asked and for a moment he looked sad.

"No, just trying to woo a client," he said. "See you tomorrow."

On my way home the bypass was clear, there were only a few marks on the ground to show where the accident had been. The wreck of the lorry had gone, the crash barrier had been replaced and traffic flowed normally in both directions. All the blood had been cleaned away; it was as if the policeman had never existed.

Sure enough, by the time I got home, Cath had left for her night shift. There was a meal ready to be reheated and a little note by the microwave: 'hope you had a good day, love you, Rick', she had written, 'don't forget the tablet, sleep well tonight'. Even though there was a line of kisses, she had still managed to get an instruction in. Nurse to the last.

I took the second tablet after I had eaten; the first one had taken about an hour to work, this time I felt tired almost immediately. I never made it to the shower; I only just got to the bedroom before sleep overtook me.

CHAPTER FOUR

ECIAS

VANESSA PARKED the buggy outside Whistles, the big red-roofed shack that was the bar-stroke-restaurant-stroke-company-store-stroke-everything else in Richavon. She had relented and driven slowly down the hill, taking it easy on the switchback. My stomach was grateful, perhaps our exertions had calmed her down a little. I certainly felt a lot more relaxed than I had done two hours ago.

As we had swung around the last bend, we could see that the ship had landed, off to the left of the buildings and between the town and the farm compound. That part of the settlement was surrounded by a tall metal fence. It was the only place in Richavon that was; it had to be to stop the local animals from wandering in among the machinery, eating the crops and mingling with our non-native stock. A collection of nearly noiseless equipment worked the earth and processed crops, milk and meat. There was a building in the corner with freezers and stores for our produce and the supplies that were being unloaded from the ship.

Before we went into Whistles, we walked over to the Burgstrom office. The title made it sound grand, it was just another prefabricated hut. Richavon was a collection of prefabricated huts and trailers, single and double storied. Some of the more enterprising folk were building log cabins; there were a few in various stages of construction. The rest of us were far too busy for carpentry.

One day, a gang of lumberjacks would turn up, build a sawmill and make a fortune; there were plenty of trees for them to cut. There was still a market for good quality lumber, a lot of planets had no trees and it was just as good a material to build with as metal and plastics. In some ways it was even better.

The office was empty; I left our report chip, in its anti-static envelope, on the desk. Ove Strand ran the planet on his own, without any staff; as he was fond of reminding us. We rarely saw him in here, if he wasn't off somewhere he was in Whistles, which we all called his real office. He would be on the ship now, reporting and getting things organised. He had the knack of appearing to do very little, yet it was impossible to find anything that he hadn't done, once he had said he would do it. If a job went in his notebook, it was as good as completed. He was a very capable man; I thought that he was wasted on Ecias.

"Right, that's the job sorted, how about a beer?"

"I thought that you'd never offer." Vanessa put her arm around my waist, together we went into the bar.

"Hey, it's Dan and Van," shouted Marcus as we walked in. The room was dark after the bright sunshine. He was employed by Burgstrom, the manager of Whistles and in control of the booze. He was also the general wise guy that every small town has. "How come you're all wet and covered in mud?"

"Wrestling practice," said Vanessa with a straight face. "Get us a couple of beers."

Marcus lifted two bottles from the cooler. "I don't need to know anything more," he said. "Not that I'm not jealous." Vanessa laughed. Marcus was unattached, Vanessa wasn't his type.

"We're not going to run out of beer either," he said. "The supply ship's got here in time this month." He grinned. "Good thing, there were only a few of these babies left."

We opened the bottles and drank. The beer was cool and very welcome, even more so now that we knew we wouldn't have to ration them.

There was hardly anyone else in Whistles, everyone who wasn't working had gone down to watch the ship land and try to be first to get to the mail. Unloading was a communal thing; we would have a couple of beers and go down to help later in the second shift. We nodded to the other customers, people we knew vaguely. There were fishermen and their partners, one or two of the farm workers. We only really met any of them once a month; it meant that we didn't know them that well, but they were always friendly. We had all undergone the same psychological evaluation before we had been allowed to join the settlement, to try and make sure that we all fitted in together. There were characters among us but nobody really got on anyone else's nerves. And when there were only a few of you, any contact was nice.

Supplies from home, a few luxuries, all played a part in keeping us contented. They were an important part of our lives. We had plenty of food, one of the first things the original settlers had done was clear land for the farm. Conditions were perfect for growing all our own crops, the climate meant that most vegetables and grains grew well; the soil was fertile and free of pathogens. There was a sort of grass in the spaces between the trees; it provided grazing for the animals that the first few ships had brought.

The farmers had found it easy to work the land, although the hours were long the work was not physically tiring, they had plenty of machinery to help them. As well as the grass, the other native plants were mostly edible as far as the cows and sheep were concerned, we had milk and meat. Until we got a proper harvest going, with a surplus to our bread making needs, there was no spare grain for making beer. There was no equipment for doing it either. Nor was there anyone who wasn't needed for something essential with the time to make it.

As Marcus was fond of saying about anything that arrived on the ship, "Stuff from home is important, it's more than just a bottled drink or a video with news and sports reports, it keeps us tied to Earth."

There were sure to be a few more settlers on the ship, some new faces to liven the place up. More arrived every month, some even stayed. They would be welcomed, as long as they pulled their weight and joined in. Those that couldn't take it or didn't fit in could always leave next month. With the ship's arrival, Vanessa and I would get a new area to survey, based on the satellite scans and the analysis of our previous reports. We would be out of here in a couple of days, before we had the time to make any new friends.

Richavon was a small settlement on the edge of the only large landmass on the planet Ecias. It occupied at least half the surface of the world, the rest was sea and ice at the poles. The planet was surprisingly Earth-like, atmosphere and temperature were acceptable, like a lot of the planets that had been discovered so far. After all the talk of Earth being a rarity, it was nice to find that a lot of star systems had at least one body that we could live on. Gravity wasn't an issue here either, and the sight of several moons of differing sizes in the sky had become normal to us.

The landmass, which had no formal name yet, straddled the equator, extending into the higher latitudes in places. The way the planet was inclined meant that there wasn't much difference in the seasons. It was all pleasantly temperate, with variable rainfall and little in the way of extreme weather. The seas were joined at a narrow gap where the land didn't quite make it all the way around the globe; in a feature that we called the Canal.

Animal life on the land was varied and sparse, compared to the sea. Apart from the birds, there were insects and a few mammals; all the species we had found so far were harmless, at least to us. We had seen dead animals, found evidence of attacks but had never spotted a predator. We had seen no snakes or large carnivores, no tracks or nests. There had been nothing at all to threaten us as we explored. Even the pollinators appeared to have no stings. There had to be something, a top predator somewhere. The ecosystem needed balance and there were certainly predators in the sea. Maybe we just hadn't found them in the vast forests, apart from Vanessa and me there were few people exploring. Perhaps they had seen us and despite the lack of fear in the other fauna, were keeping out of the way while they assessed us.

The majority of the planet's animal life was situated in the seas. There were huge whale-like creatures and lots of different species of fishes, good eating when you could subdue them; they all seemed to have lots of teeth and attitude. A small fleet of fishing boats went out daily from the harbour that had been constructed from huge plastic blocks filled with water. The boats harvested the seas to supplement our diet, using sonic stunners; the fish would have made short work of nets, unless they had been made of heavy wire.

The land under the forest, from what we had found so far, was filled with an abundance of the minerals that civilisation needed.

That was our job, why we were here. Vanessa and I worked surveys on the land, mostly to our own timetable; so long as we had results for Burgstrom on every monthly departure, they were happy.

Burgstrom was the company who paid us, they had a big investment in the planet and everything on it, even though I wasn't an analyst, I knew that they would be very happy with the figures we had come down to send off this time. Hence the celebratory beers.

We were on our second bottle when the first of the new arrivals came in. Led by Ove, there were about fifteen of them. A mixture of men and women, young and old, they all looked a little shell-shocked to be here. Maybe we had looked like that ourselves when we had arrived.

"This is Whistles," Ove announced in his best corporate voice.

"It's where we meet up when we're not working, but let me make one thing very clear, we do not get drunk. Marcus is in charge of the place, he works for me and will not serve anyone who he thinks has had enough beer or starts causing trouble."

"Hello, everyone," said Marcus. "Ove's right, upset me, get drunk or pick a fight and you're gone. No arguments, no second chances. Just the next flight off at your own expense."

A couple of the crowd looked annoyed to hear that; let them be. We had a good thing going, we worked hard and once Marcus got to know you, a little extrovert behaviour was ignored. But the pep talk made Ove and Burgstrom feel better.

One of the new arrivals looked around at the place and shook his head. "This is not for me," he said. "I'm getting back on the ship." He turned and walked out, followed by taunts and jeers from a small group who seemed to be together. The rest just stood and watched him go.

"Good," Ove sounded pleased. "Anyone else want to save themselves a month and go now?"

There were no takers, just a lot of shuffling and looking downwards.

"Right," he continued. "Marcus will get you beers, or soft drinks, there's nothing harder. The upside is that there's no money here." That got people interested; they looked up and took a bit more notice of the idea of free beer.

"These two fine people," Ove waved at us, "are Dan and Vanessa Waldon. They run surveys and prospect for Burgstrom. They're usually up in the sticks, so you'll only see them once a month, when the ship comes in."

We raised our bottles in salute; there were a few muttered greetings. I noticed that the group who had shouted at the departing settler had stayed together and moved to the front. There were three of them. All large and heavily bearded, they looked like miners, or maybe they were the advance party of lumberjacks. Standing apart from the rest, they were looking at

Vanessa. And I mean looking. She spotted it and looked straight back. If they had picked on her to ogle, they might be surprised at her reaction. Ove was still doing introductions.

"And over there are Terry Malvern and Linda Chan, with their partners. They run the fishing operation." Quickly Ove introduced the few others present.

One of the new arrivals, a short, stocky man came over to us. "Hi," he said. "I'm Vince Kendall. I have a message from Burgstrom for you. I think that we're going to be working together." He handed over an envelope.

"Typical," said one of the group, loud enough for us all to hear. "Loverboy gets all the luck." The other two laughed.

"Watch your wife, mate," another said. "We've seen him in action, he'll be after her."

"I could be stuck here for a month with that," added the third.

The tension was rising; I could feel my neck going red as I decided what form of reply would be appropriate. Would words be enough, or should I do more? Vanessa squeezed my hand as I started to get up. Ove sensed the tension as well. "Come on then," he said. "Let me show you the hostel, get your accommodation sorted out."

He ushered the group from the bar and I relaxed. The three glared at me and blew Vanessa kisses as they left.

"Those three were trouble all the way out," Vince said, as Marcus passed him a bottle.

"I don't like the look of them," Marcus said. "They seem like the sort that I might have to explain a few things to."

"Can't see them staying," added Vanessa. "Not with that attitude; it might intimidate some people but it just annoys me." She opened the envelope and pulled a couple of sheets of paper from it.

"They're plant hunters," said Vince. "They're working for a big drug company, I can't remember the name. They held court on the ship every night. According to them, they're going to find a cure for just about any disease in what's growing on Ecias."

"You want to tell me what they meant?" I asked. I didn't like the look of them; this man would be with us for the next month, away from civilisation. If there was a chance he was some sort of ladies' man I wanted to know. Not that I didn't trust Vanessa, I'd seen her handle unwanted attention in the past. With her wrestling and martial arts, she could look after herself, he wouldn't get very far. I felt secure in our relationship, what I didn't want was a month of ill feelings, an atmosphere. It would be so much easier to know where we stood from the start. He was about to answer but Vanessa interrupted.

"Looks like he's right," she said, reading the note. "He's with us." She read on. "Where's Anna?"

"She's not here, at least not on this ship, maybe next month. I'll tell you all about it later."

"Shouldn't you be down on the ship?" Marcus reminded us. "Pedro and the boys will want a beer too you know."

Marcus was gently reminding us of the way things worked. "You can tell us when we get back," I said to Vince. We finished up our beers and went down to the ship, along with Linda and Terry and the others. There was still unloading to do.

On the way down to the ship, we talked about Vince. Vanessa told me that the letter from Burgstrom said that he was a geologist. He had our next set of surveying schedules for us. Apparently, because of the nature of the ground and what they wanted us to do, there was a lot of extra work involved. Burgstrom wanted us to take samples as well as getting all the readings from our drone. Vince and his girlfriend Anna had been sent to help us dig holes and do some blasting. They were both qualified in the use of mining explosives, the same as we were.

"Why is it just him?" Vanessa wondered aloud as we shifted pallets of stores and equipment onto trailers.

"Maybe she couldn't travel, perhaps she was ill," I suggested.

"It could be awkward," she said. "Especially if what that man shouted out was true."

"He said he'd explain. Rather than listen to a loud-mouth, perhaps we should hear him out."

"We can always sneak off for a bit of privacy," she suggested with a gleam in her eye.

CHAPTER FIVE

WE FINISHED UNLOADING; the huge hold of the ship was just about empty. There was a line of vehicles and trailers outside, their engines idling. They were filled with the things we had plenty of, frozen fish, some plants and a few rock samples sealed in plastic for analysis.

We returned to Whistles, riding on top of a trailer of large and small wooden cases, 'Property of Kalesh Pharmaceuticals' was stamped all over them. 'Fragile' and 'Bio-hazard' stickers were everywhere.

"They must belong to those plant hunters," Vanessa said. "Looks like they've got a full-scale chemical analysis set-up."

"Unusual," I replied, "most stuff goes away for testing."

Vince had vanished when we got back, we were hungry after all the exertions of the day, we hadn't eaten since lunch and it was now dark.

We ordered food and Ollie, the cook who Marcus employed, went and did her thing. Her real name was Olivia, bizarrely there were two Olivias on Ecias, she opted to be called Ollie or just Ol. The other, a fisherman's wife, was known as Liv. Ollie had come from a big hotel to work on Ecias, she said that she was looking for a challenge; anything that she cooked tasted superb. Apart from a few things that came on the ship, all the ingredients were fresh; most of it had been in the sea or the ground less than a day ago. Tonight, she was serving fillets of a local fish we called 'fang' largely because over half its length was a tooth studded mouth. The back end, so to speak, was the most amazing creamy white flesh, delicious with herbs and a little vinegar. It came on a bed of local leaves, with some new potatoes and garlic, to remind us of home. After a month of concentrates and berries, it was delicious. All that was missing was the white wine; we made do with another beer each.

As we ate, Ove came back with a few of the new people; the three plant hunters and Vince were not among them.

He introduced them to Ollie and she told them what she was cooking today. Their faces fell a little when she said 'fang and salad'. Then they saw our plates, caught the aroma of what we were eating. Suddenly, they all wanted some. She would be busy for a while.

Ove came to sit with us for a moment. "I don't like the look of those three," he said. He had spotted the potential for trouble.

"Don't worry, they'll be off tomorrow, we're ferrying them and all their gear to a spot near the Canal. That's where they want to start working."

"They seem to have plenty of gear," I remarked. I didn't want to get drawn into discussing their attitude. I was prepared to let it all go, if they kept it at banter and stayed out of our way. If we met up away from prying eyes and they started up, it might be a different story.

"I know," he shook his head. "It's a nightmare, we're going to need both lifters for most of the day to get it shifted. Why the ship couldn't have dropped all their gear where they wanted it to be is a mystery to me. That's where I've been, talking to my boss about it."

"What did he say?" It was unusual; Burgstrom was normally a well-organised outfit. You had to be, with the time it took to get anywhere, even with the trans-light engine things had to be done in sequence, with maximum use of resources.

"I told him that the land where they want to set up camp is a wide strip of grass between the beach and the forest, there was plenty of room there to land a ship. I was surprised that the team didn't suggest it themselves."

So was I, it made sense, especially if they had any delicate equipment. Now it had to be handled off the ship, onto a lifter and off it again, there was more chance of breakage, as well as the waste of time.

"Was Ingerbrightsen embarrassed to be questioned?" asked Vanessa. Ingerbrightsen was the boss above Ove, a hard man to impress.

"His first words were, 'I knew that you'd be on the blower to me about that. It was our foul-up. We loaded the ship in the wrong order, we would have had to take all the cargo off at the site to get to it. Then reload half of it'."

"So you would have had to send the lifters out to the Canal anyway?"

"Exactly, not really our finest hour. Kalesh is a new company, they want to work with Burgstrom on several worlds, searching for useful plants and stuff. We haven't made a good impression."

"Neither have they, with those three," Vanessa said.

"Maybe that's why they're riled?" I added.

"Maybe," Ove agreed. "But that's still not the way to behave. You don't come in and start upsetting people. Burgstrom told me that I have to be nice to them. I don't like the attitude. Whatever, they're over there for at least a fortnight, setting up. Then I guess they'll be doing what you do."

"Can't you just leave them there?" asked Vanessa. I realised that meant we might bump into them in the forest, if we were both surveying the same area. That was good, the rules didn't apply out there. The forest was my backyard.

"I'm sorry if they upset you," Ove said. "Burgstrom only gave them a three-month licence. I can make sure they don't come back after that."

She shook her head. "I'm not especially upset, although there were three of them, that's a bit more intimidating. It was more what they said, they've planted a seed. This fellow Vince should be with his girlfriend and she isn't here. It was just what they said about his behaviour."

Ove nodded. "I see what you mean," he said. "I put everyone in the hostel, you'll see him in the morning and you can ask him then."

We left Whistles and drove the short distance to our trailer, it was a copy of the one we kept up in the hills, it was a lot easier to have both than to keep moving one around. This one lived on the edge of the town, where it met the forest. It was far enough away from everyone else's living quarters to be private. Space wasn't a problem, we had the whole planet to choose from.

"I have a feeling that things are going to change, and not for the better," Vanessa said as we prepared for sleep. I had locked the door; I'd never done that before.

"How do you mean?" I asked even though I thought I knew what she would say. The three men and their comments had unsettled her. I wasn't used to seeing her react like that to a bit of banter, which is what I suspected it was, banter, a bit of jealousy, annoyance at being messed around, nothing more.

"I don't know, just a feeling."

"We don't get involved," I said. "We're out of touch where we are."

She snuggled up to me in the bed. "I know," she said. "And I like it like that. The trouble is, having this bloke around for a month is going to be a strain, if his girlfriend was with him it wouldn't be so bad but..."

I understood exactly what she meant, it was our little world, we could do what we wanted, and now this man might spoil it.

CHAPTER SIX

NEXT MORNING, as we drank black coffee, Vanessa looked at me with a puzzled face. "You had a dream last night," she said. "You were moving about and muttering, it woke me up."

"I don't dream like that," I replied. I never had before. Then I remembered fragments. "OK so I do now," I told her. "There was a road, and a crash, someone got hurt."

She laughed and came over to punch me on the shoulder. "My driving's getting to you," she said. "I knew you were scared."

"Must have been," I answered, trying to see the picture in my head. All I got was the smell of damp earth, blood and oil, all mixed up. It wasn't nice. "I'd appreciate it if you don't give me any more nightmares."

As we prepared to face the day, there was a knock at the door. I unlocked and opened it. Vince stood outside, with a pack on his back and an eager face. His boots gleamed and what I could see of his gear all looked brand new.

"Hi," he said. "Marcus told me where you were; I walked over to see you. Are you ready to start work? I've been up since I don't know when checking all my gear, I'm too excited to eat."

"Vince," I said, "come in for coffee. Have a bacon sandwich.

There are two important points you need to know. First, you're working with us and you do things our way."

"OK," he said. "And what's the other?"

"You're working with us and you do things our way," said Vanessa, who had come to the door.

"But that's the same, you said there were two things."

"Yes, well it's that important that it needs to be said twice," she said with a straight face.

He tried hard not to laugh, in the end he gave up. He dropped the pack by the door, kicked his boots off and came inside. Vanessa handed him a coffee and made him a sandwich. "Got any milk?" he asked, looking at his cup.

"We drink it black," Vanessa said, "it saves having to carry milk powder around with us."

"Oh right," he said, "that's sensible I guess." He took a bite of his sandwich. "Sorry," he mumbled, while he was chewing. "I'm way too enthusiastic, Anna is always telling me to calm down."

Here was the perfect chance to find out what all yesterday's fuss was about. "Why isn't she here with you?" I asked.

"She's sick," he said. "We were on Helor, working for Burgstrom and she caught some sort of bacterial infection. She's in quarantine." He saw our faces. "Don't worry, it's all under control, she's not gonna die or anything but they want to keep her there until it's sorted. I had to come on my own. And before you ask, I wasn't infected, I got lucky. She should be along next month."

And that led us into the other question. "So what were those three on about, what you were up to on the ship?"

"Oh that," he said with the weary tone of someone who had been trying to explain it without much success. "They knew about Anna from the start, we got talking when we boarded, when we all met up. They were friendly enough then, even sympathetic. Then they changed, there was an argument about their equipment, they kept going to the hold, speaking to the crew, and to their bosses. One evening, they heard me telling

Fearne, one of the stewardesses on the ship, that I was missing Anna. We were laughing and messing about. They must have decided that it would be fun to spread a rumour that I was after her."

"And you weren't?"

"No, I was just telling her about Helor, what they didn't bother to find out was that I knew her. Anna knew her better than I did but she was a friend of us both. It was all just banter."

Three frustrated men had seen him chatting to a friend, maybe giving her a hug. They had jumped to jealous conclusions and here we were. I had been right; they were just stirring up trouble.

"I'm not after you," Vince said to Vanessa. "No offence," he added quickly. "I'm sorry if I'm gonna be a spare wheel, I'll try and keep out of your way."

She smiled at him. "Fair enough, none taken."

"Now that's sorted," I said, "let's get into Whistles, we can plan the job and get the stores loaded into the buggy."

"What's that hanging off your pack?" Vanessa asked him as he swung it onto his shoulders.

"That's my EPIRB," he said. Emergency Position Indicating Radio Beacons were a mandatory requirement for everyone on Ecias. At first, Burgstrom had wanted to implant chips in all the settlers, so that they could see where we were. They said it was for safety, which was reasonable. Then the unions and the usual agitators had got involved, there had been a fuss about what would happen if we were sacked, who would pay, civil liberties and anything else they could think up. Of course, the ones making the most fuss were safe behind desks, on Earth.

In the end, as a compromise, we got these small boxes. They had the added advantage that there was a button we could press, under a sealed cover, if we needed help. If we didn't carry them at all times we were in trouble. It was another way to get the next shuttle off Ecias, as it was for our own safety we complied. Ove could monitor our position, in real time, from his office. If he wanted to. He said that he didn't bother much.

"Top tip, Vince, keep it inside, it could snag on a branch and rip off, then you'd be in trouble if you needed rescuing."

"Oh yeah," he said. "Good point." He reached around and unclipped the pouch, transferring it to his trouser pocket.

We drove back into town in our buggy and stopped outside the back of Whistles. As we walked around to the front, we could see that the supply ship had gone, the settlement's two lifters sat in the square by the pile of boxes. The three plant hunters were there, supervising loading. They had a large vehicle as well, painted black with tinted windows. It sported a roof rack and a trailer. They ignored us, we returned the compliment. It was quiet inside, Ollie and Marcus were deep in conversation, they waved a greeting as we sat at one of the tables. Vanessa took her tablet out.

"We need to get organised before we set off," I told Vince. "We don't just go racing into the forest. There's a lot to do first."

"We need to plan and set up a reporting schedule," added Vanessa. "If we don't keep to it Ove will come looking for us."

"And organise our supplies and equipment, load the buggy up," I took over.

"Make sure we don't take any gear we can't carry, once we leave the buggy, we're on our own," she had the last word.

Vince looked mystified at what we were saying. Surely he had done fieldwork before? Vanessa spotted it as well. "It's not like we can just drive up to the spot, Vince. There will be plenty of hiking to do."

"Hiking, what on foot, with packs? On Helor we just drove around, mind you it was mostly desert. Don't we have horses, pack animals?"

I was about to tell him that it was so old-fashioned, that we had moved on. Vanessa was trying not to laugh at the thought of swapping her buggy for a horse. Then I thought about it, actually it wasn't a bad idea. Horses could take us over the ground where the buggy couldn't, they could carry loads of gear, feed on the grass. It was brilliant. We knew that the plants could support cows and pigs, horses would be easy. Why had nobody thought of it before?

"Great idea, Vince, I can talk to Burgstrom about horses next time we're back. Till then, it's just us."

Vanessa had started making notes. She asked Vince for the chip he had brought. He handed it over, she paired her machine with it and downloaded its contents.

"Our start point is quite a way out," she said. "We'll have to stop off at the crater tonight, then somewhere else the night after that. We leave the buggy here." She passed me her tablet. The map showed the road that hugged the coast; Richavon was a point on one edge. The road headed west, or at least towards the setting sun, past a landmark called the crater, the result of a meteor strike. A red line showed the route to a place more than halfway to the Canal, at the foot of a hill. Great, we were headed towards the plant hunters.

"Is that the first sampling point?" Vince asked. Vanessa shook her head.

"Nope, that's where we leave the buggy and start the real work. We fly the drone from there and follow it. Where it lands, that's where we dig."

"We have most of the gear we need in the buggy," I said. "We just need to pick up our rations and your bits and pieces."

"They're all in my pack," he said, "with my tent and personal gear, but I haven't got any food."

"We only take concentrates, protein bars, coffee, the rest we forage or hunt and kill."

Once again he looked shocked. "It's a bit different to Helor."

"You're not wrong there, Vince, welcome to proper surveying. Vanessa can give you all the details while I get the rations, I'll be back in a bit."

As I was leaving I bumped into Ove. "I've got some paperwork from Burgstrom for you," he said. "Come with me and I'll hand it over."

I followed him to his office. He had a large padded envelope for me. I knew that it would contain update chips for all our devices, personal messages and company notices. I hated paperwork; at least the updating was automatic, you just paired the chip with your device and it did it for you. Personal messages were good, a chance to see what friends and family were up to. Company notices were a waste of time, they were only good for starting fires and other important camping duties that required paper.

I left him and went to the store around at the back of Whistles. I pulled out a box of daily ration packs. Inside were thirty days of concentrated rations for four people, contained in small, vac-packed pouches. There were basics, protein powder, chocolate, vitamin tablets, a few useful items, matches and suncream. That would be more than enough for us. I took the box and put it in the buggy.

That was us, we were ready to go. It was a good six hours' drive to the crater, our destination for the night, nobody drove after dark, animals wandered around unseen, they were drawn to light and would step out in front of a vehicle, mesmerised by its headlights. So we only drove in daylight.

As I walked back towards Whistles, the loading had stopped; the black vehicle was on one lifter and about a quarter of the boxes filled the loadbed of the other. They were ready to go; everyone must have gone for coffee before taking off.

I arrived at the bar to see that Vanessa had her arms around Vince, they were wrestling. They pivoted together, seeking an advantage, the loss of balance that created a chance to throw. Vanessa was taller, which gave her a reach advantage, Vince was stronger and had a lower centre of gravity, making him harder to topple.

They seemed to be evenly matched for skill, but Vince hadn't learnt her tricks, so it was no surprise to me when she pretended to slip, recovering as he committed and threw him. I saw that the three plant hunters were there, they looked on; shouting encouragement. Then they spotted me and turned, all gleeful smiles at my surprised face. It went quiet, Vanessa helped Vince stand, he was winded from the fall. They sat on opposite sides of our table, they were smiling, out of breath.

"Hi, Dan," Vanessa said, she was panting and flushed. "We were talking about what we did for amusement. Vince said he liked to wrestle, we were sparring, I was checking out his moves."

"That's what they all say," one of the three said with a sneer. "I'd watch him, if I were you; pretty lady like that. Did you know that he was after a stewardess on the ship?"

"He hasn't wasted any time moving in here," added one of the others.

The largest one, a particularly ugly specimen with a broken nose and a bushy beard, came up close to me. "Of course, stuck up in the mountains together," he leered through black and broken teeth, "she might appreciate the variety."

I was about to reveal my own moves. Unlike Vanessa, I had nothing subtle. I would just deck him. Before I could do that, Vanessa took her own sort of direct action to defuse the situation. She got up, grabbed me and kissed me violently. I couldn't see what was going on, I was far too busy. It took my mind off thoughts of physical violence, maybe that was her idea. I could hear more cheering though.

Vanessa pulled away and let me up for air. She wiped her mouth with the back of her hand, looking at the surprised faces.

"Tell you what," she said with a shudder, "I'll stick with Dan. Vince will just have to look the other way and get over it. At least you three will have each other for company." She raised an eyebrow. "I expect you'll enjoy that."

There was silence. It was broken by one of the lifter pilots.

"Come on, you lot," he said. "We have the first load of your gear on board, if you don't want to walk, get on the lifter with it."

Muttering, the three left, the last one out pointed his hand at me, in the shape of a gun. He pretended to shoot me as he walked to the door.

I sat down. "She always catches me out with the pretend slip," I said. "She's tricky."

"I'm embarrassed," Vince said. "Not that she beat me, just that they would have to come in then, I haven't helped. There's some real trouble brewing with them."

"At least we're off out of the way soon," I said. "Perhaps when we get back they'll have gone."

As Vince was talking, I could hear a buzzing in my ear, the lifters were taking off, but instead of getting quieter as they moved away, the sound got louder. I looked around but couldn't isolate the source.

CHAPTER SEVEN

EARTH

THAT WAS A FIRST; I had actually slept up to my alarm. I hadn't achieved that for weeks. I stretched and realised that I was laid out on top of the bed. I still had my clothes on. And my bladder was near to bursting. I hadn't had a drink last night. I occasionally had a couple of beers before bed, falling asleep so quickly had robbed me of the chance.

Had I dreamt? I remembered a bar and a cold beer, a crowd of people. That was more like my usual dreams. I had been back on Ecias, there had been some excitement but it was all still a bit hazy. Not being able to recall all the details must be a side effect of the tablets. I could mention it when I had my follow-up with the consultant. I had a shower and got dressed, no bacon sandwich for me this morning, just cereals and black coffee.

Cath arrived back just as I was getting ready to leave for work, she looked tired.

"Hi, love," I said. I made her tea, put my arms around her as she poured her cereal, tried to show her that I'd missed her. "How was your shift?"

"Awful," she replied. "We were short-handed, the agency sent cover but when they arrived they were useless, one of them walked out during the handover, the other was a lazy cow with a big mouth. Plenty to say but not a lot of use when it came to getting anything done. And she's back again tonight, oh joy. I'm off to get some sleep, drive safely and I'll see you later." We kissed and headed off in opposite directions.

The drive in to work was slow but uneventful. It was a cold morning; I had to scrape ice from the windscreen before I could set off, a weak sun poked through thickening clouds. It looked like it might rain again before too long; maybe it was cold enough for snow? I went through town, it was no quicker than yesterday but less eventful. I was at my desk early, Molly was already there. Deanne arrived fashionably late, as normal. I was trying to think of something new and exciting to say about oven cleaners when Hughie appeared from his unofficial bedroom, straightening his tie.

"Good news, people, we might have a new account," he said proudly. We all looked up. New work was a chance to do something different. Which one of us would he choose for the project?

"What's it this time," said Deanne, "more cat food? Or maybe we've gone up in the world and now we're doing dog food."

"It's better than that," he said, trying not to grin. Deanne, being junior, got most of the cat food. "This could be the big one. A drugs company wants copy for a new range of medicines and health supplements that they're bringing out. Rick, I want you to lead, with your inside knowledge of the field."

That was a laugh. "My wife's a nurse," I said. "It's hardly like I was a doctor in another life."

"Whatever, she'll be in at eleven," he said. "We can take her to lunch after we've pitched."

There were groans from the others. All of us had wanted the job. Hughie tried to dish the work out fairly; Molly was up to her ears and Deanne, being new, was at the bottom of the list for new clients. She had to prove herself first on the routine stuff; mind you, with the quality of her work, she wouldn't be long catching us up. And if this was for a big company, she didn't have the experience.

"Alright," he said, "while we're at lunch, you two ladies can get takeout, on me." They both cheered.

We all got on well, this had always been Hughie's way, one of us went to lunch with the client and the other two got takeout. It was another reason why he was such a good boss. I started scribbling notes about the possible angles for health products, things I could suggest for their campaign. I didn't know what the products were; but I had done health adverts before, maybe I could adapt them. From about half past ten, we kept glancing at the doorway, in case whoever it was turned up early.

Promptly at five minutes to eleven the door opened and a woman walked in. Tall and slim, she had a grey suit on over a plain white blouse, with dark brown hair to her shoulders. She came over to me, my desk happened to be nearest to the door.

"Hello," she said, leaning forward. She shouldn't have done that, my eye was drawn downwards. She coughed. I hurriedly looked back up. Oops! That wasn't a good start. I could feel my face flush.

She seemed to find it funny. "I'm from Phay Medical," she said in a soft lilt. "I'm looking for Hughie."

Her eyes were brown, like her hair, the lashes full. There was something about her, some indefinable vitality in that face, the clear skin glowed with health and there were the merest hints of freckles around her pert nose. If she was using the company's products, they were doing her good. She was vaguely familiar, as if I had seen her face somewhere.

Hughie had come out of his sanctum. "I'm Hughie," he said. "Pleased to meet you."

"Hello," she replied, looking him straight in the eye and holding out her hand. "Esther Phay."

I realised that I knew the name, Phay. It was on the bottle of sleeping pills I had from the consultant. I was testing one of her products. I debated whether to mention it but decided that it might be good to keep it quiet. At least until I knew a bit more about her and Phay Medical. If we were going to be working together it could become an issue. She might think it was a conflict of interest and not want to use us. I would tell Hughie later, see what he thought.

"Ms Phay," Hughie was on his best behaviour, "please come into my office, you too, Rick, we can discuss your company's requirements."

We all went into his office and sat around the conference table. He fussed with coffee; Esther said that she liked hers black and strong, I got the same. He loved to do this, he reckoned it showed his humility, I always said that it showed that he was too cheapskate for a proper secretary.

When we were all comfortable, and had exhausted talk of the miserable weather, she produced a folder of glossy photographs from her bag. Unusual in these days of tablets and digital presentations, they showed pictures of packets of medicines, from throat soothers to painkillers and stomach settlers.

"These are our over-the-counter range," she said. "At Phay we've produced a new collection of natural remedies made exclusively from plants and minerals. I've seen all the old-style advertising, we need an original idea for marketing these products, hence our coming to you. The company we normally use are too set in their ways to come up with anything modern."

That put paid to my idea of rehashing an old campaign with a name change, I would have to start again. I quickly turned my notebook over to a fresh page, in case she looked at my notes, I had written 'rehash Prima job?' in big letters. If she saw that, after my earlier embarrassing moment, it would give her the wrong impression.

"That seems straightforward enough," said Hughie. "Rick here is our expert on this sort of thing; I'll leave you in his capable hands."

She spread the pictures out on the table; looking at them together you could appreciate their quality. "Can you use these?" she asked. "Or do you want to take your own?"

Our hands touched as we both moved the pictures about; it was as if I had been plugged into the mains. I might have thought I recognised her before, suddenly I felt that I knew her. The memory of a hilltop, wet grass and laughter in bright sunshine came into my head. She appeared not to notice, I could feel myself flush again at the memory. I moved my hand away, avoiding any further contact. What was going on?

Once I had the pictures arranged in groups I got out my pen and started making notes. We needed an angle and I had some ideas. "How important is the natural aspect?" I asked her. "Do you want to emphasise that they're not laboratory designed and engineered chemicals?"

She looked at me. "Phay only works with plants and natural ingredients," she said proudly. "We have no genetically engineered products, so yes, in today's market we feel it's a good selling point."

"Even though the rest of the market is trying to convince everyone that man-made is better?" interrupted Hughie. This was his style, he would ask the awkward questions to find out how committed the customer was, to gauge their passion for what they wanted us to do for them. It often produced an answer that nobody expected. Caught on the hop, the most reticent person will often say what's really on their mind.

"If you don't believe in us, then we're wasting our time," she snapped and got up. Her face had gone red, the freckles more pronounced. That wasn't the way it normally went, I could see that any business relationship with Phay would be a roller coaster.

There it was again, a feeling in my mind that I knew her. She was as tall as me and slim, the cut of the suit made her look almost boyish. Brown eyes and long hair, there were any number of women that looked like that. But I couldn't place her among our circle of friends. Then I realised, she was like Vanessa. That was just crazy, how could she be like a woman I only knew in my dreams? When I was awake, Vanessa wasn't really my type at all. Cath was not as tall as me and more curved, with short black hair and blue eyes. That had always been my type.

"Rick?" said Hughie. "Come back to us, you look like you're dreaming."

I snapped back to the present, I had to focus on reality. "Sorry," I said. "That's the mainstream view, surely you must have noticed. It's what we're up against, I have ideas and I can work around that, use it to your advantage."

She relaxed. "Good," she said. "I apologise if I got excited, it touched a nerve. That's exactly what was said when we started, we were told we were mad going the natural way, but we think it's better to use ingredients that have been around for as long as we have. The long-term effects of new chemicals can't be predicted." She sat down again.

You had to hand it to Hughie; he had found her driving force, the passion that he wanted. Now we had established that, we could concentrate on the job. As long as I could stop myself comparing her to Vanessa and remembering what we got up to on Ecias, we might be able to work together.

As we talked I could tell that she really believed in what she was doing. She told us that she had started Phay Medical with her father, after he had left his job with a big drugs company. It wasn't specifically mentioned but I got the impression that it was over the very thing that she was now so passionate about.

"Do you produce other drugs?" Hughie asked her, which was a relief. I thought that I was going to have to ask and reveal my use of the sleeping pills. Now I could keep quiet and listen.

"We have a couple of licence applications for prescription medicines," she said. "Again they have all-natural formulation; there's no conflict of interest with the ones we want you to advertise."

"Can we link?" I asked. "You know, we make these prescription drugs, trusted by doctors, now we bring you these over the counter remedies."

"We'd rather you didn't."

Her reply surprised me, and the speed at which it came out. Alarm bells went off in my head. Why didn't they want to mention the link? Were they unsure about the drug I was taking?

"Fair enough," I said, trying to stay calm. "But it adds credibility. You know the line, doctors trust us, so can you."

"They're not on the market yet, they may not gain approval, then it would look a bit silly. Let's just see what you come up with without using that," she said. Her temper was quick; she was going to be a handful to work with. Maybe I was getting worried about nothing, it was logical, I can't have been the first or only test subject.

"And that's lunch," Hughie said, before either of us said too much, or anything that we might regret. "And we try not to talk shop at lunch."

We left the office; heading to the local restaurant that Hughie always used for business lunches. As we left, Molly and Deanne were already sorting through menus.

CHAPTER EIGHT

WE TOOK a cab to the restaurant, even though it was only a few minutes' walk. I had been right, it was now raining steadily. Esther produced a small umbrella for the dash to the cab. "I'm always prepared," she said. "Old habits."

When we were seated and enjoying a glass of wine before our meal arrived, we talked about her background. She was happy to tell us what she had done; a lot of it was plant hunting in jungles and rainforests. I found myself feeling envious of her life, I had always wanted to get away from the office, from the rat race in general and explore the planet. I noticed that she had ordered water instead of wine.

"I'd have loved to do that," I said. "Just go off and explore, see what I could find. I guess that you never really know what a plant can do until you analyse it."

She smiled. "There's a lot more to it than just wandering around picking flowers," she said. For once the tone wasn't confrontational, this was her field and she was explaining it. "You have to have a rough idea what to look for, local knowledge is essential, and that means there is as much asking questions and getting information as there is actually exploring and sampling."

It still sounded like fun, then she gave an insight into its darker side. "There's a lot of superstition, and mistrust, especially in some of the more remote places. The natives have been ripped off and it's important not to upset them. You have to be tactful and fit in, not charge around upsetting everyone. You need to know and respect their traditions, let them tell you how they use plants for healing, how they're prepared, all that sort of stuff."

"It sounds fascinating." Hughie added, "How did you get into that?"

"I trained in Botany and Pharmacy, because of my father. He loved the outdoors. When I was little, I used to go with him, we would head off into the country for the school holidays and he would show me the plants, tell me which ones had been found to do what. It made me want to discover something that would help everyone. He was working for Hilliar then and they sponsored me to learn."

She sipped her water. "It wasn't just daddy's girl getting a plum job," she said. "If I had failed I was out, that was made very clear to me. It made me fight, to achieve on merit."

"And what happened then?"

"Hilliar were a big company, even so, they were unable to compete with the companies that had huge R & D budgets and chemical facilities for drug synthesis. Hilliar tried to make a virtue out of being natural. Then there was boardroom shake-up, the boss was replaced by Darshan Kalesh, he was a chemist and he quickly made it clear that plant hunting was far too time-consuming and hit-or-miss. In his brave new world, all drugs would be designed by computer, using genome mapping and virtual testing. Natural was out and synthetic was in."

You could tell that recalling the tale had upset her; she looked like she would cry. Wiping her eyes with the back of her hand she continued. "We had just discovered that a mayfly, of all things, produced a chemical in its mouth to enable it to eat a certain sort of algae."

"Hang on a moment," Hughie interrupted. "I thought that mayflies didn't eat."

She looked at him in surprise and annoyance. I thought that there would be another explosion.

"It's a hobby of mine, trout fishing," he explained. "I see lots of mayflies, they fascinate me. I read a book, it said the adults didn't eat, with their short lifespan, they have no proper mouths."

"You're part right," she said. "That would have been Casper Holworth's book. The way he explained it confused everyone. The adult mayflies don't eat but the nymphs eat algae, some species are even carnivorous."

"I see, sorry to interrupt, please go on," he said.

"Well, where was I...? Oh yes, we found that the chemical they produced is a natural soporific."

"A what?" I asked.

"Oh dear," she said. "I forget that I'm not talking to other pharmacists sometimes, a soporific is a chemical that induces sleep."

I thought of my tablets, was mayfly spit making me sleep?

Esther was still talking. "The new brooms at Hilliar were glad to see my father go, with all his tree bark and insect secretions. It was made clear that I was expected to go as well, not that I wanted to stay. We made the decision to set up our own natural company. It took time and money, we found backers who wanted to get away from the genetically engineered products; there's a growing body of thought that we're storing up problems for the future."

"I can see that," said Hughie. "You mean that we don't know if there will be any long-term side effects yet?"

"Exactly," she said, attacking her food as if it were an enemy. I noticed she had ordered steamed fish, new potatoes and salad. There was a strong smell of garlic. "In twenty years, people might just start falling over because of what we're doing now with synthetic drugs."

It was an interesting idea. "What about trials?" I asked, thinking of my own part. "Surely they highlight problems."

"Yes they do, but they're not long enough," she answered. "Everyone's too impatient for a return on their investment to wait and see what happens long term. With all drugs, not just the synthetic ones, I think we should be testing for a lot longer than the two or three weeks that we do now, of course that would make them uncommercial. Which is why it'll never happen."

"Anyway," said Hughie, "we seem to have strayed, we were supposed to be keeping off shop for lunch."

"You're right," she said graciously. "But it flowed from what we were talking about. How about you, Rick? I know about Hughie and his fishing, what do you get up to?"

I was on the spot; compared to her my life was boring. "I like music," I said, "from the seventies and eighties, I go to tribute concerts with my wife, she's a nurse. I'm partial to a good action movie, lazy Sundays, a quiet pint. All the normal things."

She nodded. "I wish I could slow down sometimes," she said wistfully. "Time passes and I never seem to get the time to relax. But you must have dreams, isn't there something you really want to do?"

The brown eyes seemed to get bigger as she looked at me, I was stuck for a reply, hearing her mention dreams, it felt almost as if she knew. It was unsettling, especially with her not knowing that she reminded me of them. I muttered something about travelling to the places that I advertised; that seemed to satisfy her. She turned to her food and we ate in silence for a while.

After coffee, she looked at her watch, said that she had to leave, she had another meeting. The waiter called her a cab.

"I'll look forward to seeing what you come up with," she said, handing me her business card. "My numbers are on there, call me." With a swirl of her hair, she was gone. Phew!

I could see that working for Phay would keep me on my toes; on the walk back to the office, I said as much to Hughie.

"You can handle it," he said. "Give her a few good ideas, show her you're not intimidated, she'll be eating out of your hand." He was jubilant; it looked like we had landed a big client.

"If we get this right, Rick, the world will notice us; we'll be up there with the greats."

I spent the rest of the afternoon working on getting it right, using her pictures. I had an idea about her plant hunting past. Could I work it into the copy somewhere? There was a memory from my dream, something to do with plant hunters. Talking to Esther I could see the good they were doing but in my dreams, I felt that they were not nice people. Esther had said they had to be sensitive and integrate, mine were anything but. I racked my brains for more of my dream; it might be useful in my work.

When I got home, Cath was dressed in her uniform, ready to head out. "How did you sleep?" I asked. If she thought it was funny that an insomniac wanted to know about someone else's sleep she never mentioned it.

She hugged me. "It was fine, tonight is my last shift. It's all been changed around. A week off, then I'm going to do some days to cover the school holidays."

I hated the way her shifts seemed to change at short notice, usually as a response to another staffing crisis. It made things difficult when it came to social events and holidays. Goodness knows how we would manage when we had the children that we both wanted.

Mind you, a week off sounded nice, I had some holiday owing, perhaps we could get a short break, even though it was winter. I might be able to get a late booking somewhere warmer. I would have to ask Hughie for the time off. It might be difficult with this new work though. It seemed like something always came up when we had the chance for a bit of alone time.

"If I can square it with Hughie, where do you fancy going for a few days?" I asked.

Her eyes lit up. "Can we?" I nodded, she hugged me again.

"Anywhere warm, you sort it out. I didn't ask you this morning, did the tablet work last night?"

"I slept all night," I answered. "In fact I was out of it before I even had chance to get undressed. The alarm woke me up, I was on the bed, fully clothed."

She looked relieved. "Great, he said it would take three nights, you've done it in two. But you'd best carry on like he said, have another tablet tonight."

"Aren't you going to question his advice? I know how nurses like to think they know more than the doctors."

She laughed. "That's because we do. Not this time, it's experimental, I've tried to look it up on the hospital computer, there's nothing about it. I'll have to go along with it this time."

Then I remembered my big news, the coincidence at work. "The strangest thing happened at work," I said. "You'll never guess what!"

She didn't look particularly interested, she thought that my work was boring; trying to persuade impressionable people to part with their cash wasn't as glamourous as saving lives. "Go on," she said in an 'if you must' sort of tone.

"The company that make the tablets, the ones the doctor gave me..." She nodded, more interested. This was medical, it mattered. "...Hughie's only gone and got us a job with them."

"No! Really? Phay Medical, they're at the forefront of research, real leaders in new stuff."

"I know; they're developing herbal remedies, over the counter stuff and I'm doing the advertising campaign. The boss, Ester Phay, came in and gave us the job. We went to lunch; she's keen for us to do her company's advertising."

I got another hug for that. "Well done," she said, laughing. "At least it's not cat food. Oh, I forgot to ask you, when you started telling me about Phay, did you dream last night?"

I told her what I could remember, bits and pieces about a bar and an alien landscape, that I was called Dan. For the first time I mentioned Vanessa in more than just a 'there were people in it' sort of way. I actually used her name.

Her ears pricked up at that. "Vanessa? You never said anything about her before. Was she pretty?"

I should have played it safe and said no. I should have changed the subject and talked about mayfly spit. There was no way that I was going to mention that I was sleeping with her in my dreams.

"I can't remember," I said. Instantly her mood changed, the eyes narrowed and she looked annoyed.

"She might have been then?" There was venom in her voice.

"C'mon, Cath, it's a dream! She was tall; she had brown hair, that's it. She's not as pretty as you."

"That's the right answer." She hugged me again. Then her face turned serious. "You watch yourself," she said as she left. "No messing about. Even if it's in a dream, *Dan*, it still counts!"

I tried not to look too guilty as we parted. I ate my dinner, wondering if I hadn't said too much.

I wasn't taking any chances with the tablet this time; I had a shower and got into bed before I took it. I knocked the bottle over as I put it back on the bedside table and was asleep before I could pick it up and put the lid back on.

CHAPTER NINE

ECIAS

VANESSA, Vince and I were up in the mountains, three days' drive along the coast road and a hike away from Richavon. We had shared the driving; Vanessa was on her best behaviour, she hadn't managed to scare Vince more than once or twice. Wait till we come back, I thought. He had offered to drive before we left, then changed his mind when he saw the state of the road.

We stayed at a campsite called the Crater on the first night, arriving before the light had gone. Because this part of the road was well used, there were half a dozen cabins arranged around a clearing, the result of a meteor strike. They were kept supplied, for travellers to get a wash and a decent rest. Water fell from a hole in the rocks at one end, forming a small stream that meandered through the crater, attracting wildlife.

We were the only humans on the site, we ate outside and watched as our single lantern picked out a small herd of Ghost Deer. They were clear in the artificial light, in daylight and surrounded by the forest they were so well camouflaged that you could only see them when they moved. Large bats flashed in and out of view as they hunted the insects which had been attracted to the light.

Vince said little, he was awestruck by the beauty of the place.

When he did speak it was in a hushed whisper. "It's incredible," he managed to say. "Apart from Earth, which is nothing like this, I've only been to Helor. That's just a desert, there're a few trees and not a lot else."

We slept in comfort, then we were on our way at first light. We drove all day, stopping only for meals and leg stretching, by dusk we had done well, there were no more campsites, so we just pulled off to the side of the road and pitched our tents between the trees.

The next morning, we woke with the sunrise. Breaking camp after breakfast, we carried on driving. We were getting close to the point where we would start the real work. Just before lunch, there was a bleep from Vanessa's tablet. She slowed down and found a place to stop, clear of the road. "We're here," she announced. "Now we can get started."

We got out and I set the drone up. It was fitted with ground penetrating radar to map the geology. All the difficult stuff was down to us; we just had to go to where the drone told us and dig. The search grid had been set by Burgstrom, on the chip that Vince had brought with him.

Vanessa had loaded the information into the Drone's memory on the journey. I powered it up and it launched, buzzing quickly out of sight. It would fly to our first sampling point and send out a homing signal for us to follow. We left the buggy in sunshine; the solar panels built into the chassis would keep the batteries topped up while we were gone.

We were at the bottom of a steep hill. On the other side, the ocean stretched away, the coast on either side faded from sight in a heat haze. It would be a hard climb, we had a mountain of equipment to take with us. Once we had secured the buggy, we got all the gear out and split it into three piles. Then we loaded our packs, trying to distribute it equally. Vanessa took an equal share, no concessions for her. I hadn't even dared suggest it. As well as the essentials, she had various bags hanging from her pack. They were filled with things we might need – 'just in case bags' she called them. 'Be prepared' was one of her mantras.

Vince had forgotten some of his surveying kit. "There's some of the sampling gear missing, tubes for the drill and a few other bits," he said. "I must have left them back in Richavon."

"Don't worry. We can call for a drone from Ove," I said, when he started getting worried that he had screwed up. "He can find them and send them out to us."

"Don't do it yet," he said. "I'll look like a fool who's never done this before, we might have enough. I'm not even sure where they would be. I thought that I'd got everything. I'd have to hunt through the boxes I left behind. Let's wait and see if we need them first."

I had a receiver on my wrist, set to the drone's frequency. It must have landed because my display showed me an arrow. All we had to do was follow it. It didn't show a distance, which was probably as well, it was enough to know that it was uphill.

"This is where the horses would come in handy," Vince said as we started to climb. I had to admit it would be easier, we could have a mount each, with one for the gear.

To start with, the trees were widely spaced, with room and light underneath to allow for easy passage through a patchwork of tall grass and small bushes. As we got further away from the road, we found clinging vines hanging between the trees, blocking our way. We had to cut our way through, which, together with the gradient, slowed us down. This part of the landmass was different to our previous areas of exploration and it was handy to have Vince with us for the extra muscle power. A bonus was that the shrubs we found as we got higher produced a large yellow fruit. We saw evidence that animals had been tucking in and when we tried them we could see why. They were sweet and delicious.

After a calf numbing march up a steep slope and along a rocky ridge, we had arrived at our first sampling point. The drone was sitting on a rock, one of a jumble showing above the surface. They were crusted with moss, but we could see the strata clearly. As it was getting late we set up our tents and rested overnight, before starting on the real work. Vince diplomatically pitched his tent behind some trees a short distance away from ours. After a meal together we settled down, in the quiet we could hear noises from Vince's tent. Was he watching a movie or talking to someone? It was impossible to tell.

Next morning, we woke to another clear, warm day. After breakfast, we spent the morning chipping rocks and drilling holes, using the portable gear that Vince had in his pack. While we were doing that, Vanessa turned the drone on. It lifted off and buzzed away; we watched its progress on our receiver tablets. It would head to our next site and busy itself taking all the pictures and scans it had been programmed to do. Then it would land and shout 'here I am' at us until we found it. While it did all that, we took samples of the rocks where we were. It was a simple method of working, one we had used before and we were used to it.

After a couple of hours, we had finished our work. We hadn't needed to dig or drill too much here. Everything we needed was chipped from rocks on the surface and secured in labelled bags. We took the chance to eat, then started cleaning and stowing the equipment. The drone sent back a message to my receiver; it had landed at our next site for sampling. As there was still some daylight left, we set off through the forest towards it. Our route followed the ridge for a while, then we turned and went into a steep-sided valley. Thick brush and the land obscured the sun, it got cold. The lack of warmth and light had not hindered the flora, it was as impenetrable as on the other side of the hills. We kept warm cutting a path.

"Are there any dangerous animals in here?" asked Vince.

"We've never found anything larger than a deer," answered Vanessa. "There are no snakes or poisonous insects either." I was too out of breath to say much.

"Surely there must be some predators?" he said.

"I agree," Vanessa answered. "It's logical; there are predators in the seas. We've never had a chance to look properly for them on land. We've seen evidence of predation, half eaten carcasses. They must be out there somewhere, one day we'll find them."

"As long as they're not looking for us," he suggested, looking around with a slightly apprehensive expression.

The conversation made me realise just how little we actually knew about Ecias. We had mapped the planet from space and by drone, built a road but actually explored less than one per cent of it.

It was my turn to lead; I was hacking through vines that were a few centimetres thick, they sprayed sticky sap over me every time I cut one. It made the machete harder to swing and I had to keep stopping to clean the blade. Vince and Vanessa were close behind; I could hear her explaining the things we saw. I stopped in a gap between the vines, a tree had fallen and made a small clearing. "Time for a break," I suggested, sitting on the trunk.

We sat and made a hot drink. Vince was getting used to black coffee, once he had come to terms with having to carry his own milk powder if he wanted it white.

"It blows my mind," said Vince. "Every step I take, I'm the first person to be here. I wish Anna was here to see it all with me."

"We don't notice anymore," said Vanessa. "It's just our home, I'm sure she'll be here soon."

"I was talking to her last night," he said. That explained the noise we had heard. "Telling her all about it, and all about both of you. She's getting stronger all the time."

Over the following days, we settled into a routine. We took samples and investigated where the drone told us to look. We followed it around the country as it worked ahead of us. We dug and drilled, even blasted a few times to measure the echoes from the rock below. We took core samples, packing them in the containers that Vince had. We carried everything that we needed in our packs and apart from our concentrated rations, we lived off the land. As fast as we used up our supplies, the core samples and bags of rock took up the empty space. I laid traps every night and kept us supplied with small rodents, about the size of rabbits, which we butchered and grilled over a brushwood fire. They tasted like a strange cross between lamb and chicken, with a hint of the herbs and leaves that they lived on. I even managed to catch a couple of the geese, just for variety.

We had forgotten about the plant hunters, so had Vince, not only that, he had cheered up about Anna not being here. In fact, he was counting down the days until she would join him.

It was a tough trek through the forest; neither of us had been this far out from Richavon, it was a good distance past the point where our other trailer currently stood. If only we had been closer, we could have detoured, had a shower and spent a night in comfort but we kept moving further and further away from it and Richavon.

Vince pushed us, it was clear that he wanted to get finished as soon as possible, so that he could get back in time for the supply ship's arrival. As the survey progressed, we found that we were headed in the general direction of the place where the plant hunters were based, on the shore near the Canal. I began to hope that we wouldn't meet up with them as we trekked through the forest.

The road we had left the buggy on went all the way to the Canal, that was another two days' journey, although we would normally go by lifter. We had finished the road for when we could set up a second settlement. The Canal was an ideal place for one, a grassy plain and a natural harbour. In some ways it was a better site than Richavon; it was a mystery why the first settlement had not been there. Ove didn't know the reason, it had been before his time here.

As we worked the forest, we were almost certainly the first humans to have been here, Vince was right, the silence and feeling of being alone was quite wonderful. At least it was for Vanessa and me, neither of us was really fond of groups and social situations.

Although it was great to have his help with the sampling and the drone electronics, the way it had been set up meant that the schedule had been designed for four people, which kept the three of us busy. Because of that, and his genuine attempts to avoid being a nuisance, we never felt stifled by Vince's constant presence.

He never stopped saying how he loved it on Ecias. He insisted in calling me 'professor' – a title I never used unless I really had to. Not that I was embarrassed by my doctorate, I just didn't like to show off about it. And there was never a need when it was only Vanessa in earshot, she wasn't impressed by it, she was one too.

He picked our brains for all the information we had about the planet, he said that it was to help Anna catch up. He would always pitch his tent in a separate clearing from us, we would meet for our evening meal then he would go off on his own, giving us privacy to wash and be together. He said that he was messaging Anna and telling her everything that he had learned about the place. It was very thoughtful of him to give us the privacy and we appreciated it.

"I've got some good news and some bad news," he said one morning. "Anna's better now. Trouble is, she missed the ship by a day. She'll be on the one after that. I've been describing what she's going to see, sending her video recordings. She can't wait to be well enough to come out."

One night in our tent, lying close to Vanessa I whispered, "I don't mind Vince being around, do you?"

"He's a great guy," she agreed. "I'd be happy to work with him again, with Anna as well, when she arrives. We've got so much more done working like this. Burgstrom would be crazy not to renew his contract."

I could see what she meant but preferred the solitude. Still, if Vince and Anna together behaved the same way that Vince did on his own, it would be OK. And I liked his idea of horses, it could save us a lot of effort.

"I've been thinking about the horses," I said. "The planet's going to open up, we all know it. We might not like it, but once we get a bit more organised here, the place will be ripe for development as a resort. There's money in tourism."

Vanessa shuddered. "What? All those loud visitors, demanding drinks by the pool and frightening the animals away?"

"I don't want them around me, but there's plenty of land. They could set up on the other side of the world. I just think that it would be great to have a holiday from some over-polluted city on Earth, riding a horse through this wilderness. If I was stuck in some boring job I'd jump at the chance."

"I suppose they could always set up little camps in the woods, keep it select," she said. "In a way it would be nice to give people the chance to see it." She paused. "As long as I don't have to get involved or share it with them."

We lay in silence for a while, I was thinking of the first time I had seen Ecias; I had grown up in the sort of place I had described, dirty, crowded and polluted. I had been lucky and had travelled around a bit before I had come here. Even so, the first time I had seen Ecias, it had still been breathtaking. I imagined seeing it after a life of grime and dirty air; it would be just as good. Then riding a horse through the forest, camping in solitude; who wouldn't jump at the chance?

Vanessa brought me back to reality. "There's one thing that bothers me in your vision of paradise. Those three we saw in town last time, stirring it up."

"I know," I replied. "The last thing we need is a group that don't fit in."

"I suppose," she said, "if they give any grief, Ove and Marcus will sort it."

I hoped she was right. They had 'explained' things to

awkward people before. "That or the place will get to them and they won't stay."

"Besides," she added, "as we're out of the way most of the time, we won't have much to do with them."

That was all very true, but deep down, I knew that what had happened in Richavon was bound to affect us in the end.

CHAPTER TEN

THEN ONE MORNING, we woke and had breakfast. Vince never appeared. We went over to where his tent had been. It was gone, along with his pack. His EPIRB and position fixer were lying on the grass. We were due to move out, the drone was already at our next location.

"Where's he gone?" wondered Vanessa.

"Don't you mean when?" I asked, pointing to the faint circular mark on the ground. "Look at the grass, where his tent was."

Vanessa got down on her hands and knees. "You're right," she announced. "The grass isn't flattened, like it would be if he had slept on it. He's been gone since last night."

What could we do now? We cast around, assuming he had gone in the other direction to our tent still gave us a large area to search. We found no sign of where he had entered the trees, no evidence of which direction he had taken.

"We can't go blundering about," I said. "We just have to carry on and hope we find him."

"Without his gear, he'll never find his way back to us."

We recalled the drone; we had an hour to wait until it arrived. Its batteries had charged up in the time it had been waiting for us, so it had plenty of juice. Vanessa stripped the GPR package and reprogrammed it to search infrared. We flew it in ever increasing spirals from our position, hoping to pick up his body heat. It was using a lot less power without the extra weight. We found plenty of animals moving about but no humans, not Vince or the plant hunters. Our survey was abandoned as we searched. We had to find him, I for one didn't want to admit to Anna, or Ove for that matter, that we had lost him, even though technically, he had left. We were the experts here, it was down to us.

"We're going to have to tell someone, organise a bigger search?" Vanessa said after we had spent nearly all day flying the drone with nothing to show for it. It was time for our regular message; normally we just said that we were all OK, what were we going to tell Ove tonight?

"We'll look again tomorrow," I suggested. "Just say that everything's normal. If we don't find him tomorrow, then we'll tell Ove."

We reported 'situation normal' and left the drone to fly all night, while we tried to sleep. In the morning, it had found a place where Vince had camped, right at the edge of its range. There was still a hot spot where he had boiled water to make a drink. He must have been moving non-stop, it looked like he was on the way to the Canal. What was he doing? We set out to follow him, carrying his EPIRB, so it would look like we were all together. Now that we knew where we were going and that he was alive we didn't bother telling anyone. We were moving out of our survey area but we could work around that, make up some story about the terrain or an equipment problem. We could use the lack of Anna, say there was more for us to do. No-one would be too bothered, we had our plan and there was plenty of time. If we missed the ship, our results would just have to wait for the next one.

When we got to his campsite, it was deserted. He hadn't returned, but it was clear that Vince was using it as a base. All his gear was here, he must have been travelling light.

"You realise that we're getting close to the sea here," Vanessa informed me. She was reading from her mapping tablet. "And not too far from where the plant hunters are based."

Had Vince set out to get revenge on them for something that he hadn't told us about?

CHAPTER ELEVEN

WE STAYED with Vince's equipment, working on the theory that he would come back when he was hungry. We sent the drone back to where it should have been, just in case Ove decided to check up, and settled down to wait.

Twenty-four hours later, Vince staggered into the camp, his clothes were torn and he looked like he was on his last legs. We made him coffee and gave him protein bars.

He slept for twelve hours. When he woke we gently asked him where he had been.

"I'm embarrassed to say, I got lost," he said. This didn't really tie in with the fact that he had left our camp in the first place.

"That doesn't make sense," Vanessa said. "You left us. Why did you go?"

He got agitated. "Please don't report it. I can't tell you, there was something I had to do."

"Is it to do with the plant hunters?" I asked.

He hedged, looked down at his feet. "No. Nothing at all to do with them." He said it very quickly, the words coming out in a rush. I wondered if he was protesting too much. "I had a secret job, Harald Burgstrom asked me to do it, there's something the surveys had spotted that they wanted me to look at, alone. I needed to get it done, I should have told you I was going but I figured I'd be back in a day. It took me so much longer than I expected to get through the forest."

"Fair enough, but why can't you tell us?"

"Because I told Harald Burgstrom that I wouldn't," he said. "Trust me, I'll tell you later. It's complicated. I wish Anna was here, she was supposed to help me. For now, let's just say I was doing something important for Harald, off book, and leave it at that."

"If you want us to keep the secret," said Vanessa, "you'd better get your finger out and help us get the rest of the surveys done, or we'll all be in trouble."

We started to head back to our next survey spot. Later that night, when we were alone, we talked about Vince's absence. Despite what he had said, it still didn't make sense. Harald Burgstrom was the big boss, why had he sent Vince to do a secret job while he was with us? We would notice he had gone; we had noticed. He had gone off without his safety gear, which meant that he had to have another position fixer somewhere on him. What was there, near where we were? The only thing we could think of was the plant hunter's camp, but he had said that it wasn't to do with them. Had the previous surveys found something valuable, maybe some rich seam of rare minerals? If they had, why weren't we trusted to have a look? We talked about it till we fell asleep but got no answers.

Because of the time we had spent looking for Vince, and the work we still had to do before we could come down from the mountains, it became clear that we hadn't got anywhere near finishing the programme that had been sent to us. We were going to have to think of an excuse, we could say it was because we were one person short; or we could blame the difficulty of the terrain. It wasn't a total lie, very often we had to spend ages clearing the ground before we could dig and it all took time. I radioed Ove and told him we would miss the supply ship, he said he would pass it on to Burgstrom and sent a larger drone with extra food packs for us.

To add to the mystery, I started to think that we were being followed. It was hard to describe but I had a feeling that we weren't alone. Living in a place with so few humans, their presence was more noticeable. It was unlikely that anyone would sneak around, nobody would hide, there were so few of us on the planet that any meeting was normally celebrated. I mentioned it to Vanessa; she kept her eyes open. Then we spotted a large Sawgrass, a deer-like creature. Startled, it ran off into the trees, bellowing. She laughed. "I'll bet that's what's been following us," she said. "Looking for scraps of food."

"Are they dangerous?" asked Vince.

"No, they're herbivores, harmless but they love to eat sweetened grains, like our protein bars, and chocolate, so they hang around. If you feed them you can't get rid of them, they communicate with the herd somehow. Before you know it, there's a whole load of them around you. I've not seen one that big before though."

It showed us that we knew so little about the planet and the way the ecosystem worked.

We were in a clearing when the monthly ship arrived. We watched it pass overhead with mixed feelings. It meant another month had passed; there would be the usual celebrations in Whistles tonight. Vince had already told us that Anna had missed this one, I knew that he had been messaging her but since his solo expedition, he hadn't said much about her.

"It's a shame that Anna won't be there when we get back," Vanessa said as we saw the ship vanish behind the trees.

"It's only another month," he said. "Last time I talked to her, she was OK, she was hoping to be on that one but she was still too weak. The doctor wouldn't let her fly. At least the infection's gone. She'll definitely be on the next one."

The work had kept us busy. Then one day, when we set the

drone to fly, it announced that we were at the last place in its memory. We had finally finished all the work, investigated all the sites it wanted us to look at. When we had sampled here, the drone would home onto our buggy and give us a direction to walk.

Twenty-four hours later, the drone signalled to say that it had arrived at our buggy, we set off towards it. It would take us two days to walk back to it, then another three days driving down the road until we arrived in Richavon. We could hand in our results and relax until the next ship arrived. The delay had worked in our favour; Ove had told us there was no new job for us on the ship. It meant that we could have a break.

Vanessa had been hoping for some time off. She wanted to borrow a boat and explore the islands that lay off the coast near Richavon. Perhaps we could do that. We saw the ocean in the distance on the second day, after climbing a steep ridge, it almost felt like the drone was sending us on the longest way around to get back to our buggy. We rested at the crest, looking down we could see the scar of the road, clinging to the coast. It was the first disturbance we had seen in the landscape for so long, it looked like sacrilege, like this pristine place had been defiled.

We had an energy sapping downhill hike, then we were back at the buggy, exactly where we had left it. The drone sat on the bonnet. We stowed it and threw our packs into the rear compartment.

"Let's get going," said Vanessa. "I'm driving." It wasn't worth arguing, I got in the back, Vince took the front passenger seat; he would soon learn that it wasn't the best place to be for the journey. Vanessa had behaved herself on the way out; it was too much to expect that she would do the same, now that home, a shower and a cold beer were within reach.

"Don't you want a rest, a drink?" he asked.

"We can rest tonight, we can get a good few miles in before dark."

She sat in the driver's seat and switched on. The engine

wouldn't start. Sat behind him, I could see Vince's shoulders slump. It was a long enough drive, walking it would be ten days or so. We would have to call and ask for a lifter to pick us up. That would be embarrassing, a cause of mirth in Whistles either way if we couldn't get it fixed.

"Don't worry," I told him. "Vanessa is a pretty good engineer; she'll soon have it working." We got out and sat on the side of the road, out of the sun while Vanessa lifted the bonnet and peered inside. I tried not to watch her rear too intently as she bent over the engine. In no time, she straightened up and dropped to the ground. Laying on her back she wriggled her way under the chassis.

"What's up?" I asked her.

"Inverter's gone," she said, her voice muffled.

"What, broken, uncoupled?" My knowledge of the electric engines that powered the buggy was rudimentary, compared to my ability with broken drones and mining gear. I knew that the inverter regulated the power supply from the batteries and solar panels to the drive motor but that was about it. I could find it under the bonnet, I knew how to change one but I couldn't tell you how it worked. She crawled back out and stood, her face was a mixture of puzzle and disbelief.

"No," she said forcefully. "It's *GONE*, it's not there."

How..." I started, but she interrupted me.

"It's missing, it's bolted onto the side of the engine, there's two cables attached to it as well, with screw connectors. It can't just fall off. Even if it did manage it, we would stop, instantly. Anyway, I checked the buggy over before we left Richavon, it was firmly attached then. And it got us here. As it's not laying under the buggy, it must have been taken off by someone."

CHAPTER TWELVE

WE WERE all silent for a moment as we absorbed the fact, it looked like someone had done this, someone had wanted us stuck out here. Who would do that? And why?

"Do we have a spare in the survival kit?" Vince wondered.

"No," she replied. "Sorry but it's not a part that fails, or falls off."

"So what do we do?"

"We'll have to call it in, Ove will send a spare out by drone, it'll home on our EPIRBs."

Vanessa made the call and we waited. After an hour or so, Ove sent us a message, the drone was on the way, it would be with us in another three hours or so.

"That's put paid to our travelling far tonight," Vanessa said. "We won't get many miles done before it's too dark."

"I'm going to do some more filming, for Anna," Vince announced. He took his camera from his pack and strolled off into the trees.

Vanessa and I sat by the side of the road, looking out over the forest below, stretching all the way down to the dazzling blue ocean. The sunlight made an orange line on the water. Claudius was high in the sky. It was a perfect moment. I was reluctant to spoil it by talking about the missing inverter. Instead, I put my arm around her. "Happy?" I whispered in her ear.

She wriggled closer. "You know I am," she said. "I'll be even happier when I've had a proper shower, one of Ollie's specials and we can finally have a night to ourselves."

I was just contemplating that when I heard a noise. "That can't be the drone already," I said. It wasn't, another vehicle was approaching us. A large black enclosed vehicle came around the corner, heading towards the Canal. All the glass was tinted, impossible to see through. It gave it a sinister appearance. It stopped beside us and a window rolled down with a whine. I already knew who was inside.

"Car trouble?" said the driver. It was one of the plant hunters, I could see another one beside him; the third was probably in the back, hidden behind the tinted glass.

"No, we're fine," Vanessa said. "Thanks for asking, we're just enjoying the view."

The man looked at her. "So am I," he said.

"Where's lover boy?" asked his mate, leaning across. "You worn him out, or have you killed him and dumped him in the woods?" There was laughter.

"You're funny, guys," I said. "Didn't you ought to run along, it'll be dark soon." They glared at me.

"You wanna make sure your buggy starts, before we go?" the second man said.

"Shut up," snapped the first and they raced away, scattering dust and stones, fishtailing the vehicle in their haste.

"Friendly bunch," Vanessa said.

I realised that I was tense, primed to fight. "Do you think that they knew something? That bit about the buggy starting."

"Just banter," she replied, but I could tell that she didn't believe what she was saying.

"Have they gone?" Vince stepped out from the trees, camera in his hand. "I heard all that, got it on film too, I didn't want them to see me filming, that was why I kept out of the way."

"Keep that footage, Vince," I said. "We can play it to Ove, see what he thinks."

When the drone arrived, it was the work of a few moments to fit the inverter. Ove had attached a message to the packaging: 'Bring the broken one back for repair', it said.

"Didn't you tell him it had gone?" I asked Vanessa. She shook her head. "Nope, he'd never believe it and we'd spend hours arguing. I can explain it when I see him."

By this time, it was getting dark. "We might as well stay put till morning," I suggested. "Camp here and set off at first light."

"If we push it, we can maybe get to the crater in a day," said Vanessa, hoping for an excuse to drive faster than usual, if that was possible. I didn't reply, I thought that it was too far.

The journey passed as a blur, maybe that was down to Vanessa's driving. We didn't make it to the crater, there had been a rockfall, blocking the road. It must have happened after the plant hunters had passed, unless they hadn't gone that far. It took us half a day to clear a path. We camped one night and spent one at the crater, the cabins had been resupplied since we had set out and there was fresh food in the fridges. We had long showers, dined well and were able to shut ourselves away from Vince for a night. Vince seemed to have run out of things to say, he was fretting about something.

It can't have been the missing gear, we hadn't needed it. Anna was OK, she would be here in a couple of weeks, so it wasn't that either. Perhaps it was to do with his secret mission. I left him to his thoughts and concentrated on trying to arrange things so that I would be at the wheel for the last section of the road, but Vanessa was ready for me.

She treated Vince to the drive to the hilltop where we had admired the view. He had sat up front all the way, and from what

I could see of his back, I think he enjoyed the slide around the bend, past the logs. When we stopped at the lookout and gazed down on Richavon, he told us that he had been quiet for the last few days because he had been thinking about what he would do next. He said that he had decided to stop on Ecias, at least for a while. He had planned to do a year's fieldwork somewhere, with or without Burgstrom.

"Here's as good a place as any, it's better than Helor and I can't imagine finding anywhere else I'd like more." Once he had told us that, he perked up, it wouldn't be long till the next ship arrived and brought Anna. "She'll love it here, and you'll like her," he said. "She's seen all the footage I've been taking, she can't wait to meet you all. I've just got to convince her to stay here with me, it shouldn't be hard."

We stopped outside our cabin. Vanessa went to have a leisurely bath, do some laundry and generally be domestic. She would come into town and meet me in Whistles with a list of the supplies we needed for our cabin. We had two weeks off now and could do what we wanted. Anything that wasn't in the stores could be ordered now for delivery on the ship after next, which would not have left yet.

Vince and I carried on into town; we had the results of all our work to hand in, the data from the drone and all our samples. I wanted to give everything to Ove personally, there were things I wanted to talk about, the inverter for one. If Harald had given Vince a job, Ove might not have known so it was pointless to mention that. I parked up and Vince grabbed his pack and went off towards the hostel. "I'm having a shower," he said. "I'll meet you for a beer later."

Ove was away when I arrived, his office was empty. I left all the samples and the report chip on his desk. There was time for a swift beer in Whistles, he might be there anyway, if not, Marcus or Ollie would know where he was.

Whistles was empty; there was no sign of anyone. I helped myself to a beer, sat in the corner and let my thoughts wander.

I hadn't seen all the results, but I had taken a quick look as the data was dumped onto the chip to accompany our bags of samples. From what I had seen, we had found a lot of interesting stuff in the mountains. If the analysis checked out, it could mean that the planet was viable as a long-term investment for Burgstrom. And despite any misgivings that Vince had, the arrival of the plant hunters was a good thing as well. Medicines were big business and with every planet, every new ecosystem, new remedies were being found.

The problem of antibiotic resistance had been solved, at least for the time being, with the discoveries from Tontranix; a planet claimed by the electronics company whose name it bore. They had originally discovered rare metals; in clearing the ground for mining operations they found plant and bacterial life that had unleashed a whole new class of drugs. Rumour was that it made them as much money as the mining operations they had intended. It was ironic that Vince's girlfriend might well have been saved by the work of plant hunters, maybe even the very people who he disliked so much.

A noise in the stockroom woke me from my thoughts, I had been considering a dream I barely remembered. There was something about a drug company in it; it must have been triggered by Vince and the newcomers.

"Is that you, Marcus," I called out. When nobody answered I got up and went through into the stockroom.

There was some sort of argument in progress. I could see Marcus was on the floor, it looked like someone had knocked him out. Vince was stood with his back to me, facing a stranger. A tall, bearded man. I couldn't see his features properly in the shadows, he looked like one of the plant hunters. Hadn't we seen them two days ago, heading away from Richavon? I realised that we had only seen two in the black vehicle, this must be the third. He had a gun, pointing at Vince. I stayed out of sight.

"What have you done?" Vince asked the man.

"You should have kept your nose out, lover boy," sneered the man, he was definitely one of the plant hunters, it was what they had all called Vince, ever since they had arrived. "He saw what he shouldn't have, like you've just done."

"What are you on about, I haven't seen anything. I was looking for some of my equipment. What do you want with him, or with me?"

"All I wanted was to retrieve some of our gear; it's ended up in here somewhere. You should have kept your nose out, stayed with the woman and that bloke of hers, now it's too late for you to walk away."

"You can't point a gun at me," said Vince. "I'm—"

His words were cut off as the man shot Vince, twice. Vince was pushed back by the impacts; he fell without saying another word, an untidy heap of limbs on the hard floor. Blood started to pool.

I stepped back in shock and knocked a stack of boxes over. Instantly, the man turned. He started to come towards me, gun raised. "Who's there?" he said. He fired. The bullet buzzed past my ear. I felt its heat. I heard it smack into the doorframe.

That was enough for me, I was out of there. I turned and ran for the back door, I could see the trees. Safety was twenty yards away. I stumbled out into the daylight, and just kept going. Running away from the horror of what I had just seen. I was waiting for the bullet that was coming my way. One dug up the ground about a foot from me, another went past me into a tree trunk, then I was out of sight, blundering through the bushes. I heard shouting behind me, a man's voice, "Stop him, he's just shot someone."

I kept going, deeper into the undergrowth, the branches and spiky leaves pulling at my clothes. I didn't care where I was headed. I went on, deeper into the safety of the trees. I didn't know what I was going to do. I could hear voices behind me as I pushed through the undergrowth. The branches held me back, pulling at me. I was so busy looking over my shoulder that I tripped on a root. I fell and it all went black.

CHAPTER THIRTEEN

EARTH

"WAKE UP. THAT'S ENOUGH." Cath was shaking my shoulder. "I know what's going on; we're going to sort this out, right now."

"What do you mean," I said, I felt confused, out of place. It was dark; just now it had been a bright sunlit afternoon. I had been running through Richavon. Then I remembered, this time it was all so clear. There had been a murder, I had to go back and tell Ove. No, the murderer had a gun and he was coming my way, I had to... wait a moment.

I was in my bed. Then I realised. I had been dreaming. The dreams were so much clearer now; it had all been so real. I still felt shock at what I had seen. At least one person was dead; I couldn't accept that it was only a dream. I was even out of breath for goodness' sake.

Here it was another dull grey morning and Cath was in uniform. She must have just got back from work. I hadn't set my alarm. It was Saturday; I didn't have to go to the office. I looked around; I was in my home with my wife. This was the reality; the only thing was, it felt less real to me than what had just been happening on Ecias.

Cath stood in front of me, her face stern, arms folded. I

thought that she was concerned about me. It was about time that I opened up and told her all about it. I couldn't cope with all the thoughts in my head anymore, I had to tell someone.

I sat up in the bed and took a deep breath. "You're not going to believe this, but I have to tell you," I began.

"OK," she said sarcastically. "Let's hear it, and it'd better be good."

I thought her tone was a little strange, putting it down to her having been up all night. The way I felt, exhausted and confused, it felt like I had as well. I started to tell her everything, Ecias, Vanessa, the murder I had just witnessed.

"You're right," she said, as I stopped for a moment. "I don't believe a word of it. You seem to have forgotten that it's only a dream, now according to you it's all real."

"But when I'm there, I don't know that it's a dream, it feels real."

"Well if it's real, that means that I'm the dream," she said, anger colouring her cheeks, "and given what you reckon you're getting up to, I find that particularly insulting. You're obviously here, with me."

"But just now, before you woke me up, I was there. I was running for my life. How can you tell what's real?"

In answer she stepped forward and slapped my face, hard. It stung, her wedding ring scratched across my cheek, just under my eyelid. It brought tears to my eyes. I tasted blood.

"What the hell was that for?"

"If you felt that, you're here, with me. You're not with some long-haired figment of your imagination that you're screwing on another *planet*. How do I know that's not just what you want to do to someone you know here? Maybe you already are?"

This was all going so wrong; how could I convince her it was just a dream? Cath had got an idea into her head, I knew what that meant.

"Come on, Cath, I wouldn't do that, I love you. I'm just as

messed up as you are, but I need to talk to someone. I can't keep it in my head any longer, it's driving me crazy."

"What about this then?" she said. She showed me her phone. She had found a picture of Esther Phay on the internet.

"She's the new client, isn't she?" She was shouting at me now. "Esther Phay, or is she Vanessa? She's got the long hair and brown eyes; she's got it all. Hell, the name's even the same. I wanted to hear your story, your sorry excuse, before I tell you what I think this is all about."

What could I say, my dreams had started before I had met Esther, but I hadn't told Cath all the details before now. I'd never mentioned anything about Vanessa before last night. What did she mean; the name was the same?

"I found the picture at work last night," she said. "I was telling the rest of the staff about your job with Phay and as it was quiet we had a look at them on the web. I found Esther Phay; now I can see that she's close to your description of this *Vanessa*."

"So are lots of people. Look, Cath, I don't know what you've got into your head but it's not like you think." I wanted to explain, I should have said something weeks ago. She didn't give me a chance.

"We did some more digging after I saw that picture; do you know what else we found?"

Had she got the whole nursing team looking into what they thought I had been doing? I could just imagine a bunch of them, bored on a night shift, working each other up. I didn't answer, so she carried on.

"Tina found it, the nurse I thought was bolshie when I met her. Well, it turns out she's alright; she just talks a lot when she's nervous." She stopped for effect. "She found the proof."

This was crazy, what proof? Nothing was happening, at least not on this planet, in this reality. Esther Phay and I had only just met, it was all just coincidence.

"There is no proof," I said, "because nothing's going on."

"Oh yeah?" she mocked. "How do you explain this nothing then? You've heard of Jonathon Swift, the author?"

Of course I had, but what did he have to do with anything? She never gave me a chance to answer. "He invented the name Vanessa," she said, her voice rising in pitch. Her face was red. "It was all to do with some woman he knew; funnily enough she was really called Esther. Esther came first, then Vanessa."

She took a deep breath, she was sobbing, my instinct was to put my arm around her, to tell her that she had got it all wrong, that it was all a coincidence. I moved towards her and she backed away.

"Keep away from me! Esther and Vanessa, two names for the same person. I guess you thought that was clever? Did you think I'd never spot it? As if that wasn't enough of a clue," she spat out the words. "Jonathon Swift wrote *Gulliver's Travels*, which just happens to be about a man's journeys to other worlds. That's pretty blatant! How could I be so stupid, it's a subliminal confession, you're having an affair with Esther Phay. You're pretending that she's called Vanessa. Pretending that it's only a dream. It all fits."

I didn't know where to begin, coincidence didn't really cover it.

CHAPTER FOURTEEN

WE SPENT the next hour arguing, really screaming at each other. The trouble was, I could see where Cath was coming from, no matter how much I insisted that I had seen Vanessa in my dreams before I had met Esther, it didn't make any difference. She had got it into her head that it was all some sort of cover up. That it had been going on for months. And just like she was with medical things, once she had an opinion, that was it.

How I wished that I had just said something more about Vanessa before I had mentioned Esther Phay. I mentally cursed the nurse who had found that little fact about the names. I'd read *Gulliver's Travels* as a child, probably seen it on the TV but that was about it. I knew nothing about the author, apart from the fact that the book was supposed to be a sort of satire on the rotten state of the nation at the time.

In the end, Cath locked herself in the bedroom. I could hear a lot of noise, I thought that she would be going to sleep but she appeared to have forgotten that she had been up all night. After about an hour she came out, dressed in jeans, wearing a thick coat and dragging a suitcase. She announced that she was going to stay with her mother for her days off, and for the foreseeable future.

"I need to think," she said, before I could protest my innocence again. "I don't want to listen to you or have anything to do with you. I'm sure I know what's going on; I need to decide what I'm going to do about it. Perhaps you can sort out your head while I'm gone, have the balls to admit it, even if it's only to yourself." The door slammed behind her and I heard her car start and pull away.

I looked in the bedroom; her side of the wardrobe was half empty, the drawers open with clothes scattered on the floor and the bed.

How had I got myself into this mess? I was trying to rationalise it all in my head. I was still worried about Vanessa's safety on Ecias, now that there was a murderer about, had he killed Marcus as well as Vince?

I had to catch myself; it was only a dream, wasn't it? It had all felt so real. While I was asleep I was Dan on Ecias, Cath waking me up had proved that it wasn't reality though. Unless Ecias was real and this was the dream. I felt my face, felt the blood on my cheek.

If this was a dream then it was as realistic as Ecias was. Here must be the reality, Ecias was the dream. I would probably be back there tonight when I slept, all would be well. I looked at my face in the bathroom mirror, there was a swollen cut under my eye, a thin line of blood had dried on my chin. I was getting a headache.

The pain convinced me this was reality, Ecias was the dream. It didn't matter what happened there, all that was important now was getting Cath back. I was worried about her, driving after a night shift and an argument, I remembered only too well what had happened to Claire.

In the back of my mind, a small voice kept saying, "Vanessa's in danger, Dan; it's all up to you."

But I didn't go back to Ecias that night, maybe it was because I was in a state of shock over the way Cath had reacted. Or maybe it was due to the half bottle of whisky that I went out and bought because I was feeling sorry for myself. I was a beer drinker by choice, but I needed the hit of alcohol, without the volume.

OK, so I could understand her being annoyed at the way things looked, but leaving me? And without giving me a chance to explain. It seemed to be an overreaction, Cath might have been impulsive, I just hoped that she wasn't stupid enough to believe it once she had calmed down. I'd always got on well with her mother, maybe she would talk some sense into her?

In the end, I never got as far as taking one of my tablets or clearing up the mess in the bedroom. I drank the whisky on an empty stomach, wallowed in disbelief and self-pity for a while and fell asleep on the sofa.

I slept soundly and dreamlessly, not waking until late on Sunday morning, with a sore head, a crick in my back and an empty feeling in my heart as well as my stomach.

It felt like half of me had been ripped away, Cath and I had been long term lovers long before we had been married; we had been an item for years. Why couldn't she see that it was all a great big coincidence?

I had to admit that it was incriminating, though. The first thing I did was to look on the web. All the stuff about Jonathon Swift was there. He had tutored a woman called Esther Vanhomrigh, making the name Vanessa from the Van of her surname and Essa, another version of Esther.

That was damming enough in its own right, and enough to raise her suspicions even if I had have told her about Vanessa before I had mentioned Phay. I couldn't believe my situation. If I had tried, it would have been hard to make things worse for myself. There was no room for me to manoeuvre; every angle I could use to try and explain only led to the same conclusion.

I made myself coffee and sandwiches, then I spent the rest of

Sunday typing out my dreams of Ecias on my laptop, as much as I could remember. I had been meaning to do it for a while as the dreams had got clearer. I found that doing that made me recall more and more, it might have only been a dream but my subconscious had created an incredibly detailed world.

I remembered the interviews with Burgstrom, including the psychiatric evaluations. The acclimatisation tapes we had listened to on the trip from Earth. All the facts and figures about the planet, where it was, when it had been found. My life there was six hundred years from now. Humankind had expanded across the galaxy. Ecias was one of several hundred inhabited planets. It orbited the star called 61 Virginis, in the constellation Virgo. Travel faster than light was a reality, I could remember how it worked; the engineer on the ship had explained it all. It was such a simple concept, it made perfect sense. I wrote it all down, along with the name of the largest moon orbiting Ecias, Claudius. I considered stopping to check the information but didn't want to interrupt the flow.

I wrote lists of the birds, animals and fishes of Ecias, the trees and plants. I remembered the taste of the ones we had eaten, the rodents and fish, the giant prawns, the fang, the deer which we called Sawgrass because of the way it moved its head when eating. I described the geese in detail, how I had hunted them for food when we were hungry in the forest. I mentioned Denise Harabus, and other significant names from the past of my future.

And I wrote about my job, the drone flying, hiking and rock sampling that was my reason for life on Ecias. My trailer in the woods, the one in town, Whistles and the people I knew. I included the plant hunters, Anna and Vince. I described Vince's death and my reaction.

And of course, I wrote about Vanessa. How we had met, on a survey operation on a planet called Robus. I had initially thought that she was well out of my league. She had laughed at my clumsy attempts to chat her up, then we had been assigned to work together. Somehow, we had clicked. I remembered her passion for wrestling and martial arts, her ability to do more physical labour than most men, her appetite for beer and her love of danger. I remembered the mole on her stomach and her love of silk underwear, incongruous under the dark boiler suits and simple white T-shirts that she always wore.

The information poured out of my head and onto the screen. I lost track of time, it was past midnight on Sunday by the time I had put every last detail that I could remember down. As soon as I thought I had exhausted a scene, more information came into my head.

When I read it back, I saw that I had even put down the shapes of the trees and their Latin names, which was crazy. We'd hardly been taught the English names for trees at school, never mind learning them in Latin. Even technical surveying terms had tripped from my fingers. I would have to check them up online, but there was no way that I should have known any of them. In the end I gave up reading it and went to bed.

I looked for the tablets, the bottle was gone. I remembered then that I had knocked it onto the floor; it would be under the clothes that Cath had scattered in her haste. I was contemplating looking for them when I fell asleep naturally.

For the second night, I slept reasonably well. The only thing was that my sleep wasn't filled with dreams of Ecias. I felt disappointed when I woke. I had expected to be there, I wanted to know where I had run to, and what had happened. I needed to know that Vanessa was safe. With all of the memories that writing it down had stirred up in me I was sure that I would have been back to get all the answers.

But nothing happened; the alarm woke me on Monday morning. Now I had work to face, together with awkward questions about my weekend.

CHAPTER FIFTEEN

I PRINTED my notes while I got myself ready to face the day at work. I wasn't going to tell Hughie or the others that Cath had gone if I could help it. I would have to think of how I could get around the painful truth. As the pages kept coming from the printer I realised that my life in my dreams was so much more detailed than any dream had a right to be. I did more on Ecias than I did on Earth, in less time. I couldn't work out how I spent weeks there in a single night.

I stuffed the pages in my briefcase; I might get a chance to look at them if it was a quiet day. I needed to check out all the technical terms as well as the Latin. And do a lot more research on dreams.

I was determined to act as if nothing much had happened over the weekend. At least the tablets seemed to have reset my sleep pattern, which was about the only good thing to have come of the whole mess.

When I arrived in the office, Molly told me that Hughie was out all day, wooing clients at a trade fair, he had taken Deanne with him, for experience. I did an hour or so on the Phay posters, but I couldn't settle, the papers in my bag were calling me. Molly was involved in something in Hughie's office; she needed the big table to lay out her latest project.

I took the chance to go online and look up some of the surveying and technical terms that I had written down. If Molly noticed and said anything, I would tell her that it was research for Phay.

I typed the first thing I had written that I didn't understand into the search engine. It was a surveying term. Real Time Kinematic. The internet told me that it was a signal enhancement method for GPS position fixing, somehow in my dreams, I knew that. I had only got to the second word when the auto-complete filled in the rest. To say that I was surprised to see that it was real and matched what I thought it was would be an understatement. Where had I got the knowledge of that from? It wasn't a subject that had ever interested me.

But more concerning was the fact that as I went on, the technical terms that I typed in gave fewer results, most of the ones connected with drones and spaceflight either came up unknown or with lists of theoretical references.

Apparently, I was dreaming in detail of things that hadn't been invented yet, things that were just ideas in research. Yet in my dreams, six hundred years from now, they were functioning. Spaceships traversed the galaxy using a method of propulsion that was as much a dream on Earth as my life on Ecias was. I hadn't even started on the Latin names. I didn't need to rush, I was sure that they would all match up as well.

Molly came out for lunch; the sandwich man came around and we bought from him. She was quiet, I knew that she was friendly with Cath; perhaps the two of them had talked over the weekend. I tried to find out.

"Are you alright, Molly?" I asked. "You're a little quiet today."

"I'm fine," she said. "I'm just worried about Hughie. It's Claire's anniversary this week, when he goes to Randalls for their big party. I know he's upset."

I'd not realised that it had come around so quickly, where had the year gone?

"How's Cath?" Molly asked. I tried not to look guilty.

"She's fine, just finished nights, she's gone to see her mother for a few days."

"That's good, I like Cath. You look after her, Rick; you don't know how lucky you are with her."

There was no trace of anything but genuine feeling in her voice. She had never said anything like that to me before, the memory of Claire's loss must have prompted it. She can't have spoken to Cath. I nodded. "I will, she only went on Saturday and I miss her already."

The two of us had a leisurely lunch, after that I gave up on my list and got on with designing the posters for Phay. I realised that I could use the ideas that she had given me and combine them with the things I had written for a travel company job that never materialised, maybe I could even use a bit of the Ecias stuff as well. If it was all there, in my mind, giving me so much grief, then it might as well make itself useful.

In the end I came up with the concept of portraying Phay as a group of intrepid plant hunters, scouring the globe for natural remedies. I used silhouettes of people, looking in obscure landscapes as a hook for the project. I made up about ten rough posters, one for each product. Each was based on my dreams, using the exploration of Ecias and the discoveries on Tontranix as a tag for the drugs. 'We've explored the world for you', the posters said, 'and found these new natural remedies'. Cheesy but effective, the pictures were superimposed on tropical landscapes and ocean views; they implied freshness, exotic roots and mystical healing powers.

I added the drug boxes and a few descriptive words to my pictures. I printed out big copies and put them on Hughie's desk, with a note. If he liked them, he could pass them on to Phay. We would have to see what Esther thought. Hopefully, we would soon be rid of her contract and I could prove to Cath that I wasn't seeing her.

Molly announced that she was finished for the day. I decided that I was too; she said that she would wait in the office until Hughie returned. "He needs a proper meal, he forgets to eat for days sometimes," she told me. I had never taken much notice, he ate when we ate, we went to lunch with clients, but thinking about it, the number of takeaway wrappers in the bin decreasing.

I left Molly and headed home deep in thought, would I sleep tonight, would I go to Ecias, what had happened there since my last dream? I hoped against hope that Cath had changed her mind, that reason had prevailed. She might be at home waiting for me.

When I arrived the lights were off, the heating hadn't come on. Her car was missing. The house was cold and empty.

In a way I was glad. I hadn't tidied up the bedroom; Cath had dumped her stuff all over the place while she was packing, it needed putting away. Knowing her, she would come in ready to talk, then get side-tracked and angry that I hadn't bothered keeping the house clean. We would end up arguing over that, all our good intentions wasted in trivia.

I folded her clothes and put them away, tidying as I went. When I had done, I expected to find the bottle of tablets on the floor. But they weren't there. I checked the clothes; to make sure that I hadn't folded them in together. There was no sign of the bottle, or the lid. Cath must have taken it, or hidden it, there was no other explanation. I remembered knocking the bottle over when I had taken the last one, she must have decided that I wasn't having any more and removed them.

I shouldn't have been bothered one way or the other, I was sleeping properly without them, what was more worrying to me was that I hadn't gone back. It was crazy, but I found myself feeling emotional for the place. I wanted to know what had happened. Was that weird, did it make me mad? And what would

I say to the doctor when I went for my follow-up? How could I explain what had happened without him thinking that I was crazy?

Thinking of the doctor, he had told me that it would only take three days to break the cycle of insomnia, and he'd been right. He had told me to take all the tablets and I hadn't. What was more unsettling was that I hadn't dreamt since Friday night, it was now Monday. Surely, I would return to Ecias soon, unless it really was all just a random thing, caused by lack of sleep, the tablets, stress, boredom; who knows what?

But I didn't go back on Monday night. I fell asleep without any help, again I didn't dream, or if I did, I didn't remember it. I stayed firmly on Earth. When I woke on Tuesday I felt fine and rested.

I arrived in the office to find Hughie in a good mood. "The stuff you gave me yesterday," he said, "Molly showed it to me when I got in last night. I sent it off to Phay and they came straight back, even though it was late. They liked the ideas, well done."

"Did Molly wait for you last night?" I asked. He looked at me suspiciously.

"No, she never does, I mean she left me a note to look at them." He had answered far too quickly. Not only that he looked away from me as he said it. The sly old... surely they weren't? Molly was a bit older than both of us, still very attractive but... It was none of my business. And it was me who had left the note, not Molly.

Molly had her head in her screen, it would not be polite of me to question her, best to leave it. I had the support of the people here, no sense in stirring things up, Molly and Hughie were both single adults, what they did was their business. And talking about it in front of Deanne would ensure that everyone in town knew by tonight. Apart from that, I didn't know Molly's situation, she never gossiped, or let on about any sort of home life. In fact, she never had much to say about anyone. She was a gentle, kind soul, a lot like Claire in that respect. I'd hate to upset her with unfounded rumours.

"Thanks, I'm glad you liked them," I said, and then I had a thought, perhaps I could ask Esther for some tablets if I started waking again. I still had more than a month to go before my follow-up appointment.

"How's Cath?" asked Hughie and I wondered if I should tell him.

"She's fine," I answered. "She's got a couple of days off, she's staying with her mother." It wasn't the whole truth but it was as near to it as I felt like sharing. And it was what I had told Molly.

"Great, we should go and get drunk somewhere," was his reply, just what I wanted!

"Not tonight, maybe tomorrow," I said, putting him off, the last thing I needed was a drunken night out with Hughie. I'd only end up regretting it, or saying too much after a few drinks.

"I'm away tomorrow," he answered. "I've got to go and see Randalls; I'll be away for a couple of days."

Randalls, Molly and I had talked about it yesterday. Apart from the obvious connotations, it was a good idea, at least business wise. Randalls was a big client, a manufacturer with a big budget. This was Hughie's yearly reward, a corporate knees-up. He would probably get some new work as well; it also meant that we could do some more chilling in the office, sitting around chatting and indulging on the takeout while he was gone.

He never said anything to indicate that he knew what this was the anniversary of. I thought I caught him looking sad as he went into his office. Was it really a year ago that we all had said goodnight to Claire, little knowing it was the last time we would see her alive.

There was nothing much for me to do while we waited to see what Esther would say. I spent most of the day polishing up my portfolio and sneaking a look at my list of Latin names. In every case, the genus was right but a lot of the species and all of the variety names were unknown. Considering that gardening and Latin were about as interesting to me as surveying, it was downright weird to find out how much I knew about all three subjects.

By the time I decided to call it a day and head off home, I was beginning to reach some very disturbing conclusions. One of which was that somehow, I was seeing the future. If that wasn't bad enough, the other option was worse. I was mad, and inventing things in my head.

I didn't dream on Tuesday night either, that was the fourth on the trot that I hadn't. Not only that, I woke up a couple of times. Any effect that the tablets had must have been wearing off. Or maybe it was stress. I wanted to talk to Cath, to try and explain but I hesitated to call her. I wanted to tell her that she was right; it looked like it was all a dream. I couldn't see how, but the Phay thing had to be a coincidence. It wasn't just that, I had been told not to stop taking the tablets. Cath knew that, why had she taken them? Was it to stop me going to Ecias? I needed to know. And I think that the Hughie thing was playing on my mind, what if the last time I had seen Cath was when we were arguing?

CHAPTER SIXTEEN

WEDNESDAY WAS a relaxing day in the office, without Hughie to keep us focused we sat around and chatted most of the time, had a leisurely lunch and finished early. I had to buy food on the way home. I had run out of everything fresh. I didn't know whether to get enough for both of us, in the end I just bought a few basic things for myself.

Then, on the Wednesday night, not only was it difficult getting off to sleep, when I finally did drop off I had a very blurred glimpse of what was happening on Ecias. It wasn't like the usual immersive experience, more like as if I was watching a film, instead of being a part of it.

I was moving around in the forests near Richavon. I could see the buildings through the trees every now and then. Vanessa was searching for me. Although I couldn't tell what was happening, it was obvious that I hadn't gone back into town. I could feel fear; it must have been from being shot at, it felt like I was being hunted. I was hiding, living in the forest, eating berries and drinking from the streams as I kept moving, close to Richavon but out of sight. And Vanessa wasn't alone, just about everyone was there, side by side in a long line, searching through the trees. I must have kept going after I had regained consciousness and now I was being sought. Was it to kill me or was it for some other reason? Why couldn't they find me? I must have dumped my EPIRB.

I came across the plant hunters at some point in my wanderings. They were camped in a clearing, I managed to get close to them. I could hear them talking, they were in a good mood, laughing and drinking what looked like whisky from plastic tumblers.

"So the plan's on track then?" one said. It was impossible to tell them apart, all dark haired and bearded, they wore grey boiler suits with 'Tontranix' embroidered on the backs. I knew who Tontranix were, could that be the name of the company that they really worked for. I was sure that the boxes I had seen had said something else, Kalesh or some other company.

"I never thought they would have let all our stores in unchecked." They passed the bottle around. "Not just the hooch but all the supplies for the main party."

"That was a stroke of genius, getting the load mixed up; it kept them away from the camp, distracted them from examining the crates."

"We're all set for the next bit of mayhem then, destabilising the system here will be easy, Burgstrom will never know what hit them. Once we have them all running around and chasing shadows, we can call the reinforcements in, we can get phase two moving."

What were they on about? Was this an invasion, a takeover? This was all information that I had to give to Ove.

"That Vince almost screwed things up though, I'm sure that he was on to us."

"He got what was coming to him." Looking at the one who spoke, he was the one I hadn't seen in the vehicle, he can't have been with them that day on the road. He must have been the one that shot Vince. The others joined in the laughter. "We were lucky, he should never have disturbed me and perhaps I shouldn't have shot him but it all works in our favour."

"What about the other person who disturbed you?"

"I knocked the barman out, he never saw me coming. It was like rush hour in there! Just when I thought I could get away, another one turned up. That was the fit woman's husband, Vanessa and Dan or whatever their names were. I recognised the shirt. I put a bullet or two past his ear, to encourage him. He ran away, the coward. I didn't want to kill him, he's more useful alive. We can implicate him; it'll take the heat off us."

"Yeah, it was a bit of luck him being alone with you and the other man unconscious. He makes a perfect murderer, especially after Vince and his wife were smooching like that. It'll be easy to convince anyone that he did it."

"And all we have to do is say we were together, alibi each other, the beacons back at the camp will prove it."

"Have you dumped the gun?"

"Yup, I hid it in the log-pile behind their cabin."

"We're in the clear," another muttered. "They'll think that Dan killed him, when he's out of the way we can grab the wife, we could share her around for a while, it'd be fun."

"Bit of a bonus," said another. "She was wasted on him. If we get them looking for her too, that'll be more distraction." There was laughter while they argued who would get to go first with my wife.

That made me very angry; I just wished that I had a gun, or a voice recorder. Perhaps I could circle back to my place, pick up the gun he said that he had dumped there. The way they were talking made it sound like I was being set up. I crept slowly away, I needed to give myself up, to see Ove and tell him that I hadn't killed Vince, convince him to check out the plant hunters. It sounded like they worked for Tontranix, who were planning to take over Ecias.

The image faded as I woke up.

I lay there, alone in the early morning and shook, so much for my idea that it had all been a series of dreams, life on Ecias was proceeding, maybe not how I wanted it to, but it was carrying on, my dream life was carrying on. I knew then that I had to get back regularly. I had to see the story through to the end. I knew that I was innocent of killing Vince; all I had to do was prove it to everyone else. Not only that, I had to ensure Vanessa's safety, there was no way that I could let those three get their hands on her.

I couldn't rely on the possibility of dreaming. Cath had taken my tablets. The effect of the ones I had taken was wearing off. Esther Phay seemed like my best and only hope of getting more, to guarantee that I could return every night and sort things out.

I typed notes of all that I had seen and heard as soon as I was washed and dressed, adding it to the file on my laptop. Printed copies went into my briefcase.

CHAPTER SEVENTEEN

THURSDAY AT WORK was the best day I had had for ages. The three of us were doing the bare minimum of actual work while Hughie was away at Randalls. There was lots of laughter and joking, it cheered me up after the last week, the shock of Cath leaving and the dream shock of finding that I was being set up for a murder I hadn't committed.

Why couldn't I have dreams of sandy beaches and fun? It occurred to me that I had, that the arrival on Ecias of the plant hunters had spoiled everything in that world. When I came to think about it, the arrival of Phay had coincided with it all going wrong on this world as well.

I stopped analysing what I had just thought. If I had control of my dreams, it was me whose subconscious had introduced the plant hunters, the question was, why had I put them there?

The three of us had been enjoying a Chinese banquet for lunch and I was trying to remember things that one of the sleep counsellors had said about why we dream, when the phone rang.

"Creative Concepts," I answered it.

"Hi, it's Esther Phay," said the voice I recognised so well. "Can I speak to Hughie please?"

"Sorry he's not here. It's Rick, can I help you?"

"Rick, ah yes, it's actually you I wanted to talk to, about your work so far. I'm very pleased, well, I should say that the company is very pleased. There are a few things to iron out, nothing major, before we get on to the timing and placement. Can Hughie and you meet me later today?"

"Hughie's away until next Monday," I said. "I don't have the power to control those things, I'm just the copywriter."

"That's a shame," she replied. "I'll be away myself for a couple of days from tomorrow, I wanted to get this sorted out before the weekend if I could. Tell you what, can you come over and let me explain what I want, give you our point of view. Then if Hughie knows what we want, and what we're willing to compromise on, he can set it all up in my absence. I can just check it over when I get back."

It sounded reasonable to me. "Sure," I said. "I can come over now if you want."

"I'm off to see Esther Phay," I told the others. "I'll leave you to lock up, see you tomorrow."

"Be good," said Molly. "Don't do anything you shouldn't," added Deanne. I laughed as I left. With the amount of trouble I was already in, I wouldn't dare. Perhaps I should have taken one of them, as a chaperone.

Phay Medical had offices in town, with a huge underground car park, which was handy. I rose up in a lift into the reception area, where I was met by Esther Phay. Dressed in another dark trouser suit with a white blouse she looked every inch the top executive. Her hair was tied back, exposing cheek bones that could slice bread, just like Vanessa had.

"Hi, Rick," she said, shaking my hand. There was the same spark in me that I had felt before that she still didn't notice. "Come up to my office and let's get started."

We talked for an hour or so, coffee flowed. We sat opposite each other at a huge glass topped desk, she had poster sized versions of the work that I had produced, laminated so that she could write on them. They were already covered in black marker lines and notes. She knew a lot more than I had expected about advertising, her queries and suggestions were logical. I had to keep my wits about me to keep up with the stream of ideas. In the end we changed a few things, but I managed to persuade her that others were best left alone. She was intrigued when I said that we could interchange the drugs and captions on the pictures. She hadn't thought of doing that, which surprised me, she had cottoned on to so much else.

"I'm happy with the work you've done, and what we've achieved today," she said, as we finished debating the last of the posters. I was particularly pleased with it, a sunset over a forest, the shadow of a man stretched across the scene, a box of throat lozenges and the words 'We found nature's best for you'.

OK, it was cheesy but it captured the message that I wanted to convey. She leant back in her chair and stretched her arms out over her head, slowly. Her back arched. I tried to keep my gaze somewhere else.

"Tell me," she said, "where did you get the idea for the campaign?"

As I looked across the table at her, I realised that she didn't just remind me of Vanessa, she was identical to her. Even the dark blue trouser suit looked like the overalls she always wore, together with the white vest underneath. At that moment the low afternoon sun broke through the clouds and illuminated her head, like a halo. I almost blurted it all out, then I stopped myself. Ecias had got me into enough trouble with Cath. I had no idea what her reaction to that sort of admission would be, so I decided to go for the official version.

"I thought that it fitted with your ethos," I said. "The intrepid natural plant hunters eschewing modern gene splicing and molecular engineering to use the gifts of nature."

"Very poetic," she said. "And as it happens, exactly right. That's our philosophy, and it always will be." She lowered her arms, got up and moved around the table. "Can I let you into a secret?"

"Sure." I wanted to move away, without making it obvious, her closeness and her resemblance to Vanessa was making me feel very uncomfortable. I was stuck in the chair as she stood over me; the swell of her chest under the dark blue jacket was level with my head.

"I've never told anyone this before," she said. "My father believes that one day we will travel to other worlds."

Oh hell, had she guessed somehow? Was this a hint, maybe she shared my dreams? No, that was getting silly.

"That's hardly a secret; I think that we will too."

She looked flustered, suddenly not the assured business-woman. "I'm explaining it badly; he thinks that in the future, companies like ours will send plant hunters to harvest medicines from other worlds."

"It sounds possible," I said, thinking about the three plant hunters that had caused so much trouble on Ecias. "But surely it won't be for years."

"Oh no, it'll be hundreds of years from now, but when I was little, he used to say that one day, part of my DNA would carry on, it would explore an alien planet, it got me so excited."

This was getting really spooky. Again I wondered if she was playing with me, her comments were all made as if she knew and was trying to get me to admit it. I was about to try and say some-thing to lead the conversation in a different direction when I was saved.

Her secretary put his head around the door. "Excuse me, Ms Phay," he said. "It's six and we'll be shutting up now."

"Thanks, Vincent." She glanced at the clock on the wall. "Look at the time," she said. "Your wife will be cross that I've kept you so late, with the rush hour traffic as well."

"How do you know about my wife?" I meant to say it quietly;

with all the tension I felt it came out as a sort of accusation. She looked at me, puzzled.

"I'm sorry, you should have been told. We do a vetting check on all our contractors; it's a standard thing, what with industrial espionage and all that. We know about you and Cath, she's a nurse, right?"

I felt insulted, violated even, by the casual intrusion. Not that we had any secrets, but she hadn't mentioned it when we took the job. Maybe she had told Hughie and he hadn't passed it on? If she knew that about me, what else did she know? Did she know about the drug trial?

"I'm in no rush," I said. "Cath's at her mother's so I'm home alone." As soon as I said it, I regretted it. I was so wound up with thoughts of Vanessa and me on Ecias, her proximity had unsettled me. Not only that, it felt like Esther knew about it too.

"That's good, you can come and have dinner with me," she said. "I'm home alone most nights myself. People don't seem to stay in my life for long." There was little I could do to get out of it. I seemed to be in another one of those situations where you can't escape, whatever you do. 'Be good,' Molly had said. I was in danger of breaking that one. I had to make sure that I made a better job of following Deanne's advice.

As we left the office the secretary gave me a disapproving glance. "Let's go to my favourite restaurant," she said. "They keep a table for me, you'll love the place." She asked me if I knew where the 'Avon' was.

Did I know? I had wanted to take Cath there for ages; I was saving up for an anniversary treat. And she had a table reserved there permanently, how the other half lived.

"Did you come over by taxi?" she asked as we waited for the lift.

"No, my car is in the underground car park," I replied.

"Great," she said. "I'll let you drive."

Fortunately my car was relatively clean inside, she relaxed into the seat like she was at home. When we arrived, I handed the keys to the doorman. "I'll put it around the back for you," he said, shaking his head at it, clearly he was used to driving better. He managed to move it without stalling and we went inside. There was a queue for tables. Esther was spotted and greeted like a long-lost friend by the maître-d.

"Hello, Ms Phay," he drawled, washing his hands with invisible soap, "and your companion, let me show you to your table."

We dined on seafood, fillets of white fish with a salad and steamed potatoes. It was the same as we had eaten at our lunch, when Hughie was there. "My favourite," she said. "It's the only animal flesh I'll eat."

We talked about nothing much, the weather, the other diners, just small talk really. I started to relax, before I knew it we were on coffee.

Then I ignored Deanne's advice, I offered to take her home.

"Come up for a nightcap," she suggested, and I wondered if that was all she had in mind.

With the state of my marriage, the last thing I needed was any more problems. I was already committing adultery with Vanessa in my dreams; as far as Cath was concerned I was doing it with Esther Phay in reality as well. I didn't need to prove it to her. But I still felt unable to leave; it was almost as if I was committed, like a moth heading towards a light.

Her apartment was in an expensive block, overlooking the river. The lobby was all marble, a uniformed security guard and lots of cameras. The lift was carpeted and bigger than my living room. The apartment door opened onto a hallway, ahead was a room with a huge picture window.

"Go through, make yourself at home," she said. "I won't be a moment." She disappeared and after a moment I heard water running, she must have been taking a shower.

I looked around the apartment; it was decorated in a simple style, the sort that costs so much for so little. It was like a show house, impressive but not homely. There was a bookcase, filled with textbooks on botany, organic chemistry and bound volumes of medical journals.

And there was a glass topped display case, with insects mounted on card, like they do in museums. They all had little printed labels; one in particular caught my eye. The lighting in the case made its wings sparkle as my head moved closer to look at it. It was a mayfly; according to the card it was attached to, it rejoiced in the name *Ecdyonurus Criddlei Iascani*. Maybe this was the one that provided the drug I was taking. It would give me something to talk about when she returned.

The card had been typed on an old-fashioned typewriter, the letters were unevenly spaced, some were clearer than others. But five leapt out at me, E-C-IAS. I shook my head, that was just crazy. It was like when you own a blue car, all you see are blue cars. I was finding references everywhere; my brain must be working overtime to make these connections.

I turned away from the display case and looked out of the window, down on the city, it looked like an ants' nest, filled with lights moving in ordered patterns as the cars followed the roads, stopping and starting with the rhythm of the traffic lights. In the darkness there was no sense of nature, just man's presence.

"Sorry, I wanted to get changed out of that suit," Esther called from behind me. "I like to leave working clothes behind when I get in and be more feminine." As she came into the room I smelt oranges, mixed with some sort of musk.

I turned; she had let her hair down and was dressed in a simple black dress, tight and very short. I could see a vertical line on her thigh, surely she wasn't wearing black stockings under it? She wore shiny black high heeled shoes. She looked incredible as she walked to a table by the bookcase and poured herself a drink of something. I averted my eyes as she bent over the table. "Want one?" she asked. I got the feeling that I was out of my depth.

"No thanks, I've got to drive," I answered, eager not to give her an excuse to get me to stay. She shrugged her shoulders.

"Of course, I'll get you a coffee, it was black wasn't it, I remember from your office." She left again, I heard the rattle of a coffee machine.

She came back in with my coffee and placed it on a table beside the large leather sofa that dominated the room. "Come here," she said. "Let's sit and talk."

We sat side by side on the sofa, she drank her whisky and I sipped my coffee. I wondered if I could take the chance of asking for some more of the tablets. I couldn't help notice that the dress rode up as she made herself comfortable. Its movement proved that she was in fact wearing stockings. Surely they hadn't been under the suit? If she had got out of the shower and dressed like that for me, I was in over my head. If she had checked me out, did she know that Cath had gone?

"Can I be honest with you, Rick?" she asked. I wondered what she would say next.

"It depends." I was cautious, what would she want? Her attire and attitude screamed a message at me. 'Get out, while you can!' it was loud in my head. If I was following Deanne's advice that's what I should do, never mind what she was about to tell me.

"I know you're on the trial of Calpropogin, can I ask you how it's going?"

Of course she did, she knew everything else about me. I still clung to the hope that I could get more tablets from her. I had to think of that, it distracted me from thinking about her, about what was under the dress.

"They worked on the second night," I said. "But since I've stopped taking them the problem has come back."

"Why did you stop?" she demanded. "The recommended course is two weeks; we need subjects to take the full course as part of the trial. The consultant should have told you that."

"The consultant said it should work in three days," I began and she frowned.

"Well that's true but he shouldn't have prejudiced your subconscious. Let me guess, Cath, being a nurse, decided that you'd had enough."

I had to admit that she was right, but not for the reason that she thought.

"You should take the rest," she said. "Tell Cath that I said so."

Now I had a choice, could I tell her that Cath was gone and that she had taken the tablets with her? But then I would have to tell her why she had gone. Or did she know? She seemed to know everything else about me. Was that why I was here, because she knew that Cath had gone and thought that I might be available? If I was available, would she give me any more of the tablets in return?

I tried to be loyal. "I'll tell her you said so."

She nodded. "Good. Are there any side effects, some people have reported sweats and hallucinations?"

"No," I said, I reckoned that as the dreams had started before I had taken any tablets, then they didn't count as hallucinations.

"OK, how about any lucid dreams?"

That was slightly more difficult. "What are they?" I asked.

"They're dreams so real that you think they are real," she replied. "But at the same time, in your dream you know that they aren't." She had slipped into expert mode, she spoke like a lecturer would. "A lucid dream is defined as a dream during which the dreamer is aware of dreaming. During lucid dreaming, the dreamer may be able to exert some degree of control over the dream characters, narrative, and environment."

I hesitated before replying and I think that she realised that there was something there that I wasn't telling her.

"Please." She took my hand, there was that jolt again. This time, in my mind, I saw Vanessa's rear, sticking out from under the bonnet of the buggy. That didn't help me one bit.

"You need to tell me," she urged. "It's vitally important."

Put like that, I suppose that I had to, she made it sound like it was important to the drug trial. And to be fair, it probably was. I'd had the Vanessa dream in snatches before I'd taken any tablets, but just two had clarified them and made my life there feel so much more real. OK, so I didn't realise that I was dreaming whilst I was on Ecias but I certainly felt like I was in control of my life there.

"Do you promise that you won't think I'm some sort of madman?" I asked her.

She kept her hand on mine. "I promise," she said, her voice had dropped almost to a whisper.

It all came out in a rush; I told her everything, all my dreams. I told her about my life on Ecias, about my life with Vanessa and everything that I could remember. I got so wrapped up in the details that I even told her about the sex, and that Vanessa was a lot like her to look at. As I did, her eyes widened and she looked more and more surprised.

She stopped me before I could describe the shooting of Vince. "That's enough," she said. "I don't want to hear any more."

She must have come to some sort of decision, she pulled away and stood. She reached under her arm and I heard a zipper. She shrugged her shoulders somehow; the dress fell around her ankles. My eyes took in the pearl silk lingerie, the suspenders and the stockings. Then I saw it. There was the mole on her flat stomach, near her navel where I remembered it on Vanessa. In my mind I was kissing it, like I had so many times.

She moved a lot closer to me, stood still and raised her arms again, arching her back like she had in her office.

"Is this what you see in your dreams?"

"Yes," I croaked.

She reached forward and pinched my left forearm, it hurt but I tried not to shout. I didn't want to break the spell.

"Are you still here?" she asked.

I nodded and gulped. How much more could I stand, my resolve was fading. I tried to think of Cath, of tablets, of anything. She moved her hand and took mine, pulling me upright.

"Then it's not a dream," she said. She wrapped herself around me; her body in the silk lingerie was burning hot. I felt her breath on my neck. "You're doing it in your dreams, try the real thing," she whispered.

I was frozen to the spot, my arms at my sides. I knew that I shouldn't have been here, I should be off as fast as I could run but oh... I was tempted. Her hands were at the buttons on my shirt, urgently she fumbled with them, then she reached down.

CHAPTER EIGHTEEN

I PULLED AWAY. "I CAN'T," I said. "I'm sorry."

The spell was broken; it was her turn to be embarrassed. Suddenly she needed to cover herself. She picked up her dress and ran out of the room, the shoes clicking on the tiled floor. I breathed in for the first time in the last five minutes.

"It was wrong of me," she said, reappearing covered in a long silk dressing gown. "I thought that I felt something. I got it wrong, you shouldn't be sorry, it's me who needs to apologise."

That wasn't strictly fair. "It was me talking about Vanessa," I told her. "What we did, it can't have helped the situation."

She laughed, just like Vanessa did, but this time I knew it wasn't her. The tension was broken.

"You're a gentleman," she said. "Cath should appreciate you. Are we still friends?"

What could I say? "Of course we are, always."

"Good, I'd hate our business relationship to be difficult." She looked relieved. There was an awkward silence. We sat at opposite ends of the sofa, both looking ahead, avoiding eye contact.

"I think it would be best if I went," I suggested after a moment of silence.

She nodded. "Sure, take another tablet tonight. Please keep me informed." She paused. "Professionally of course."

I got home, relieved to have escaped with my honour intact. Deanne and Molly would have been proud of me. Whatever else she might think of me, I knew that I could still look Cath in the eye and tell her that I hadn't done anything with Esther Phay. She didn't need to know how close it had been. Then I wondered if Esther hadn't had her own agenda, she had said that she spent most nights alone, perhaps she had thought that I was available. At least she hadn't screamed at me to get out or threatened our working relationship.

There was a pile of post on the mat, it looked like a bunch of junk and bills. I'd look at that later, right now I had more important things to consider.

I should take another tablet, Esther had said. That was the problem. I couldn't take another one; Cath had made sure that I couldn't. I had already looked everywhere for the bottle. I hadn't been able to ask Esther for more.

I was far too awake for sleep to come naturally. In desperation I searched the bedroom and the bathroom again. I was hoping, praying, that Cath hadn't taken the bottle with her. Maybe she had just hidden them somewhere.

But I couldn't find it. Wide awake now, I ripped the house apart, even looking in places that I knew it couldn't possibly be. On my second or was it third time in the bedroom, I was on my hands and knees looking under the bed. In amidst the empty suitcases and bags of summer clothes, I found one tablet that must have fallen out when I had knocked the bottle over.

I gratefully swallowed it; I'd worry about what came next later.

CHAPTER NINETEEN

ECIAS

IT WAS the cold that woke me, that and the shouting. I was in a cave on the side of a hill, morning mist made the visibility poor. I could make out tree trunks but the view across to the sea, the view that had once seemed so captivating, was absent. I heard the shout again. "Here he is."

Vanessa appeared through the gloom.

"Dan," she said, she sounded anxious, her posture was wary, what was the matter? She had no reason to be frightened of me. I got up and moved towards her, she backed away.

"Stay there," she said. "Where have you been?" The sun behind her through the mist gave her a glow, like an angel.

"Moving about, waiting for them to leave," I said. "How long have I been out here, I've lost track?"

"Almost a week. When I last saw you, you and Vince were on the way to Whistles. When I arrived, Vince was dead, Marcus was unconscious. Ove said that he had heard shots, someone else saw you running away." She peered at me. "You've cut your face, under your eye, it looks infected. What do you mean; waiting for them to leave, who?"

She might have had all the facts, but she had come to the wrong conclusion.

"The plant hunters, one of them killed Vince, then he tried to kill me. That's why I've been keeping out of their way. Wait a moment; you don't think I killed Vince do you?"

Ove arrived at this point with two of the workers from the farm complex. They both carried cattle prods. Ove had a pistol in his hand.

"Dan," he said, there was no 'hello' or 'where have you been?' There was no friendship in his tone. "We know what you did. Do you still have the gun?"

"I don't have a gun." I remembered that the men had said they had hidden it behind our cabin but I kept quiet. "You can search me if you want."

Ove nodded and one of the farmers patted me down. He stood back and shook his head.

"Will you come quietly?"

So they did think it was me. "Listen, Ove," I said, "it wasn't me, I know who it was, I can point him out to you."

"Don't make it worse for yourself, Dan." He shook his head. "I'm sorry, I thought that you were a good guy but I'm forced to take you into custody for the murder of Vince Kendall and the attempted murder of Marcus Hayman. The authorities have been informed and are sending a police team to gather evidence. Now will you come quietly, or do I need to get these two to restrain you?"

"It wasn't me," I repeated. "I've just told Vanessa; it was one of those plant hunters."

"They're all over at the Canal," he said. "I've checked their EPIRBs; they're moving around over there, probably doing what they said they would."

This was crazy, I had seen them, here, only a few days ago. "They're not, they're in these woods. I don't even think that they're plant hunters. I heard them talking, they have some sort of plan. They had Tontranix boiler suits on, it's serious, they were talking about a takeover! You have to listen to me."

He shook his head. "I don't think so, is that the best story that you can come up with? You've had a week. If you were so innocent, then why did you run?"

"He was shooting at me, the plant hunter," I said desperately. "What did you expect me to do? Vanessa, tell them it wasn't me." I pleaded with her.

She stood silently. "I can't, Dan. I wasn't there, I thought that you liked Vince, I never thought that you'd kill him." She turned and walked away.

There seemed to be little point in arguing any more. "I won't make any fuss," I said. The two farmers, big tough men, were beside me as we walked back through the trees. They took me back into town in the back of a buggy. I was sat between them. Nobody spoke.

When we arrived the town was deserted, everyone must have been out trying to find me. We kept going, into the farm complex, through the safety fence. It was designed to keep animals out, now it was keeping me in. They threw me into a small room in the basement of the stores. It was the old administrative office, the place where Marcus threatened to put the drunks until they had sobered up. It had a chair, a desk, a camp bed and some office equipment, that was about it. There were two windows, high up; I would have to climb up on the desk to look out. When the door clanged shut I heard the sound of a padlock.

I sat there and considered my options. Ove had asked me why I had run. The answer was obvious to me, because I was being shot at. Why hadn't I just waited until the coast was clear and given myself up?

The trouble was that I couldn't remember much about where I had been or how I had hidden for so long. They should have found me straight away with the signal from my EPIRB. I took it from my trouser pocket, it wasn't working. There was no power switch, it was supposed to be on all the time, the battery was inside, it was sealed. The green light was off; I must have broken it when I was moving about in the woods.

I could claim that it wasn't me as much as I liked. And that I had heard the three talking in the woods when I had gone on the run. I needed hard evidence and if I was stuck in here could hardly go out and gather any. What I needed was Vanessa to get it for me. And for that, I needed her to believe me.

I banged on the door.

One of the farmers came to the other side, I heard his boots. "Shut up," he said.

"I need a drink," I shouted through the steel door, "and something to eat."

He laughed. "No chance, you can rot in there, after what you did. Why kill Vince? He seemed like a good lad, did you catch him and Vanessa at it while you were up in the mountains?"

Was that the story that was going around? It would give me a motive, but only if Vanessa didn't deny it. They had been wrestling in the bar before we had left but I had no reason to... I could see how it must look though, the three of us had spent time together, one woman and two men. Now one of the men was dead, it had to be jealousy, that was how minds worked.

"Did Vanessa tell you that?" I shouted.

"Of course not; it's just obvious to me. Now shut up, I'm not supposed to talk to you." I heard the boots as he moved away, the scrape of a chair as he sat. I could imagine him sitting in the sunshine, free. I sat on the bed and tried to think.

About an hour later the door opened. Ove was there, carrying a cup and a plate on a metal tray. He also had a bucket, with a lid. He came in and the door slammed shut behind him.

"Here you are," he said. "Maybe I should have brought this over sooner but I had paperwork to do, messages to send to Ventius."

Ventius was the nearest planet with a big city, administrators, police, civilisation. I'd never been. Vanessa had, apparently it was a bit of a dump. Now the authorities there would decide my fate.

There was a meal on the plate, the cup full of coffee. I was starving, I shovelled it down quickly, using my fingers to pick the food up. Ove obviously didn't trust me with a knife and fork.

"Listen, Ove," I tried again. "I'm innocent. OK, I shouldn't have run but I was scared, I thought I was going to be shot. They shot at me, three times, I can show you the bullets in the door and a tree. While I was in the woods, I heard some things you need to know." My words had the same effect as last time.

"Save it, I don't want any of your stories. Save it until the police arrive."

"But there's a plot or something, I overheard them talking about a plan and that Burgstrom wouldn't know what had hit them. They were wearing Tontranix boiler suits."

"Yeah right, like I said before, is that the best you can come up with?"

I wasn't going to get anywhere with him, he had clearly made his mind up. I had to try another tack.

"How's Marcus?"

"At last, I was wondering when you would ask. It shows your caring side." The look he gave me was not a friendly one. "He's awake but he can't remember anything, so he's not going to save your arse, he doesn't know who hit him, they sneaked up from behind."

"It wasn't me," I said. "What about the cameras in the storeroom?" I knew that Marcus had CCTV covering the stores, I had helped install them.

"You turned them off, didn't you?"

"No," I shouted, this was turning into a nightmare. I had been set up for this. While we were arguing, what were the real culprits up to?

"Why did you run, then?"

"I've told you, the man who shot Vince, he saw me and shot at me; three times. I ran from him."

He looked dubious, had he heard the shots, maybe he was counting them in his head. I knew Vince had been shot twice. Was I finally getting through to him?

"The police will be here in four days, the day after the supply ship," he said. He went to the door. "I have a settlement to run, I can't let you try and talk your way out of it. The police will sort it all out." He banged on the door and the farmer opened it.

"Can I see Vanessa?" I asked as he left.

"I'll think about it, she's really screwed up. She can't process the fact that you did what you did."

I was going to repeat that I hadn't, I saved my breath. He went out and I heard the lock click behind him.

The rest of the day passed slowly, I searched the room for anything useful. Not that I was intending to escape, I just wanted something to do. I found a case of bottled water and moved the furniture, so I could use the bucket without being seen from the door. There was a computer terminal but it was password protected. I had three unsuccessful attempts to login, then it locked me out. I found a first aid box and tended to the cut on my cheek, there were antibiotics and I took some, washing them down with the bottled water. I would have to take them for a week, to make sure they worked.

With nothing else to do I found a pad of paper in the desk drawer and wrote out as much as I could remember, to keep it from being distorted by the passage of time. All about what I had seen in the storeroom, the conversation I had overheard and the gun they had hidden. It won't have any of my fingerprints on it, I thought, at least I hadn't tried to go and get it. Already my recollection of things was getting hazy. One thing I did know. If the cameras in the storeroom had been turned off, then Vince's killing must have been more than just a random act.

When I had finished I fired up the copier and made three extra sets. One I placed in the filing cabinet, behind last year's stores inventory, it would never be found there. I folded up the originals and put them in my pocket. The other two sets I left on the desk, one set was for Ove, the other was for Vanessa.

It got dark outside, I used the bucket, laid on the bed, tried to sleep.

Next thing I knew it was morning, I had dreamt, a rare thing for me, I had been some sort of past world, in an apartment, looking out on a city below me. A woman's voice in my ear kept saying, "The fly, how did you know?" Before I could puzzle it out, the door opened.

Vanessa came into the room, she had brought me a bacon sandwich and a mug of coffee, it smelt incredible. The door shut behind her. "Is it safe?" she asked me as I ate.

"What do you mean? Do you think I shot Vince, do you think I would hurt you?"

"I don't know what to think, the police are coming. Ove has told them what he thinks happened. He said I could have ten minutes with you, if I wanted."

"And you believe him?"

"Vince was shot twice," she said. I knew that. "We've found a pistol, around the back of our trailer. Ove has got it, he said that the police will test it for fingerprints when they get here."

I knew that my fingerprints wouldn't be on it. "Did you tell him that I don't have a pistol, only the rifle I keep for hunting?"

"I said that as far as I knew you didn't have one," she replied. Why was she talking like that, so formally? Then I realised, there must be a recorder somewhere, she was trying not to say anything that might be used to incriminate me.

I gave her two of the sets of papers that I'd copied. "This is what really happened," I said. "Read it when you can, there's a set there for Ove as well."

The door opened. "Time's up," said a voice, a different man was guarding me today.

"I will," she said. "Don't worry." I moved to kiss her but she backed away, turned and left.

Time passed, Ove had told me that Marcus was OK, I was relieved about that. I liked Marcus; surely he would stick up for me? People would rally round, wouldn't they? I had been here a year, got on with everyone. Trouble had only started when the plant hunters had arrived. They had wound Vince up, tried to imply that I would be jealous of him and Vanessa. But anyone who knew me would see through that.

Ove brought me a meal in the late afternoon. He seemed happier, or at least not as unhappy to be in my presence. "I've read your statement," he said, "very detailed. Pity it doesn't agree with all the evidence but at least it's something."

"What bits of it don't agree?" I asked.

"I don't think that it's appropriate to talk about it," he said, glancing up at the corner of the room. So that was where the microphone was. I got the message; I would be better off keeping quiet until I got the chance to speak to the police.

"Is there anything else I can do to relieve the boredom?" he said.

"Can you let me use the computer?"

He shook his head. "No, we can't have you on the network. I've been told by the police to keep you isolated."

"What? You mean I can't see anyone until I've seen the police?"

"If it makes you feel better, I don't agree. So here's what I'll do. Vanessa can bring your meals in, but she'll have to be quick. At least you'll see her twice a day."

"Thanks," I said. "Can you empty the bucket?"

He laughed. "Sure, we have a replacement outside." He knocked on the door. "Bring it in," he shouted and the farmer wheeled a chemical toilet inside. He must have scavenged it from one of the spare trailers. It would be a lot more comfortable than the bucket.

They left, the door slammed.

CHAPTER TWENTY

THAT NIGHT, in my prison, I had another dream. This one crept in on the edges of my consciousness; I was in an office, then sitting on a sofa, telling Vanessa about a dream, about some tablets. It was all muddled up and made no sense. It must have been caused by the stress I was under, maybe it was the infection.

Vanessa brought my breakfast. "I've read your notes," she whispered. "I hope it's all true, I want to believe that it is."

"Listen, Vanessa, this is all so crazy, I almost wish that I could wake up, wish that this was all some crazy dream."

She laughed. "Well if this is a dream, what does this mean?" She reached over and pinched my right arm, hard.

"That bloody hurt," I shouted. Vanessa laughed.

"Sorry but it proves a point, you're not dreaming, you're here alright."

I had to concede that she was right. This was just getting me nowhere, if it was a dream, then when I woke I wouldn't have been in the cell.

"Come on out, Vanessa," said my guard. "I can't let you be in there any longer, Ove's orders."

"See you, Dan," she said, this time she kissed me. That made me feel better as the door closed behind her and I heard the lock click.

There was nothing else to do. I spent the day doing stretching exercises, napping and rehearsing what I would say to the police. I looked at my notes and made some amendments. I could understand why Ove wouldn't let me have the computer password, even though I only wanted to watch some videos. Vanessa didn't bring my evening meal over; the door opened a crack and a tray was shoved through the gap. "Thank you," I shouted but there was no answer. When I had eaten there was nothing to do but sleep, it was getting dark outside.

Daylight woke me up; I was still in the cell. Despite my hope that it was all a bad dream, it couldn't have been, whoever heard of falling asleep in a dream and waking in the same place more than once. The isolation was getting a bit much; there was still a wait before the police turned up. I wondered if I would be allowed to go for a walk.

I got up and went to the door. "Let me out," I shouted, hammering on the panel with both my fists.

There was silence.

"Hello," I shouted.

"What do you want?" the guard's voice said. "You've really messed things up, the supply ship's been delayed, we're in lockdown and the police are on the way. There's no beer left, thanks a bunch."

Oh, that was bad. I wasn't really getting the rest of the population on my side. My arms hurt, I looked at the mark on my arm where Vanessa had pinched me. There was something about it that didn't feel right.

CHAPTER TWENTY ONE

EARTH

I WOKE TO THE ALARM, I was back on Earth. It was time to get up and get to work. I rolled out of bed and headed for the shower. Memories of last night, Esther's apartment and my behaviour flooded back. They were all mixed up with bits of my dream, my captivity on Ecias.

While I was washing I ran my hand over the red mark on my right arm, where Ester had pinched it last night. It was red and very sore. Then I realised, Esther had pinched my other arm, my left. I looked down; there was a red mark on it too, a different shaped one. I rinsed the soap off and studied my arms, how had I got the same injury on both of them?

It hit me like a hammer blow to my head. The shock of the only possible explanation exploded across my senses. I felt sick. I actually retched and felt myself break out into a sweat, despite the coolness of the shower. I saw it again in my mind, just like I had in that room on Ecias. Vanessa pinching my right arm in the dream I had just awoken from.

What the hell was happening to me? This wasn't possible. Ecias was a dream; you couldn't injure yourself in a dream. I must have done it somehow, last night, when I was searching for the tablets. Except that I couldn't remember how, all I could see was Vanessa, hear her laughter at my yelp of pain.

At that moment, I was sure that I was going crazy. I racked my brains for a logical explanation, it didn't take me long to accept that there wasn't one.

I took photographs of both arms with my phone, then I set the timer, propped the phone on the table and got a picture of both arms together. They would be stored, date stamped, on my cloud, preserving the moment with no possibility of forgery. Looking at the pictures, I could see that both of the bruises were different, one had been made by someone with long fingernails; there were distinct marks in the flesh. Esther had long nails while Vanessa kept hers clipped short. She hated it but it stopped her getting dirt under them or breaking them in the hands-on environment of Ecias. The pinch that she had made had no nail marks. What was happening to me? It should have been impossible but the evidence spoke for itself.

As I dressed I realised that I had spent so long gazing at my arms that I was running late. I put two slices of bread in the toaster and looked through the letters that I had found last night.

Most of them were rubbish but there was one official looking one. When I opened it, I found that it was from a solicitor called Simon Walsh, who claimed to have been employed by Cath. In legal language it advised me that proceedings for divorce 'on the grounds of adultery over a period of several months, causing irretrievable breakdown', had begun. At least it didn't name Esther Phay directly.

Cath had wasted no time getting in touch with a solicitor. I had expected her to call me after a few days with her mother, who I'd always thought was a lot calmer. I'd hoped she would have talked Cath out of doing anything hasty. According to this, Cath must have decided that I had been unfaithful since my first dream, since the first time I had mentioned my alternative life. She had been characteristically quick to act.

The last paragraph suggested that I retain my own solicitor and encouraged me to pass on the information in the letter to them. Did we really need to take this road? It all seemed a little hasty.

I was surprised to find that this didn't hit me as hard as seeing the pinch marks had. At least it was logical, its familiarity was almost a relief. Up to that moment, Ecias had seemed more real to me than London did. Not only that, if solicitors were involved; I could have my say, they would have to listen to my story.

Before that, who could I confide in? Hughie was still away, Molly and Deanne were out of the question, anyone else that I knew also knew Cath. They would all be biased one way or the other, I needed a neutral. And what might happen at work, would there be some sort of reaction from Phay? Esther had said we were still 'friends' but in the cold light of morning, who knew? She might feel wronged or frustrated and decide to take it out on Creative Concepts in some way.

I ate my toast and went to work. I was still trying to act normally. At least Hughie wasn't there, he had one more day at Randalls and we would see him on Monday.

Life carried on, Molly sensed that something was bothering me and tried to talk to me about it. Deanne was hovering about and I managed to fob them off with a story about Cath and her mother being ill. It was enough to shut them up for a while. I couldn't concentrate on work, after lunch I called the company's legal advisor Clem Maslow and asked if I could meet him.

"Of course you can," he said, probably thinking it was work related and worth an hour's fees. "Come on over at three, I can fit you in between meetings. Do you want to give me a clue?"

"I'd rather not."

"OK, see you then."

I liked Clem; we knew him and Linda, his partner, fairly well. We socialised with them occasionally. Hughie called him his legal department but in reality he was just a solicitor specialising in business law who we retained. Mainly he advised on copyright and advertising, but he would know a little about the legal implications of the letter. And he wouldn't tell anyone what we discussed if I asked him not to.

There were groans from Molly and Deanne when I said I was leaving early, maybe they had planned the same and I had beaten them to it.

"Sorry," I said. "I have to see Clem. It's to do with the Phay job."

I only said that to give me an excuse to leave early and see him. Instead it raised their curiosity.

"Oh, is it to do with your meeting yesterday?" asked Deanne.

I must have gone red because she got excited. "I knew it, what's going on?"

"I can't tell you, Deanne, you'll find out when the time's right."

I left before there were any more questions, it would give them something to talk about while I was gone.

Clem's office was across town, very minimalist, and not in the expensive way that Phay's were. In fact, it was a bit rundown. If I had seen his office without knowing that he was very good at his job, I'd never have employed him for anything. But I knew he liked it that way. We chatted about families for a while, then I asked the biggie.

"Can I talk to you in confidence, Clem? It's a personal thing, nothing to do with Creative."

He frowned. "Of course, I'll help you if I can."

"I need to speak to someone; I got this." I showed him the letter from Cath's firm.

He read it quickly. "I'm sorry," he said. "And surprised. It seems a little hasty. I would have thought the solicitor would have suggested a cooling off period, or counselling, not gone all out like this."

"That's Cath," I said. "She's impulsive. She rushes in, won't let things rest."

He smiled, nodded. "Oh yeah, she gives that impression. Well, I know Linda talked to Cath a couple of nights ago, it upset her but she wouldn't say what it was about. OK, this is what you do, I don't want to know if you did it or not."

That seemed a little harsh, we were friends, weren't we?

"I'm too close to you," he explained. "I work for your employer and we're friends. Plus, it's not my area of expertise. I do know that you mustn't make any statements to anyone connected to you or Cath, or the other party, whoever that is. Keep away from them all. All contact with Cath should be formal, chaperoned is best."

That wouldn't be hard, what could I say to anyone that wouldn't make me sound certifiable?

He pulled open his desk drawer, rummaged around and gave me a card. "Go and see this man, he's an expert in divorce law, he'll get your side of the story. Your wife has already done the same, judging by what it says here."

I nodded. "Alright, what happens?"

"Well, when you've both done that, the solicitors will arrange a joint meeting where you can talk it out."

"Thanks, Clem, and just for the record, I didn't do it. I've been having some sleep issues and things have got out of hand."

He smiled. "I don't know what to say, I could make a joke about snoring, but it wouldn't be appropriate. Have you tried 4-7-8?"

"What's that?"

"It's a way of getting to sleep, I do it when I get stressed and it's great, it's all about counting while you breathe, you should try it."

His intercom buzzed. "Clem, I've got Hopkins Software in the waiting room."

"Sorry, Rick, I have to go, look up 4-7-8 and see Colin." He shook my hand. "For what it's worth, I want to believe you, Rick. Good luck."

I stood in the street; I might as well get the ball rolling. I called the number on the card, Colin Masters. His secretary said that he could see me at ten in the morning. "Are you sure?" I said. "It's Saturday."

"Oh no, that's fine," she answered. "Colin often sees his clients on Saturday mornings, he's so busy."

She didn't ask what it was about. Given the nature of his work, I suppose she had a pretty good idea.

With nothing else to do, I went home and tried to have a normal evening. I had a ready meal from the freezer. Cath had made loads for when she was on shift and too tired to cook. It reminded me of her and I wanted to call.

I didn't want to go down the solicitor route; from what I had heard, I had the impression that they often were more interested in keeping things going, keep the fees coming in, than they were in solving problems. Clem had told me not to call her so I left it. Instead, I sat and stewed. No matter how much I went over it, there was no way that I could think of that explained the bruise on my right arm. Logically, I must have done it while I was hunting for the tablets and not noticed.

By eleven I was still wide awake; I knew that I wouldn't sleep. What was that thing that Clem had told me, four-something, I turned my laptop on and had a look.

It sounded like a daft idea to me, relax and shut your eyes, breathe in and count to four, hold it and count to seven, breathe out while counting to eight. How could something like that possibly help me sleep?

I might as well try it though, I was right out of other ideas. I washed and undressed, got into bed.

"One, two, three, four. One..."

CHAPTER TWENTY TWO

ECIAS

I WAS STILL in the cell; it was the morning of the fourth day of my imprisonment. I felt hungry, it must be breakfast time.

Last night I thought that I had heard the noises of a ship landing. The question was which one had arrived? Was it the supply ship or was it the police? I decided that it must have been the supplies; after it had landed I could hear faint noises from Whistles, singing and happiness. It made me feel even more isolated.

The door opened, it was Ove. "I've got someone here who wants to see you," he said. "Come in, Anna."

My stomach lurched, this was the moment that I hadn't been looking forward to. Anna, Vince's girlfriend, had arrived. That meant that it had been the supply ship that I had heard, maybe the singing was because there was beer for the troops. The police were still to come, would they be any worse than this was going to be?

A dark-haired woman came into the room, she was shorter than me, with short, boyish hair, dressed in jeans and a shirt. "I'll leave you two to it," Ove said. He left and I heard the door lock. I thought that I was supposed to be in isolation, perhaps he wanted to hear me justify what he thought I'd done from the safety of wherever the microphone was plugged in.

She just looked at me, I had the feeling that she was trying not to walk over to me and hurt me. Her eyes were hidden by dark glasses.

"You bastard, you killed him!" she screamed. The sudden explosion of sound was as bad as a physical assault and I stepped back, into the wall. She came towards me and I put my arms up to defend myself from the inevitable blows. She kicked the cupboards, picked up some things from the desk and threw them against the wall, swore and shouted some more. But she never touched me. Then she stopped close to me and whispered in my ear, "Do you think they heard all that?"

What the hell was going on? I didn't know what to say, was this some sort of psychological torture? Was she going to make me wait for her attack?

"Don't look so worried," she whispered. "I'll explain."

"OK." I decided to go with it and see what happened. As least she wasn't strangling me.

"They're all listening out there," she said. "They think that I'm going to come in here and accuse you of killing my boyfriend."

That was what I had been expecting as well, her calmness and behaviour threw me completely. "And aren't you?"

"No, because he wasn't my boyfriend."

"Everything alright in there?" Ove called through the door.

"Fine," she replied. "I'll call when we're done."

That was another shock, the way Vince had never stopped talking about her, I had thought that they were joined at the hip. He had spent all his spare time filming Ecias for her, called her every night from wherever we were.

"Before you say any more," I said. "How's Vanessa holding up?"

She pulled a face. "Vanessa is a bit wary around me. I wonder if she thinks that I blame her for all this. There're a lot of stories going around."

I suppose she meant the story that Vince was killed by me because I caught him and Vanessa together in the forest.

"Do you know that there's a microphone in the corner." I pointed up at it.

"Don't worry about that," she said. "It's been sorted. I told Ove that I didn't want a record of what I said; all we need is it going viral because someone makes a copy. Fortunately, he agreed. Before you say any more, let me explain properly. He wasn't my boyfriend, he was my working partner, we both work for Burgstrom's security."

She pulled a plastic card from her wallet and showed it to me. I'd seen a Burgstrom identity card before, I had one myself. It looked identical to mine; it had the Burgstrom's logo, her name, Anna Durban, and a bad photo. She was described as head of Corporate Security. It was signed by Harald himself, just like mine was.

It explained so much. I had it all wrong. It must have been why Vince had been killed. He had been investigating something to do with the plant hunters and had got caught. It explained the conversation I had overheard in the woods. And why he had gone walkabout when we were in the forest. Surely Anna would tell Ove and I would be out of here by sunset.

"So you're here on a job?"

"You got it," she nodded. "We had a word that the planet was being scouted out for a takeover."

"What?" I said. After what I'd heard in the forest, it wasn't news to me, but I didn't let on too much. I wanted to see which way things were going. "A takeover by whom? Why, for goodness' sake? I mean look at the place, it's pretty but there's nothing here that you couldn't find anywhere else."

"You don't know, do you?" she seemed surprised. "You're the one who found it, the Praseodymium."

Then I understood. Praseodymium was an REE, a rare-earth element, originally used in the manufacture of engines, specifically the trans-light engines that powered all spaceships. It was also used to make toughened glass. It wasn't particularly rare, but with the exploration of the galaxy and the need for engines, a large find would be incredibly valuable. It was certainly easier to take ours than try and find your own. If we had found it, we hadn't noticed. I didn't always bother looking at our survey results, they were all stored on the chip and didn't need any input from us.

"Does Ove know all this?" I asked. I couldn't understand why we were still in here with the door locked from the outside.

"Ah," she said. "Now there's the first part of Burgstrom's dilemma. We're not sure if Ove isn't part of the problem, it's possible that he's involved with the plan. Someone's told the opposition what's here, we don't know who yet."

So perhaps I wouldn't be out of here by sunset after all. If Ove was on the wrong side, then I was staying put. And did that mean that Vanessa was in more trouble? The plant hunters had said that they were interested in her as a side project, what was it they had said, a bonus?

"The good news is that you and Vanessa are in the clear," she said. "Vince was in touch with me when you were out in the field. He says that you're a good guy, one that I can trust."

And we thought he was giving us space, he must have been reporting back. And all that filming he did, it was evidence.

"I have to be careful, even the police that Ove has called from Ventius don't know about me, it has to stay that way, at least to begin with."

It was a relief to hear her say that. "So how can I help?"

"I need to know everything about the situation here. Vince said that there were three suspicious characters, he called them plant hunters. Fearne, our agent on the ship, said they had an unhealthy interest in their equipment containers, they were in the hold every day."

I walked over to the copier and turned it on. "I have notes here," I said, pulling the sheets from my pocket, "of what's been going on, from the moment Vince arrived. It might be easier if you read them."

"Very industrious," she said. "Why did you write it all down?"

"There was nothing else to do and I wanted to get it straight in my mind. I'll make you a copy."

"OK, thanks. Vince said that the suspects seemed to be employed by a drugs company, but we think they work for an electronics and engineering company. They would want the Praseodymium."

"Tontranix," I said.

"How did you know that?"

I started to tell her everything that I knew about the plant hunters, it was all in the notes, but I told her the main bits anyway, while I made the copies. The mix-up with loading. Their crude interest in Vanessa. How they tried to embarrass Vince. How I had seen them wearing Tontranix overalls in the woods.

"Thank you, that's great," she said, pushing the papers into her bag. "I'll read it properly later. I want to hear some more now, like what you've just told me. Stuff like that is good evidence."

"Wait a moment." I had helped her, now it was her turn. "Before I do, I need something from you."

"If I can," she said.

"Vanessa isn't sure whether I did it or not, I need you to tell her that it wasn't me. And I'm worried about her, without me to stop them, she's in danger."

She thought about it for a moment. "I can't risk my cover, the fewer that know the better. I'm not able to do that yet, I'm so sorry."

"You say that you can't risk your cover, then how did you get in here? Ove must know something about you; he wouldn't let you in if all he thought you were was Vince's anguished girlfriend."

"Oh, he would, he said I could see you, as long as I promised not to hurt you. He told me that he's locked you up for your own safety. He's worried that some of the other people here will take the law in to their own hands. Vanessa is safe out there; everyone's looking out for her. It's you who would be in danger."

I understood. As far as public opinion was concerned, I was guilty already. I didn't like the feeling. "OK, I see what you mean. Can you at least keep an eye on her, help to keep her safe? The plant hunters frightened her; they kept making... suggestions. I'm worried now that I'm not around to protect her."

"I can do that, as much as I can; now, before I go, I need to know the rest."

"It's all in the notes." I felt upset. "It all seems to be me giving; I ask you for one thing, you say you can't help."

"I know, like I said I'm sorry. I have to look at the bigger picture. I will try and keep an eye on her. I would appreciate it if you would tell me what you know."

So I told her the rest of the story, how I thought that they had sabotaged our buggy and what I had heard them say in the forest.

I also mentioned the number of shots and the gun, all the things that proved my innocence. She followed along, looking at my pages and writing notes in the margins.

After nearly an hour, the door opened. "Have you finished?" asked today's guard. He peered around the room. I think that he was disappointed that there was no blood splashed on the wall, that I still had teeth. "Here's your meal, murdering bastard," he said pushing a tray along the floor with his foot.

Anna picked it up and put it on the desk.

"I'm all done for now, see you soon, Dan," she said as she walked out. The door slammed but I didn't mind. Someone believed me and I would soon be out of here. Just as long as she kept her promise and protected Vanessa for me.

Feeling more relaxed than I had in a long while, I tucked in, and when I had finished I laid on the bed.

CHAPTER TWENTY THREE

EARTH

I PARKED my car in a small square; it looked out of place, surrounded by a fleet of expensive, newer models. I was over in what my mother would have called the 'better' end of town, for the meeting with Colin Masters, my prospective solicitor. It was Saturday morning, cold and clear. I contrasted it with the weather on Ecias, which was always warm and mostly sunny. Rain was rare, heavy and soon evaporated, unlike here, where it was a constant irritant.

I rang the bell at the door of one of the large Edwardian houses that surrounded the square. It was answered by a man dressed in jeans and an open-necked shirt.

"Good morning, Mr Wilson," he said. "I'm Colin Masters, would you come into my office."

"Please call me Rick." I shook his hand. "It's good of you to see me on a Saturday."

"It's no problem, Rick. I like to meet clients on a Saturday. I have so much work and it's easier to arrange for a lot of busy people. I'm sure my secretary told you."

We sat in his office; there was a large bay window behind his desk. I could see trees and parkland in the distance. He poured me coffee from a flask on the desk. Milk for his came from a small fridge in the corner.

"OK, Rick," he said once we had our drinks. "So how do you know Clem?"

"He handles the legal stuff for Creative Concepts, and I know him and Linda socially as well."

"He called me yesterday, told me that he'd passed you on. He said that you have a letter. Can I see it, please?" I handed to over and he read it quickly.

"Standard form letter." He shrugged. "Sorry to be blunt but I see these all day. It's not as bad as it sounds, this is just the opening shot. I know Simon Walsh, he's a good man; your wife has employed one of the best. But I'm not so bad myself. What do you want me to do?"

His attitude suggested competence and neutrality, which wasn't what I expected. I had thought he would tell me that he believed me, that he would fight for me to the end, no matter how much I had to pay him. Yet here he was, asking me what I wanted. The implication was that if I held my hands up and admitted it, then that would be just the same as asking him to fight for everything.

"I want to tell my side, I tried to explain to Cath, but she never gave me the chance."

He nodded. "It's a thing I hear a lot of. In case you're wondering, I don't just represent men. Women come to me and say the same thing – 'I can't tell my side'. The trouble is, emotions run away with us and people take a position, usually before they have all the facts. Then we get to the point where nobody wants to back down, which is where I come in."

I knew exactly what he meant; I just wanted her to understand, although I hadn't helped by not telling her everything right from the start.

"Anyhow, that's what we're here for. To be impartial and rational, to offer advice, set out the legal position and try to bring calm to a difficult situation. And knock heads together, so to speak, but only if we have to."

I'd never thought of it like that, I guess my thoughts had only been that they profited from others misery.

"So," he said, "your wife alleges that you have been committing adultery. Have you?"

I looked him straight in the eye. "No!" It came out a little louder than I had expected, he flinched.

"Fine. To be honest, I want to believe you. I can't work properly if I think that you're lying. Can you tell me the whole story?"

I took a deep breath. "You're not going to believe this," I began.

"I very much doubt that you can tell me anything I haven't heard before." He sounded confident. Just you wait, I thought. I started with the rational stuff, told him about my dreams, how they had started in a vague way, then when I had started sleeping badly they had increased. He took notes on a pad, nodding and saying 'go on' every time I stopped.

I told him how Cath had become more concerned as the lack of sleep started to have an effect on my, our, lives. How she had finally fought to get me to see a consultant. How I had agreed to the trial, taken the tablets and had the clearest dreams yet. I told him that my dreams took place on a planet called Ecias, in the future. But I didn't tell him too much detail. I didn't want to freak him out from the start.

"So," he said, "do you think that the tablets are causing the dreams?"

"No," I answered. "I was having the dreams before I started the medication. The lack of sleep coincided with them becoming more detailed and then the tablets made them more vivid."

He made more notes. "Go on."

"The tablets are made by a company called Phay Medical. Creative Concepts, the company I work for, got a job advertising Phay products. When I met Esther Phay, she was identical to the woman in my dreams, my wife on Ecias, Vanessa. That was a surprise to me; I'd never seen her before she walked into our office. Cath found her picture online when I told her about the job."

"You had described this Vanessa to Cath before that?"

"Yes, but only vaguely; tall, brown hair."

"That's usually enough. I suppose that when she saw her picture she put two and two together."

"Exactly." Should I tell him about the name as well? I was unsure, it sounded so stupid.

"There's more, isn't there?" he said.

"Yes, and this is where it gets really freaky." I told him the whole Jonathon Swift thing, how it had sealed my fate. As far as she was concerned, I had invented Vanessa to cover up my affair with Esther. And jumped to the conclusion that it had been going on for months.

He put the pen down. "OK, I can understand where she's coming from," he said with a sigh.

"That's part of the problem, so can I. If only I had mentioned her before, I didn't want to when it all started. Looking back; I can see that was wrong."

He shook his head. "It probably wouldn't have made much difference," he said. "Whether you remember it or not, you must have seen her somewhere before you started dreaming. This sounds like a lot of little things that have added up to more than they are. They call it an event cascade."

"How do you mean?" I'd never heard of the term.

"Think about it, a lot of little things that taken on their own don't mean much. You have a dream about a woman with long hair. You get a job, from a woman with long hair. Two names have a common origin. Your dreams link them all together, force the research. The answer depends on each previous step occurring in sequence."

"I see, on their own they're interesting. In any other order they have another explanation."

"Exactly, if you had started work for a woman with long hair, then you dreamt about a woman with long hair, it might be more understandable. If you hadn't mentioned the dreams, or Vanessa, Esther Phay would mean nothing to your wife. She would just be a client of your company. She wouldn't investigate the name."

"But if I met Esther and then said that I had dreams about her, Cath would still be angry."

He laughed. "Well, yes she would; but unless you called her Vanessa in a moment of passion, it wouldn't seem like you were hiding something. It's all about perception."

I could see where he was coming from. It was the difference in the way you saw what was happening, compared to how someone else saw it.

"Now I'm not a psychiatrist," he said. I would have disagreed; he seemed to have a good handle on the way the human mind worked. "I can't dress it up in all the fancy language but I'm going to recommend that you go and see a real one. He might be able to get to the bottom of the reasons for your dreams. If I tell Simon Walsh that's what you're doing, perhaps that will help convince Cath that you're innocent." He looked at me. "As long as you are."

Put that way it sounded like a reasonable idea. "I'm innocent; keen to get this all sorted out. It's been a bad time. I never set out to hurt Cath. I'm certainly not involved with Esther Phay. I just want it all to go away. I'm not creating an elaborate fantasy to hide anything."

"I hope not," he said. "Although, if you're paying I suppose I shouldn't be that bothered. What I was going to suggest was this. There's a psychiatrist who we use a lot, his name is Dr Oliver Borth. Your wife's solicitors use him as well from time to time, so they will be happy to accept his findings. I can have a word with him, give him a rough idea of what you've told me. If he's happy to work with you we can arrange an appointment, all part of the service. And I'll keep in touch with the other side, on your behalf.

Any letters you get, you give to me unanswered, preferably unopened."

That made it sound like a war, 'the other side'. All I wanted was peace.

"Why unopened?" It seemed a little strange. "How do I know what's been sent if I can't open it?"

"There may well be accusations flying about, it's better if I head them off before you see them," was his reply. Maybe that was true in some cases, but Cath and I were civilised people, weren't we? There were no children to use as weapons; we only had one house and two cars, a very small amount of money in a joint account, what was there to fight over?

"Just a precaution," he added.

I shrugged. "Sure, if that's your advice."

"There is one more thing," he said. "I would advise that you speak to your boss, tell him that you can't work with this Phay person any more. Get some distance; it will help prove that you're not involved."

Even though that was going to be slightly more difficult, I could see his point. I would have to talk to Hughie when I got to work. "I'll see him on Monday," I said.

"Good. I don't think we need much more at this stage. I can't tell what's going on but I think that you're blessed, or cursed, with a very good imagination and some realistic dreams. I believe that they're called lucid dreams."

"That was what Esther called them," I said. Instantly his attitude changed. "You've discussed your dreams with her?" It almost sounded like an accusation.

"Yes, her company makes the drug that I'm taking, as part of a clinical trial. That's another coincidence. She asked me about lucid dreams, in her office, during a meeting."

He shook his head. "And you were going to tell me this when?"

"I did tell you, then we got sidetracked."

"If you want my help, I need to know everything. Was it a business meeting?"

He was uncomfortable; perhaps he was a bit freaked out by what I had said, we hadn't even got to the marks on my arms. While it was only dreams it was rational, although a bit weird. When I showed him the physical evidence and my explanation, it would make his head spin. It must be so different to his normal cases. He looked at the notes he had been scribbling.

"Oh yes, I'm sorry, you did tell me about the drug trial you were on. So the tablets were made by Phay?"

"That's right."

"Fair enough," he said. "We did go a bit off-piste there. Let's get back on track. You met her, where? At her offices?"

"Yes, followed by dinner at the Avon."

"That's not a problem, you were working for her. They're both public places; were you ever alone with her?"

"I went back to her flat, for a nightcap." He raised an eyebrow. "I told her the whole story, more than I've told you. I told her about my life on Ecias with Vanessa, how Vanessa looked like her, how it seemed so real. That was where she pinched me, to prove that I wasn't dreaming."

He smacked the palm of his hand against his forehead. "Oh great, you're telling me that you went to her flat and yet nothing happened?"

"Nothing," I said firmly. "She wanted to but I declined."

He sat back and looked at me. "Despite what I said before, I've never heard a story like this."

"I know, you should see it from my side. I can't believe the way things have all conspired together."

He thought for a moment, got up and paced around; clearly he was deep in thought. "I was going to take your case, then when you told me what you just have, I thought that I'd be better off running in the opposite direction. More than ever, I think that you need to see a psychiatrist." He paused. "But I don't think that you'll ever get another firm to represent you, with a story like that. Clem tells me you're a good, honest man. I know that I shouldn't, but I'll take your case, usual terms. If you're happy I'll write to Simon, let him know."

"Thank you," I said.

"Before we finish up, is there anything else you want to tell me, anything about your relationship with this woman that might be useful?"

Here we go, this was the bit that was going to sound crazy but I had to tell someone before the bruises faded.

"There is one more thing."

"Go on." His voice had the weary tone of a man who had heard it all. I was pretty sure that he hadn't heard anything like this.

"You remember how I told you that Esther pinched my arm, to prove that I was awake and on Earth."

He nodded. "Yes, I remember, when you were in her flat and *nothing happened*."

I ignored the sarcasm. "Well she pinched my left arm. But that night, while I was asleep, Vanessa pinched my right arm, the other one, to prove that what was happening on Ecias wasn't a dream either."

I showed him the bruises. His eyebrows went up. "I'm sure there's a rational explanation. I'm assuming that you can't think of any other way that you could have got the mark on your right arm."

He might be saying the words; I could tell that he was both-ered by what he could see. That must be more perception, I might not like it but I was clear in my head about them. To him, my explanation was impossible. He was so confused that he didn't ask for any more details. Instead, he went to his desk and took out a camera, a professional looking bit of equipment. "Move over to the window, into the light," he said. I did and he took lots of pictures, of each arm, then of both together. I told him about the fingernails, he made more notes on his pad.

"I'll get these enhanced, get someone I know to take a look at them. Meanwhile tell your boss that you can't work with Esther Phay."

"I will; he won't be happy."

"Tell him why, I'm sure he'll understand. If there's nothing more, can you find your own way out?"

That meant that on Monday, I would have to face a post Randalls, happy Hughie. I would have to tell him that the account that he thought was going to make him a star had to be dropped, and why.

I would need most of Sunday to prepare for that conversation.

CHAPTER TWENTY FOUR

I ARRIVED in the car park on Monday morning feeling decidedly unhappy about what I had to do. I had spent Sunday rehearsing what to say, how to say it. I had written various versions of the story out, trying to find one that didn't sound ridiculous or incriminating.

My sleep on Saturday and Sunday nights had been muddled, fragmented with crazy dreams. In one, Hughie was on Ecias and in the cell with me, he was very angry.

"They should lock you up for what you did to my company; all for a bit on the side," he said at one point. I told him that there was nothing going on and asked him if it was true about Molly, he went crazy and we wrestled, trying to hurt each other in that small room. The quilt and pillows were on the floor again when I woke from that one. Yet when I took a look at my body in the shower, I wasn't bruised from the encounter.

Then, in another dream, I was in Esther's flat on Earth. Vanessa walked in, it was like seeing twins, or a mirror image. They both stood in front of me, Vanessa in her overalls and Esther in the black dress and stockings.

"It's time to choose," they said together, their voices identical. "You can only have one of us, which one do you want?"

I woke on both mornings feeling exhausted, like I had been running all night. I hadn't been to Ecias and I didn't feel rested. I was none the wiser about how to tell Hughie, I would have to do it as soon as I got the chance, before I lost my nerve.

Deanne shared the lift with me. "Good weekend, Rick?" she asked, her eyes shining and full of life. "Are you OK? You look tired, like you have the world on your shoulders."

"Hi, Deanne. I'm fine," I lied. "Cath's still at her mother's and I'm missing her, I'm not sleeping well."

She gave me a look, it said that she knew I was fibbing, then it changed to a smile. "She'll be back soon, I'm sure," she said, with the optimism of the young. "Hughie will be in today, we can hear all about what a great time he had at Randalls." She rolled her eyes. "I hate hearing how wonderful everyone else's life is. Mine is so boring. I suppose Molly will be extra pleased too, now that he's back."

I saw my chance to satisfy my curiosity and change the subject. "Why?"

"They're an item, silly," she gabbled. "You know, friends with benefits. She stays over quite a lot, in the suite that suddenly appeared. You mean to tell me that you haven't noticed?"

I tried to sound surprised. "How long has that been going on?"

"Only since Claire... Molly said that they didn't before... that wasn't the reason why she... oh."

Deanne's face had gone bright red. My ears pricked up, did she realise what she had just said. That was something I would have to think about later, first I had to deal with my own news. I decided to take the bull by the horns.

"You know, don't you," I said. "About what's going on in my life?"

She nodded, all the light had gone out of her eyes. "I'm so sorry, Rick." She put her hand on my arm. "Cath told Molly on Saturday, they had a girls' day out, shopping for Christmas gifts. I bumped into Molly on Saturday evening, in town, it sort of came out in conversation. Molly was shocked, so am I. She made me promise not to tell anyone." She put her hand on my arm again. "I won't," she added quickly. She said it sincerely but I knew her reputation. I'd better tell Hughie about that then, as well as the Phay bombshell, before he found out from her.

The rest of the journey to the office passed in silence. I was still trying to get my head around what Deanne had blurted out. I had believed that Claire's death was an accident; Deanne had hinted that there was more to it. My mind raced, could it have been suicide? Could Claire have killed herself over Molly and her relationship with Hughie?

Deanne was obviously embarrassed and aware that she had said too much, normally she blurted secrets out without noticing. This one must be true. I had thought that Molly was such a prim, quiet lady as well. My heart went out to Claire, then suddenly it made me wonder what Cath was going through, what sort of mental state she had got herself into.

Sure enough, Hughie and Molly were in residence when we arrived, sitting in his office, together on the sofa. They got up and Molly smiled at me. "Hi, Rick. How's things?" she said as she came out into the main space.

"Fine thanks," I said, seeing her in a whole new light. "Hughie, I need a word before we start on your tales of debauchery at Randalls." I had decided to get it out of the way, without any preamble.

"Come in, Rick," he grinned. "Wait till you hear what we got up to, it was better than last year." He had forgotten Claire, Molly must have been taking his mind off her.

I closed the door; he saw the look on my face. "What is it?"

⁙

"You want to do what?" Even though the door was closed, Molly and Deanne looked up. Hughie had been in a good mood, until I had told him what I wanted to do. Now he was extremely agitated.

"Do you want to explain?" he said. "Why you want to walk away and dump it all on me?"

"Can you just calm down, Hughie? I'm in a lot of trouble and Esther Phay is at the heart of it."

That didn't seem to surprise him, maybe Molly had said something. "Then you'd better tell me all about it."

Here we go again. "OK, this is what's happened so far." I told Hughie the story I had concocted, how I had been having trouble sleeping, the tablets that I was taking were made by Phay and my worry about a conflict of interest. I thought that it sounded convincing.

"I see," he said. "So Cath leaving you has nothing to do with it?"

"How do you know that?"

"It's not hard to spot; Molly mentioned that she thought you were having problems."

There were no secrets here, as I had found out. "Cath thinks that I'm... with Esther." I said.

"Well I wouldn't blame you, if you were single," he said. "But you're not."

"There's nothing going on, Hughie, it's all a misunderstanding." I tried to sound sincere. I had said it to enough people over the last few days – Cath, Clem, Colin and now Hughie. But which of them believed me?

"I want Cath to come home; my solicitor said that I should back off from any contact with Esther Phay."

"Solicitor? That's a bit heavy, isn't it?" he said. "OK, I can see there's a problem, leave it with me. I'll speak to Phay; you take the rest of the day off, go home and sort yourself out, have a shave, iron some shirts, you look a mess."

"Thanks, Hughie. See you tomorrow," I said, deciding that now wasn't the time to say anything more, I didn't want to end up wrestling with him in the office. I left, glaring at Molly on my way out. She looked puzzled at my gaze, turning to Deanne as I shut the door behind me.

When I got back to the house, I didn't know where to start. Hughie was right, I was a mess. The place was a tip. I'd been home alone for well over a week and I hadn't done anything much, apart from tidying the bedroom. I saw my reflection in the mirror; I looked like I had really been locked in the cell on Ecias for a week. I was growing a straggly beard where I couldn't be bothered to shave and my hair needed a trim. I had to smarten myself up. If I was going to see a shrink looking like this he would get the wrong impression before I said a word. The least I could do was try to look sane.

I cleaned the bathroom and shaved off the beard. Clad in joggers and a T-shirt I decided to start on the kitchen. I threw a load of clothes into the washer. As I moved all the dirty cups into the sink, I was surprised to find that there was a note from Cath on the kitchen worktop, by the kettle.

"I've been home to get some stuff, you're a slob! If you want me to come back, clean the place up," it said. There was no date on it; it might have been there for a while, nothing about talking, no 'Cath' signed at the bottom. She was right in one respect though, I was a slob. I remembered what the solicitor had said and put the note in my laptop case. I would hand it to him next time we met.

I spent the rest of the day cleaning the house. I tumble-dried washing, I hoovered and dusted, I cleaned the kitchen, threw away all the rotten food. I was still clearing up as it got dark, then I ironed my clean shirts.

Instead of a shower, I took a bath, with some of Cath's stuff poured in it. The bottle said that it relieved muscle aches. I was exhausted, I was glad that I didn't have to do all that and work nights, like Cath did.

Sleep came easily, dreams were more elusive.

CHAPTER TWENTY FIVE

NEXT DAY, after another dreamless night, I arrived in the office to find Hughie pacing up and down in his office. The door was closed.

Molly and Deanne greeted me. "I like the new look," said Deanne. "You're better without the beard. And the scent, that's not your usual."

"Why are you bent over, have you hurt your back?" asked Molly.

"The ironing board was too low for me," I said. "I couldn't get it any higher, plus I'm out of practice."

Deanne laughed as the door opened and Hughie put his head out.

"Hi, Hughie," I said. "I took your advice, clean shirt." I saw the miserable look on his face. "What's going on?"

"You're bloody life is what's going on," he said. "Phay has pulled out of our deal!"

There was a gasp from behind me.

"What? Just because there's a conflict of interest? That seems a bit harsh."

"Come in here and shut the door." He looked past me at

Deanne and Molly. "Second thoughts, you two, go out and get yourselves a coffee from that stand in the lobby, clear off for an hour."

They got up and went out. I was grateful, what was almost certain to be said now didn't need an audience. Once they had gone he relaxed a little.

"I didn't get to try and justify your private life. I had a call from Phay yesterday afternoon, before I got the chance. They're the ones who're pulling the plug. They were very apologetic; lots of talk about a change in policy, refocusing the brand, that sort of thing. We're getting paid for what we... you, did. But that's it."

"Why? All that talk is just meaningless, what did she say?"

"I didn't speak to Esther, just some executive vice-president, big-chief-bugger-all." Hughie was really wound up. "You must have had some effect on Esther. I know that you went over to see her on Tuesday, Molly told me. What did you say?"

"Hughie, we discussed work, she was very pleased with what I had done. She invited me to have dinner, as she had kept me late. We ate at the Avon. I took her home; I had a coffee in her flat. We parted as friends. I can't tell you anything else, there's nothing else."

I couldn't tell him about the failed seduction, which had to be the reason for Phay's decision. Esther was miffed that I had turned her down. I didn't want to tell him about the dreams, which had been the catalyst. It wasn't me that had made the move anyway. Esther Phay had tried it on, been rebuffed and now this was her revenge.

"Coffee in her flat, and you parted as friends?" his voice was scornful. "You expect me to believe that was all that happened? Don't forget, I saw you together, when she was here, at lunch afterwards. I'm an insensitive bastard but I could feel the tension between you. If I'd left you alone then, you'd have been at it on the table before I could get the door shut."

Hughie was getting as bad as Cath. "For the last time, nothing happened, let me call her."

He shrugged. "Do what you like."

I went back to my desk. I had to think, should I call her and try to smooth things over. Even if I was off the job, surely Hughie could carry on. I hesitated.

The girls came back, Molly gave me a dirty look; she would probably be on the phone to Cath with this information as soon as she could. It was gossip gold, enough to confirm my guilt.

"Problems, Molly?" I asked, facing her down. Deanne made an excuse and headed for the toilets.

"I never believed it, when Cath told me," she said, "but after what I've heard, I'm changing my opinion of you."

"Really," I smiled sweetly at her, "after what I recently heard, I'm changing my opinion of you too."

Her face fell. Let her work it out, I thought as I sat at my desk. I was about to pick up the phone when it rang. I picked the receiver up.

"Creative Concepts."

"Is that Rick?"

"Yes it is," I said, recognising the voice.

"It's Colin. I've shown your pictures to a friend of mine, she's an expert in analysis."

I looked at Molly and Deanne, they were both pretending not to listen.

"I'll call you back."

He understood. "Sure." The line went dead.

I dialled Phay Medical, I would have to go somewhere private before I called Colin back.

"Miss Phay is away," the person who answered the phone told me. I recalled that she had said she was going somewhere for a few days. I put on my best telephone manner.

"Can you ask her to call Creative Concepts when she picks up her messages please?"

"Of course," she replied. "Creative Concepts, I'll make a note."

I went back to see Hughie. "I've left Phay a message," I said. "Esther is away. I remember that she told me she was going somewhere for a few days. Maybe it's not from her, perhaps someone else has pulled the plug."

He got up and closed the door behind me. It sounded like the door to my prison shutting on Ecias, final and depressing.

"Maybe. Sit down, Rick, tell me what's really going on. Quietly, so the girls can't hear."

How many times would I have to tell this story? "OK, you're not going to believe this," I started. "I've been having these dreams, I'm living on another planet. I guess it's in the future, but there I'm an explorer, and Esther Phay is my wife, partner; I don't know. Except that she's called Vanessa. Whatever, we have a life there."

He just looked at me. "You've been working on the travel posters far too long," he said. "Do you watch sci-fi as well?"

"You're not taking this seriously," I said. "I thought I could tell you, thought that you might understand."

He laughed.

"*I'm* not taking the tale of your life on another planet seriously? While you are? I'm sorry, it's a lot to take in, so what? You and this Vanessa, you live there and wander around doing things."

"That's it, there's nothing exciting, at least there wasn't to start with, it's just life. We get up, we do a bit of work and we go to sleep. It was mundane, as crazy as that sounds, or at least it was until the plant hunters turned up."

"Hang on," he said. "You dream about an ordinary life, no space battles, no sex with beautiful women..." He stopped, realising what he had said. "That's the problem isn't it? Molly told me some of it. Cath thinks that you're cheating and using the dreams as a cover, in case you slip up."

Was it that obvious? "That's how she sees it," I said.

"And it didn't help when Cath found that Esther Phay is similar to how you described Vanessa."

"That's right, but the spooky thing is, I dreamt about Vanessa a long time before I met Esther. I just never described her to Cath until recently, just the other parts of the dream. You couldn't make it up!"

"If you want me to believe the rest of it, I suppose that's nothing much extra to cope with. But why did Cath suddenly go ballistic? If she knew all about the dreams, what changed her mind?"

"I don't know, it was just the way it all came out. I never mentioned Vanessa until after I'd told her about Esther. It was stupid of me, it made everything sound suspicious. With all the other coincidences as well, it was enough to get her jumping to the wrong conclusion. She decided that it must have been going on for months, since the dreams started. Anyway, I've seen a solicitor and I'm going to see a shrink."

He thought for a moment. "Take some time out, there's nothing for you to do if Phay has gone, till I can rustle up another job."

"If it's alright with you, I don't want to sit at home on my own thinking about things, I'd be happier working. Can't you find me something to do?"

He thought for a moment. "OK, if you're happy to be here, I guess you can do some mentoring with Deanne. We've all been too busy, left her to fend for herself. Claire wouldn't have liked that. Help her learn."

As I left Hughie's office I saw that Molly and Deanne were sat at their desks, wide-eyed. Although I had shut the door, they didn't need to have heard everything that I said. I knew that Molly and Cath had been talking as well, maybe Molly knew about my alternative life on Ecias. When Hughie sent them down for coffee, they had probably discussed the shambles that was my life on Earth.

What would Deanne say about it to all her friends? 'Guess what, a bloke where I work dreams he lives on another planet!' I realised that maybe staying here and working wasn't such a good idea. Molly might pass anything I said to Cath and as for Deanne, well with her lack of verbal filtering, the whole town would know that I was an intrepid space traveller by tonight. It could be better to get it all out of the way.

"Listen, you two," I said. "Can I ask you to do me a huge favour?"

They both looked up and smiled. "Of course you can," said Deanne. Molly nodded thoughtfully.

"Good, you might have just heard me talking in there, telling Hughie that Cath and I have separated." They both looked shocked, it must have been because I had come out and admitted it.

"I know that you both knew before I told him. I want to clear the air, as I'm working here. We've been having some problems, it's only temporary," I continued. "I've seen a solicitor, I know Cath has, we just need some professional help to get us through this."

I watched their faces; the expression told me that they knew a lot more. Cath had probably told Molly about my dreams of Ecias. So maybe Deanne knew. Let them think what they wanted. I wasn't going to start telling them about my dreams.

"Until it's all sorted out, can I ask you both to not talk to anyone else about it, anyone who asks, especially anyone you don't know. You might think that you're helping, but can you just leave it? I'd really appreciate it if you could do that for us."

They both got up and hugged me. Molly looked guilty, what else had she told Cath? Would it be helpful, how could I find out?

"Now that you've given the big speech," Hughie had come out

of his office and was stood behind me, "can we please get some work done?"

That had cleared the air; we settled down and got busy. I pulled my chair over to Deanne's station. "As I have nothing else to do," I started.

"I know," she said, "you're going to help me."

As we worked, I could see why Hughie's wife had picked her out and employed her. She was a natural, full of ideas for catchy copy and blessed with an eye for great layout. I was learning as much from her as she was from me. We talked about everything except my life; she lived with her parents, had a boyfriend and enjoyed socialising and I got to hear about all of it. I let her ramble on, it took my mind off things. Had my life ever been that uncomplicated?

My phone rang mid-afternoon, I looked at the screen, 'unknown' it said.

"Hello," I answered without giving my name. Was I getting paranoid?

"Could I speak to Mr Wilson?" said the caller, a woman. It wasn't Phay, which was a relief.

"I'm Mr Wilson," I answered.

"Good," she said, "this is Doctor Borth's secretary, would you be available to come in tomorrow, at one p.m.?"

"Who was that?" Deanne asked as I agreed and ended the call.

"I'm off to see the shrink tomorrow," I said. "I've been having these crazy dreams and I need to find out why."

She looked interested. "Dreams? You mean like trips. Are you on drugs?"

If only it was that simple.

When we finished for the day, I remembered that I had to call Colin Masters back. With everything else that had gone on, I had forgotten to get out of the office and do it. It was too late now, I'd have to try in the morning, before I saw Dr Borth.

Meanwhile I went home, had a meal and went to bed. I wasn't missing the tablets, although it would be another story when I had to go back to the doctor and explain. At least the counting technique had turned out to be very effective at getting me to sleep.

CHAPTER TWENTY SIX

ECIAS

"HERE'S what we're going to do."

Anna had arrived with my breakfast, bringing it instead of Vanessa.

"Is Vanessa alright?" I asked.

"She's fine, happy to let me bring your food in, I think she knows that there's more to it than just me doing a favour. I think that she's starting to believe you. She offered to help me when I said I wanted to find out more, unofficially of course. And she's moved from your trailer into the hostel, I can keep an eye on her."

"Did you have a job convincing her to move?"

"I didn't have to try very hard. Like I said, she's sure that there's more going on, she feels vulnerable in the trailer, she misses you. It only took a nudge to get her to move."

I was relieved; at least Vanessa wasn't alone in the night. I was still sure that she was on the list for a visit from the people I thought of as the bad guys.

"Thank you, what progress have you made?"

"Well, I'm having another look at all the footage that Vince sent me, and the paperwork you handed over. But it checks out so far. I've tried to find the bullet that you say hit a tree. I've found the one in the door frame. Looking at the scene, it doesn't make sense. If you shot Vince, how did you fire that one and the ones that hit him? And why?"

She grabbed a sheet of paper and drew a plan of the storeroom on it, marking the door and where Vince fell with a stick figure. Then she marked the position of the bullets.

"Look," she said, "one bullet went through the front of his shoulder and hit the opposite wall to the door frame. It can't have been fired from the same place as the one you say missed you, you can't see the door frame from there. It means that the shooter must have changed position, unless there were two of them."

She had been putting a lot of work in, and so far, it seemed to be agreeing with my version of events.

"If Vince were alive and someone shot at him as he entered the room, hitting the door frame, then why would he come further in, surely he'd turn and run away and be shot in the back, outside – not be shot in the front of the chest and shoulder, over by the other wall. Vince must have been shot before the shot that hit the frame. It doesn't make sense otherwise."

"If you can find the tree, and that bullet matches the gun that shot Vince, surely that would help."

"I know, I'm working on Ove. I want him to check out the position of the three plant hunters, but it's difficult when he doesn't know who I am."

"Or which side he's on?" I suggested.

"Exactly. I did manage to get a look at the monitors yesterday; they're all down at their camp."

"Vince filmed at least two of them, when we were on the way back; they didn't know. Did you see that film?"

"Yes and I was trying to get to see everyone's EPIRB logs, that's why I was in the office. See if they matched up. If I can prove they were with you when the signal says they were in their camp, it's enough to ask for a search of the camp when the police turn up."

"Are you still not sure about Ove?"

"No but I'm beginning to think he's OK, if a little lazy in the way he runs things." Hearing her say that was a shock. I had always thought that Ove was on the ball, maybe he was being lazy about the plant hunters for a reason.

"Are the police still arriving tomorrow? Are you going to reveal yourself to them?"

"Yes I'm going to have to; I hoped to be able to say one way or the other on Ove by then."

Someone knocked on the door. "Come on, you were only supposed to give him his breakfast."

"I have to go," she said, taking my hand. "What's that?" she asked, looking at my arm.

"Vanessa pinched me, she said it was to prove that I wasn't dreaming about the way things had turned out."

"It must seem more like a nightmare, after Vince told me that this was a paradise." She looked again. "What's that on the other one? Did she pinch both of your arms?"

I couldn't answer that, the bruise on my left arm was faint; it looked like it had been done a long time ago. It was a different shape to the fresher one on my right. "I'm not sure what that is, Vanessa didn't do it. It might have happened when I was hiding up in the forest."

After she'd gone, I wondered what she was doing about the 'phase two' that the plant hunters had mentioned. I looked at my notes, it was there but had she taken any notice of it? They hadn't said what they were planning. With the police arriving, it had to be happening soon.

CHAPTER TWENTY SEVEN

EARTH

DR BORTH HAD A VERY expensive office in a modern building, discreetly situated. Unlike Colin's it was in among the offices and shops in the middle of town. I worked all the morning, left my car and walked over, stopping to buy a sandwich on the way. While I was sat in the anonymity of the shopping centre, I called Colin.

He got straight to the point. "I can't talk long, I have a client, but I'll give you the main part," he said. "I gave the pictures to a friend, she works for the police analysing crime scene pictures and forensic evidence. I told her nothing about them. She wants to see you before the bruises fade completely but based on the pictures she told me her thoughts."

I wasn't sure that I wanted to get more people in on the story; sooner or later someone would open their mouth and say something that they shouldn't. I didn't want that to spoil any chance of getting Cath back.

"I don't know," I replied. "The one on my left has almost gone."

"OK, that's fine, I understand your reluctance. She said that the bruises were made by two different people, both were made by right hands, one with longer nails than the other."

That wasn't news to me. Colin carried on.

"One person, the one without nails was physically stronger, or more determined to inflict injury. She can't tell which. When she enhanced the image, or whatever she does, her pinch appeared to have left some metallic particles embedded in the skin, that's why she wants to see you. She played with the picture but couldn't make out what they were."

I sat in stunned silence, that was just not possible. She was referring to the dream pinch on Ecias. Even worse was the fact that the analyst hadn't known that. The metallic particles could have been from Vanessa's work, or just from the environment. I had been hoping for an explanation, all I had got was deeper into the impossibility. I couldn't take it all in, not sitting where I was, surrounded by normality, by happy people Christmas shopping. I needed time to think, and I didn't have it. I was about to see a man who might decide that I was crazy.

"Let me think, Colin, I'll call you back," I said. I ended the call and lifted my right arm up, turning it in the artificial light. The bruise was fading; I couldn't see anything in it. In a daze I finished my sandwich and walked to Dr Borth's office.

The secretary asked me to wait and made me coffee. After about ten minutes a door opened and a man came out. Short and slightly crumpled, he had white hair in tufts over his ears, thick glasses and a tweed jacket. His appearance screamed shrink, or mad professor.

"Good afternoon, Mr Wilson," he said, shaking my hand. The grip was strong but I noticed that his fingers were misshapen. He saw my gaze. "Arthritis," he said. "It makes some things difficult. I'm Doctor Oliver Borth, pleased to meet you, won't you come with me?"

We went into his office, the first thing I noticed was another door, was it to a washroom? As my eye swept the room, I saw another door with 'Bathroom' written over it. Borth was watching my reaction; I suppose that the consultation had already started.

I had been half expecting to be told to lay on some sort of couch but there wasn't one in sight. We were in a room not unlike a sitting room. There were deep armchairs and a crackling wood fire. "Please have a seat," he said, going to a leather armchair on one side of the fire. I sat opposite him, in its twin. It felt like sitting down with your favourite uncle, he had a kind face and a listening manner.

"Are you comfortable?" he asked, I nodded.

"Good, don't be nervous, we're not at all like you might expect, the profession had a bad press. I just want to understand how your mind is working and see if there's anything I can do to help you."

Put like that it sounded fine, I had seen some counsellors during my insomnia treatment; in my experience they were not at all like him. They had all been judgemental. Most seemed to have an agenda, all were looking for 'blame' and once they had an idea in their heads, they were inflexible. This man seemed different, it helped me to relax, even though I still had the feeling that he would see more than the words in everything that I said. What was that saying? 'Give me six lines written by the most honest man and I will find something in them to hang him'. I was interrupted from my thoughts as he spoke.

"Colin has asked me to see you; interesting letter. He wants an opinion on your state of mind. So perhaps you can tell me, in your own time, how all this started. If it's alright with you I'm recording our conversation. It saves me having to keep stopping you while I write notes. With my fingers the way they are, I can't keep up these days."

"That's fine," I said. "I just want this to stop, I feel like I'm going mad."

He raised an eyebrow. "We professionals dislike the term mad," he said. "It's so imprecise."

"I want my wife to understand what's happening to me and to come back."

"We'll do what we can to resolve your issues," he said.

"Fine, well, it all started when Cath, my wife, went on to night shifts."

"I gather from Colin's letter that you had trouble sleeping."

I went through the whole story again, right from the change of Cath's shifts and the dreams that were initially vague. I told him about the things I'd tried, the herbal tablets, meditations and all the other ideas that hadn't worked.

"It must have been frustrating for both of you," he said as I paused. There was a small table by my side with a water jug and glasses, I took a drink.

"It was, I couldn't get into a routine. All the time that Cath was on nights, I'd have trouble staying asleep. I'd almost got to the point of being used to her absence, able to sleep when suddenly, she was back in the bed and it all started again."

"Sleep disruption is a big problem," he said. "It's a major contributory factor in so many illnesses. Have you been stressed at work?"

"Yes, I think that I have. I see images of exotic places all day and have to make up slogans, encouraging people to visit them. I see them knowing I'll never get to them myself."

He nodded. "That's stressful and can contribute to all sorts of problems, sleep disorders included. Sorry, I interrupted your flow, please carry on."

I continued, I told him about the alternative life in my dreams and Cath's reaction, her initial disinterest. Then I went on to say how she had grown more concerned as I had got more obviously fatigued, how she had managed to get me an appointment with the consultant, the clinical trial of the tablets, the improved sleep and the clearer dreams.

Then I spoke of the coincidence of Phay appearing, the names, Cath jumping to conclusions. I almost broke down as I described how we argued and she left. He didn't say anything, his expression never changed. But he was listening intently.

"I'm sorry," he said, "it must be especially frustrating, not to be believed, more so when it's by the one person who you think had your back."

"Thank you." I was almost pathetically grateful that at least there was one person who hadn't dismissed me or shouted me down. "Do you believe me?"

"I believe that you believe it," he answered. "It's a fascinating story so far. Please tell me the rest and then I'll tell you what I think."

He let me go on again for a long while, I'd just got up to the point on Ecias where Anna had appeared and I'd found out about the plot. I interspersed it with my meeting Esther in this world, the dinner and even what happened at her flat, the sex that wasn't. I wanted to show him how the timelines connected, the coincidences, the mayfly, the names. Even down to the mole on her stomach. I told him everything. It must have sounded like a complete jumble. I was describing my efforts to get Anna to protect Vanessa when he interrupted me.

"That's a lot of information. My fingers would never have kept up. Let me see if I've got this right. Vanessa, the woman in your dreams, how you've described her, she's the same to look at as the woman that you're now working for."

"Yes, and my wife has put two and two together."

"And made five," he added. "You've told me a lot about your dreams; can you tell me how real your life is when you're in one of them? Do you feel surprised when you wake and find that you're not there?" I wondered where this was going.

"It's very real," I said. "In my dreams I have a full life. I've spent months on Ecias, done so much work. I'm a geological surveyor there, I checked out some of the technical terms I remember using, they all match. I'm not a scientist so I don't know where they come from. When I'm there, I don't think of here in the same way, in fact I don't think of this life at all."

He took more interest at that point, leaning forward. "So,

when you're on... Ecias, you use a technical vocabulary that you don't in this life?"

"That's right. It's the same with the Latin names for plants and trees. And there's more. I know things that can't be true."

"Wait," he held up his hand. "What do you mean, things that can't be true?"

"I can describe how a spaceship engine works, how we can travel faster than light. It all makes perfect sense to me. If I had the equipment, I could have a good try at making one for you. And I can use a multi-sensor mapping drone, use machinery that doesn't exist." I realised that my voice was getting louder; I was getting excited as I told him, remembering more and more as I went on.

"I've looked, none of it's been invented but I use it all the time. I'm familiar with it, how it works and how it's made. Hell, I can even tell you which planet the things are made on, who invented them. I don't just use the stuff, if it breaks down in the forest, I can strip and repair it too."

If that surprised him, he never showed it. His face was blank; the eyes behind the thick lenses gave nothing away. Maybe it was the sort of thing he heard all the time, perhaps his working life was filled with tales of galactic explorers.

"Interesting," he muttered, almost to himself. "Do you live a day at a time in your dream?"

"If you mean, do I sleep there and wake there in the mornings, yes I do. In some dreams I live on Ecias for a month or more. As I said, when I'm there, I don't dream of here. Or if I do; I don't recall it in the same way. When Cath left, I tried to remember and write everything down; I found that the act brought up more and more detail."

"You mean like writing in a diary would here?" he suggested.

"I've never kept a diary but I guess so. What I mean is that the act of remembering things prompted me to remember more things." I showed him the thick sheaf of papers, the notes I had started on the day after Cath had left. There were more now, I'd added quite a lot to them, details about my findings online and the things that had happened with Anna had brought them up to date.

"Are they your notes? Can I see them?"

I passed them over, he flipped through the pages. "May I make copies?" he asked. "I can assure you that nobody but me will see them. I haven't time in this consultation to read them all."

"Of course you can."

"Thank you." He stood and crossed to his desk. There was a small multi-function printer on it, next to a computer screen. He laid the papers on the tray and clicked a few buttons. There was the noise of the machine warming up. Soon, copies started to appear in the output tray. He had to reload the paper during the operation, I hadn't realised how my rambling about life on Ecias had grown.

The machine finished. He returned my sheets to me and sat again. "Thank you, I will read them with interest. Now, tell me one specific thing," he said. "Take a day in your life on Ecias and tell me about it. It doesn't have to be a special day, any day you like."

I thought for a moment, then I recounted the last day on Ecias that I had really been happy. I told him about the journey from our place into town, the time when Vanessa and I had ended up having sex by the side of the road. Telling him that, and he never flinched at some of the details, reminded me of the first time we had driven up to the place we would call home, our prefabricated cabin in the clearing. So I started talking about that.

I told him how the cabin had been dropped in by lifter, just as soon as we had cleared the undergrowth. From that, I remembered the fun that Vanessa and I had doing it. I told him about the animals that we saw from our window, once they had got used to our being there. How we fed the local Sawgrass family muesli from our hands, how their tongues felt against our palms.

"Hold on," he said. "Do you realise you've been talking for more than twenty minutes, you've told me more about the day you moved into the cabin, all the things you did, than I can remember about when I moved to my new house. And that was only a month ago. Not only that, it's all consistent, there's nothing that you've said that doesn't follow logic, or change with repetition. It leads you to other memories as well, which indicates a consistent timeline."

"So do you believe me?"

"Well, I think if you were after a bit of extra-marital gratification, you wouldn't need to go to such lengths. I can't think of anyone else who would have bothered inventing so much detail to hide an affair. Most people would just go to another town or use a false name."

While that might not be a ringing endorsement, it was a start.

"And there is one more thing," I said. "I was pinched by Ms Phay, to prove that I was on Earth."

His eyebrows rose. "Was that when you met her, after your wife had gone? I'm sorry but there is just so much information that I'm having trouble keeping up."

"That's right, as I said, we met for business; I showed her the advertising concepts I was working on. It was late in the afternoon, her secretary was going home. Esther suggested that we have dinner. I was working for her. I couldn't really say no. After the meal, we went back to her flat."

"And what happened while you were there?"

"To be honest, I only went because I wanted to try and get some more of the tablets. As well as clarifying my dreams, they were actually doing what they were supposed to, helping me sleep. In the end, events overtook me and I didn't get a chance to ask. She started asking me if I had noticed any side effects so far, I told her my story, like I've just told you. That was when the sex reared its head. She said that if she was like Vanessa and we were doing it in my dreams, we might as well in real life. She said that somehow it wouldn't count. I turned her down, which initially annoyed her; she pinched me to prove that she wasn't a dream and then I left. We parted as friends. And then, later that same night, while I was asleep, I was pinched by Vanessa on Ecias, to prove that I was there."

"That sounds like your brain processing the information and making up a part of your dream to explain it."

"Well maybe," I agreed. "The trouble is, the pinches were on different arms, look." I showed him the marks. Both of them were fading but both were still just visible. He took pictures, everyone had pictures now. He sat quietly for a moment.

"Thank you for telling me everything, it can't have been easy. There's a lot for me to consider. As a first step, I'd like you to have a brain scan. I think that I have the start of a theory."

I had to ask him. "Do you think that I'm mad?"

"There's that word again. No, but I think you have, at the very least, an overactive imagination. Now I want you to think about the main character in your dreams, Vanessa. You've told me how Vanessa and Esther look alike. I'm going to offer you an explanation of how it's possible."

I was a little dubious, but he was the expert. "Go on then," I suggested.

"You saw a picture of Esther Phay before you met her," he said. "It might have just been a fleeting glimpse in a magazine or on the news. You could even have passed her in the street or seen her in a car. It only had to be for a split second, not even long enough for your consciousness to register. Your brain liked the way she looked and transferred her face onto the person in your dream. Then when the real Esther turned up, you got confused, associated her with your dreams, not remembering that you'd seen her before. Lay people call it déjà vu but the correct term is cryptomnesia."

I couldn't accept that. "Surely I would have remembered," I began.

"Oh no, your brain can work so much faster than you realise. The information learned is forgotten but nevertheless stored in the brain, similar occurrences invoke the contained knowledge, leading to a feeling of familiarity because the event or experience being..."

I stopped him. "OK, enough of the technical stuff, so how does that tie in with the dreams? And what about all the other things I've told you, the name, the insect?"

"Well once you have one thing, then it acts like a trigger, your subconscious starts looking for similar patterns. If I told you that you would see lots of crows, for instance, then subconsciously you would be more alert to them. In effect you would *see* more of them. Except that *see* in this case merely means that your brain would notice them more, pass the information across to your consciousness."

"Because you told me to expect to see them?"

"Exactly. It's a popular trick, used by entertainers the world over. And there really are such things as coincidences, which complicates matters tremendously."

Surely I had told him that the dreams had started before I took the drugs? I had but the effect was certainly stronger once I was taking them.

"Why did the tablets that Phay gave me enhance the dreams?"

"I don't know what's in them, but some drugs can cause what's called a dopaminergic reaction, affecting the way your neurotransmitters work, it can alter your perception and all sorts of other things. That's why they're on trial, so the side-effects can be found and evaluated."

At last we were getting to a possible answer. "So, if I had a dream, with a face that I had glimpsed and forgotten, it might have passed if I hadn't been taking any of these tablets."

He nodded. "That's right."

"But they enhanced my perception with this doper... thing and now I'm stuck in the delusion."

"It's not how I would describe it but basically, yes, that's about right."

"So why the scan? Surely when I stopped the tablets, the brain should have settled itself down. I would have gone back to normal, had other dreams about ordinary things. Can't you tell Cath that this explains it all, that I'm not being unfaithful?"

He hedged. "Let's take one thing at a time. First, have the scan. If it shows what I think it will, then we're making progress."

"And when will all this scanning happen?"

"The scanner is always busy, but I'll try to get you a slot within a couple of days, I'll send you an appointment. If you're prepared to travel, it will be quicker, the scanner is mobile. It's too expensive for every hospital to have its own. The results will come to me and I'll arrange a follow up."

"That'll be no problem, my boss is understanding. After the scan, can I go back to the solicitor?"

He smiled. "That's not my area, but once I have everything I'll pass it to him. He can arrange what to do next."

It all made sense. It was certainly something I could present to Cath.

We shook hands. "It was good to meet you," he said. "You can leave by the other door. That way you don't see the next patient, and they don't see you. It avoids any potential embarrassment. Just press the green button to open the outer door."

He pointed to the door I had noticed on the way in, it led into a short corridor, I pressed the button and found myself in the street. It was dark, how long had I been in there?

I looked at my watch. I had been with Doctor Borth for more than three hours! It was too late to go back to the office, I walked back to my car with a spring in my step, everything was going to be OK. I would have Cath back as soon as she had seen the evidence.

There were only a couple of cars left in the car park; everyone else had gone for the day. I looked up; the light was on in Hughie's office. I idly wondered if he was alone, like I would shortly be.

I got home, had a shower and sat down to eat. I had some serious thinking to do. I had told my story to so many people now, it was getting hard to keep track. Esther, Molly and Deanne were the ones who might let something slip, gossip about how weird it all was. Hughie, Colin and Borth would probably keep quiet. I had to hope that it didn't get out, if the media got a sniff of a man who thought that he lived in the future, they would have a field day. That wouldn't help me convince Cath that I was worth coming home to.

When I got into bed, I automatically started counting. Now that I didn't have the tablets, it was almost like an incantation, a magic spell to take me to Ecias.

CHAPTER TWENTY EIGHT

ECIAS

THERE WAS a lot of confused shouting, a mixture of voices in the distance. "Get the lights." "Where are you?" "Who's that over there?" were just some of the shouts that had woken me up. What was all the fuss about?

I was lying on top of the camp bed, in my prison. The night air felt heavy and oppressive, rain was coming. Something was going on outside, it sounded unplanned, hectic. There were screams in the distance, cut short. I heard the sudden burst of noise as a vehicle started up and accelerated. A woman, it sounded like Anna, shouted, "Vanessa!" My blood ran cold. I needed to get out, I had a feeling that bad things were happening.

I went to the door as the shouting continued. "What's happening?" I called, there was no answer; whoever was guarding me had gone off to investigate. I rattled the door, it was still locked.

I climbed on the desk and peered out of the window, it faced the trees and I couldn't see anything, just flickering shadows as torch beams flashed about.

Eventually, the lights stopped moving around, there was no more shouting. A calm darkness descended on the settlement. I heard footsteps, my guard was coming back.

"What's going on," I shouted through the door.

"It's all quiet," came the reply. "There was some sort of incident at the hostel. It was all over by the time I got there. I think someone was creeping around, trying to steal things."

The hostel. Vanessa was in the hostel, she had moved over there to be safer, at my request. Was there a connection? "Who shouted for Vanessa?" I asked.

"I don't know, it was all a bit confused," he said. "We'll sort it out in the morning, go back to sleep."

But I couldn't sleep. I paced and worried. It was cruel to leave me like this. I needed to know, one way or the other. Why had someone shouted her name like that?

My breakfast was late, Anna finally appeared with it.

"What's going on?" I asked her as soon as the door opened. "I heard all the shouting in the night, what's happened? I asked the guard but he wouldn't let on."

Anna hung her head, avoiding my gaze. "Two masked men broke into my room at the hostel," she said. "They told me that they were looking for Vanessa. They held me up at gunpoint and told me that if I didn't tell them where she was, they would shoot me."

She seemed remarkably calm for someone who had just gone through that sort of ordeal.

"What did you say?"

"I said that if they shot me I'd be unable to tell them, if they wounded me I'd be too busy screaming the place down to tell them. Then I asked if they could smile for the infrared camera. I'm pretty sure they were the plant hunters."

She was some sort of cool customer. "What happened then?" I asked.

"At that point they left, that was when I started shouting for help."

"I heard someone call out for Vanessa, is she alright?"

She looked up at me, her face anguished. "As I chased them out of the hostel, Vanessa came out of her room to see what all the fuss was about. She stood right in front of them; they grabbed her and threw her into that black vehicle. It drove off. There was nothing I could do."

My world fell apart; this must be the start of the 'phase two' that I had overheard the plant hunters talking about.

"This will be the second distraction, it was in my notes. You have to follow them, Anna." I pleaded with her. "We have to get her back. I overheard them talking about what they want to do with her."

"I know, she told me she was scared of them, and I remember you mentioned it. You're right to be angry, I should have done more to stop it happening. Ove's launched a drone to try and keep track of them. According to their EPIRBs they're over at the Canal, they've never left."

"Surely everyone can see that I'm innocent now."

"It's certainly helped your cause. To complicate matters, the police arrived just before sunrise, while we were still searching. There are six of them and a forensic investigator. Ove's with them now. As soon as I can, I'm going to reveal myself to them, present my evidence and see what happens. I've sent a message to Burgstrom; there's a shipload of our private security on the way, as fast as they can get here."

"This is all part of their plan, isn't it?"

She nodded. "I think this is the second diversion you spoke about, they knew the police were arriving and they wanted to get them running around, give them so many things to do that they miss the important one."

"And what's the important one?" Considering I was the supposed criminal, I was asking all the questions, but she was patient with her answers.

"I think you were right. The planet's going to be fought over,

Burgstrom against Tontranix. There's Praseodymium and goodness knows what else here. Both companies want it; Burgstrom might have it now but Tontranix think that they can take it from them. And unless Burgstrom get here quickly, they might just be right."

CHAPTER TWENTY NINE

EARTH

I HAD WONDERED when or even if I would go back to Ecias. I had even thought that the dreams were fading, becoming irregular. I could see now they had only really stopped when I was hiding from the plant hunters. Now that events were moving forward, I seemed to be there on a regular basis again. I almost wished that I wasn't. Things were getting worse on Ecias, just as I thought that they were getting better on Earth. I had been worried about Vanessa's safety, with me in the cell and unable to protect her. I expect that Dr Borth would say that was the reason why she had been kidnapped in my latest dream visit. No doubt he would say that I had projected my fear into my dream and made it happen.

Which conveniently ignored the bigger question. Why had she been in my dream in the first place?

I could chase the argument around all day. Like the chicken and the egg, I got no closer to working out which bit came first. And why I had created it.

I was on the way to another day at work, mentoring Deanne. I was coming to realise that she didn't need me, that she was more than capable of doing things by herself. Hughie had already promised her the next big job when it came in.

I was driving when my phone rang, my car picked up the call, interrupting the radio. It was Dr Borth's secretary.

"Mr Wilson, I have a slot in the mobile scanner for you, there's been a cancellation. Can you get over to Southern General Hospital by nine thirty?"

Southern General, that was where Cath worked, was she on days or nights? I couldn't remember, she had said something about swapping and doing holiday cover. I didn't want to bump into her if I could help it. 'Don't talk to her', my solicitor had said, surely hers would have told her the same. Anyway, thinking about it, it was a mobile scanner. She would be on the ward if she was working. In the end it didn't matter, I had to go and get myself scanned.

"Yes, I can get there," I said. "I'm on the way into work, I can detour."

"Thank you, I'll confirm it with them and send all the paperwork over. Goodbye." She ended the call. The radio came on again as the phone disconnected.

I called Hughie, told him that I would be in later, and why. He wished me good luck. When I got to the hospital, I found a parking space straight away, which was a feat in itself. The scanner was a huge white trailer standing in a corner of the car park. And I was ten minutes early.

I went into the trailer; the first part was fitted out as a reception area, all soft lights and comfy chairs. I introduced myself to the nurse and she checked me in. She gave me a questionnaire about my health, and an information sheet about the scanning process. The first thing I saw was a long list of things that were not allowed in the scanner: metal screws and plates, jewellery, hairpins, eyeglasses, watches, wigs, dentures, hearing aids, underwire bras. None of them applied to me.

I didn't need to read about the process, as soon as I knew that I was having a scan, I had searched online to find out all that I could. It mentioned that the space was limited inside, as far as I knew I wasn't claustrophobic, we would soon find out.

While I was writing what I could remember of my medical details, the door to the scanner opened and a man was pushed out, on a wheelchair. "There we are, Mr Marcus," the nurse said. "Someone will be over to take you back to the ward."

"I'll phone for a nurse, Tina," said the receptionist, picking up the phone and dialling. The nurse went back in and shut the door behind her. There were noises from within, as if she was adjusting something.

Mr Marcus was looking at me, I smiled. "Good morning," I said. He carried on looking at me and smiling. The nurse had a brief conversation about collecting a patient, he didn't notice, just looked straight ahead.

"Mr Marcus is deaf," the reception nurse told me as she replaced the receiver. "He's suffered a head injury, mugged in the street for his pension."

I was about to try again when the door opened. "Mr Wilson," she said. "You can go in now."

As I walked to the door, the other nurse looked at me as if she recognised the name, perhaps she knew Cath. I handed the forms to her and followed her into the other part of the trailer. She gave me a gown. "You can get changed over there. We're scanning your head with Magnetic Resonance Imaging today, strip to the waist and put the gown on."

The scanner was like a large white donut on its side with a flat rectangular box poking out of the hole. There was a bed on top of it. The nurse was studying the forms and comparing them with whatever was on her computer screen. There was no screen for me to hide behind, I took off my shirt and put the gown on. It laced up at the back and I struggled to tie the sides together. She watched me for a moment.

"Don't worry too much about that. Can you tell me your name, and the first line of your address?"

"Richard Wilson, 19 Canal Lane."

"Thank you, Richard. And your date of birth?"

"Call me Rick, March twenty-seven, 1987."

"That's great. So, Rick, just a headshot today then," she said, as if probing your head was another boring job. "We'll soon see what, if anything, is going on in there."

I was used to the apparent flippancy of nurses; I knew from Cath that they all did it, to keep from getting too stressed. "If you find a brain in there, let me know," I answered, keeping the gallows humour going.

"If we can't find it there, perhaps we could look in your trousers," she said. Even though that was the sort of remark that Cath would make, I thought it was a bit much. It might have been acceptable if we were friends, but I didn't know her. In my present predicament I suppose it touched a nerve. I just grinned as she shepherded me towards the bed.

"When you're ready, hop onto the slide," the nurse said. I wondered what else she might say, what could possibly follow that remark? She must have realised that she had said something inappropriate, she was suddenly very professional. She got me settled on the bed, with my head nearest the donut, held steady in a set of foam blocks. "It's important to keep your head still," she said, placing a small box, attached to a wire, in my hand. "Any problems, press the button."

Problems, I hadn't reckoned on problems. "What sort of problems?" I croaked, my mouth had suddenly gone dry.

"The machine can't hurt you. Press if you feel claustrophobic, if you want to sneeze or cough."

She retreated behind a screen and pushed buttons, I could hear her voice through a loudspeaker. "Hold tight, we're rolling you in now."

The bed moved and my head entered the hole. A red light shone on my nose, the board jerked about as she positioned it, by peering down I could see it on my chin.

"Keep your head still," she said. "Right, we're starting, it'll be about a minute. Her phone rang. "Hang on; I need to take this call before we start."

There was a pause while she had a conversation, I couldn't hear what was said but there was a lot of 'yes' and 'OK'. I wanted to lift my head, not knowing what was going on was disconcerting. I could see why people might be freaked out by being in the scanner. It felt unnatural, having to be immobile, knowing that all that stuff would be bombarding you.

"Sorry about that, Dan," she said. "We're starting now. There will be a series of clicks as the magnets fire, the bed will move a little between each pass."

Before I had chance to wonder why she had called me Dan, the machine emitted a tremendous clattering noise. I found it almost too loud to bear; it was like there were people hammering inside the white container that surrounded my head. Coupled with the feeling of being shut in, it was quite frightening. I closed my eyes, tried to think of other things.

Even though I knew I couldn't detect the passage of the rays, or whatever it was that was passing through my head, my senses strained to notice any sign of them whizzing through my skull, my brain. It was all very well saying they did no harm, it was my brain they were bombarding.

The noise started and stopped randomly, there was no apparent sequence to it. You could almost go mad waiting for it to start again; it was like the Chinese Water Torture. Even though the gaps between the pulses were only seconds, the silence was just as bad as the noise. While they were absent, the bed moved, jerking into a new position before they started again. She had said a minute, how long was that? I didn't want to press the button but if the noise went on much longer I knew that I would. Just when I thought that I couldn't take any more, the noise stopped. It didn't start again, instead I heard her voice. My ears were ringing, she sounded like she was miles away.

"All done," she said, as the bed slid back out of the hole.

I tried to stand, the noise had done something to my ears and I found it hard to balance, I gripped the side of the table.

"You can get changed and go," she said, bent over her screen. "Your results will be sent on in a week or so."

I got dressed and left. The other nurse was still behind her desk, there was a woman waiting. She looked worried as I staggered out of the room.

"Are you alright, Mr Wilson?" the nurse said.

I nodded, although the act set off waves of nausea in my head. "It's loud in that thing," I said.

"It's an old one," she answered, "on its last legs, quite safe though. The new ones are a lot quieter. It's a pity you moved, it means the scan loses focus and definition. That's why they had to do it twice. Didn't the headphones help you?"

It didn't seem worth mentioning that I hadn't been offered any.

CHAPTER THIRTY

I GOT into work after a hair-raising drive from the hospital. My ears were still ringing and turning my head too quickly made me feel queasy. I made myself a strong coffee, which helped a little. I was working with Deanne on improving her photo-editing techniques when the phone rang. Deanne picked it up, listened.

Initially she was nodding her head, then suddenly the other person must have said something that upset her, her face changed, she went red and slammed the phone down. She turned to me. "That was your wife," she said, her voice cracking; she was obviously shocked by what she had heard. "She's on her way up to see you, she accused me of sleeping with you, said some horrible things to me."

"I'm sorry, Deanne, she's got this idea in her head about me and Esther Phay."

"I know about that but why would she start including me in it all? She said you were a liar, said that we were all covering up for you."

"I'm going," I said, "before she gets here."

Deanne shook her head. "She called from the car park, Rick, you don't have time."

"My solicitor said that I wasn't to talk to her. What can I do?

I'm sorry about all this; I didn't want to drag any of you into my problems."

Hughie came out of his office while Molly went to comfort Deanne. "Rick," he said. "Go into my office, stay in the bedroom, I'll get rid of her."

I almost sniggered at the idea of hiding from my wife in a bedroom; it was farcical, then I realised that it wasn't a joke.

I kept out of sight of the door, heard it open, heard Hughie say, "Hi, Cath. How are you?"

"Is he here?" she said, there was no 'hello Hughie', no pleasantries at all.

"No, Cath, he's not."

It was clear that she didn't believe him, her voice went up in volume. "You're a lying bastard, Hughie. I reckon he's here and I'm sure he can hear me. I know he's hiding in your office, in that bedroom you had built there. I want him to know that I've found out more about his not-so-secret life. After I've finished telling my solicitor, well, he'd better have deep pockets."

She turned to Deanne. "Is he shagging you as well?" she asked. "Apparently he likes brown hair."

Deanne burst into tears. "There's no need to come in here and be abusive, Cath," Hughie said.

"Come on, Cath," Molly tried to calm her down. "We're friends aren't we, this isn't helping."

"Shut it, Hughie," she shouted. "I know you'll all stick up for him. How long has it been going on, how long has he been keeping it quiet? Is it as long as you and Molly? Did Claire ever find out about you, is that why she drove into that tree?"

There was total silence. It was no good, I wasn't supposed to be talking to her but I couldn't let her speak to my friends like that. She was way out of line. I stepped into view. "Hello, Cath," I said. Molly had gone very pale, Hughie was stood facing Cath, both of them were red faced. Deanne was crying.

Cath turned towards me and as she recognised me, I saw pure

hatred on her face. She was still wearing scrubs, with her coat over the top.

She shouted at me. "I bloody knew it, you were here all along." Over her shoulder, through the open door, I could see that a couple of people had come out of the other offices to see what all the noise was about.

"What's happened, Cath? I saw the note you left last week. I thought you said that you were coming back."

She was almost hyperventilating in her rage. "I was until I spoke to Tina. Remember her, the agency nurse? Last week she helped me find out your little secret, today she was the nurse in the scanner. I came over to collect Mr Marcus and saw your name on the sheet. I called Tina. She said that she'd already worked out who you were. She told me that she saw you and Esther Phay coming out of the Avon, one day last week. That you were in in the scanner this morning; she said you were having your brain scanned. I told her to make sure that she forgot to give you the headphones, and to do the scan twice. I hope it gave you a headache."

That was just nasty, and it explained the reference to my trousers. "I don't deny having dinner with Phay, it was business."

"Rick must have told you that we're working for Phay," added Hughie.

"Dinner," she spat out the words. "As soon as my back was turned. I'd only been gone a few days, because of what you and her were up to. What do you do? You're straight off to her for dinner! Do you really expect me to believe that's all it was? Tina told me that you left the restaurant arm in arm; 'they both got into Rick's car and drove off, they seemed to be the best of friends' she said."

"I was giving her a lift home," I answered. "I couldn't just leave her there could I?"

"So you admit it, you went back to her flat."

I was silent, I couldn't deny it. "I won't deny it, I took her home. It was the polite thing to do. I didn't stop."

"Hah, you admit that you went there. How long you stopped isn't important. I've just come from her office, I went to see her. She told me the same, that you didn't stop." She paused. "But then she would say that, wouldn't she?"

Before anything else could be said, two uniformed police came into the office. They stood in front of Cath. "Are you Catherine Wilson?" the female one asked.

She suddenly seemed to shrink before my eyes. Her shoulders slumped and I think she realised what was happening, she must have pushed too far, done something stupid.

"I'm arresting you for assault on the person of Ms Esther Phay, causing bodily harm. And for causing criminal damage to her office premises," the second one said, producing handcuffs. "You do not have to say anything but it may harm your defence if you do not mention when questioned something you later rely on in court. Anything you do say may be given in evidence. Do you understand?"

Cath nodded. "Yes," she said in a whisper. He moved behind her and with a practised sweep of his arms pulled her wrists together. The snap of the lock was very loud.

Together, they walked her out of the office. There was now a small crowd in the lobby, everyone who worked on this floor must have heard and seen what had just happened. And told everyone else. Hughie shut the door on them. He turned to me, he looked ten years older.

"I think it would be better if you don't come in for a while, Rick," he said. I noticed that his hands were shaking. "Take some time off. I need to decide what to do about things."

I could hardly believe what I had just seen; my life was turning bad in both worlds. On Ecias I had been imprisoned, suspected of killing Vince; my wife had been taken hostage.

Here, my marriage and my life in general was falling apart.

My wife hated me, she had been arrested in front of me accused of assaulting Hughie's client, the woman she thought I was seeing. She had said some terrible things to Hughie and the others. There seemed little chance that things would ever be right in either of my lives.

CHAPTER THIRTY ONE

"MS PHAY IS NOT TAKING CALLS," said the secretary. I'd called Phay from my car. I had sat in it for a good half an hour, in the car park at Creative Concepts. I didn't know what to do. It was all very well the solicitor telling me not to speak to Esther Phay, what was supposed to happen when you had to? Esther had been assaulted, by *my* wife, I felt responsible. So I called Phay Medical, only to be told that she wasn't taking any calls.

"Can you tell her that it's Rick from Creative Concepts please, it's very important."

"I'm afraid that you're the one she is not taking calls from. Please don't call again," the secretary said, hanging up.

I know I shouldn't have, it was the stupidest thing to do, but I went to her flat. I settled down outside the front door in my car to wait for her. An hour or so later she appeared, she was wearing a heavy coat and dark glasses.

I got out of my car, walked towards her. "Esther," I said.

"Go away. I don't want to see you, or talk to you." Her head was down and she kept going.

I stood in front of her, blocking her from moving. "What happened? Why won't you answer my calls? What have I done?" Perhaps it wasn't the brainiest question. I tried to sound contrite, even though there was nothing that I had to apologise for.

"You, nothing. I had a visit from your psycho wife," she lifted the glasses, her eyes were red, she had done a lot of crying. "She seems to think that we're having an affair."

I nodded. "I know, I've tried to tell her but it does no good."

"She was going on about your dreams, how they were a way of hiding it. And something about my name being a clue. I didn't understand it. I tried to convince her there was nothing going on between us. And there isn't, not now, not then and certainly not in the future."

"I was seen, leaving the restaurant with you, that night."

She smiled at the memory. "There might have been something then, there was some sort of spark I suppose, but..." I thought she was going to cry, she sniffed a bit and carried on. "I looked her in the eye and told her that you did nothing. The trouble is, I can't take the strain, it nearly did happen. I have to cut all ties with you. That's why I got our vice-president to cancel your contract. If my father finds out there will be big trouble, especially if he gets to hear that I knew about you being on the drug trial."

I told her what had just happened. "She came to my office, after she saw you, she's been arrested."

"Good. She grabbed me, pushed me." She pulled up the sleeve of her coat, showed me her arms, they were covered with red marks from Cath's grip. They reminded me of the pinches, only much worse.

"That's not all," she said. She pulled her coat open and lifted her blouse, her ribs were red. "That's where I hit my desk, my secretary called the police while she was trashing my office. She ran off before they arrived, said that you were next on her list."

"I'm sorry." It sounded pathetic and inadequate.

She turned away from me. "Get out of my life, and stay out." She walked off and I was sensible enough to let her go.

Stunned, I returned to my car. Cath had been stupid, let her emotions get the better of her; she must have been wound up by the nurse Tina, the one from the scanner.

Next morning, I wasn't really surprised when I got a call from my solicitors. At least I was at home, away from the office, this was one call that I wanted to have privately.

"Hello, Mr Wilson, I'm sure you know what's been going on," Colin was cheerful. "I've just heard from Simon Walsh, your wife's solicitor. Apparently, she was arrested for common assault on Esther Phay."

"I know, I was there, in the office, when it all happened."

"She'll be up in front of the magistrates the day after tomorrow. That's the first available sitting. He says that she's being kept in custody until then."

I couldn't believe that Cath was in the cells, I had imagined that she would be let out until she was required in court.

"They've charged her with assault and criminal damage," he said. "Simon told me that they were going to let her go, on bail. Her mother had agreed to take her. That was until she started making threats against you and others. She became quite agitated, they decided to keep her in custody till she calmed down. They also wanted to stop her doing anything stupid. I'll be there when she appears in court. It's possible that you'll be called as a witness. Even if you're not, I guess that you'd want to attend."

I did, not to gloat, but to try and see why she had done it, what had made her behave so out of character. My money was still on the influence of Tina. "Do you think that I'll have to give evidence?"

He paused for a moment. "It's possible. Simon says that she's not really listening to him at the moment. His advice is that she pleads guilty, there were witnesses, it's all on CCTV, it's a foregone conclusion. Plead guilty, say sorry and move on."

"What will happen if she doesn't, she won't go to prison will she?"

"No, it's minor stuff, at least as far as the system's concerned. Assault and a bit of criminal damage, it's no comfort to you but the magistrates see this sort of thing all the time. She'll get a fine, probably a conditional discharge. You might have to speak up for her character, or you might have to give evidence, give context, explain why she did it. It all depends on whether Simon can talk some sense into her."

The thought filled me with sudden panic. I couldn't give evidence. Cath's solicitor would ask me about Ecias. I'd be made to look like I was some sort of madman.

"I assume that will be OK," Colin said. "Can you get time off work?"

I thought about work. Hughie had told me to go away, Phay had told me to go away. Cath was in court, the way it looked, I'd never see her again. I wasn't even sure if I would have a job to go back to. "Oh yes, I've got all the time in the world."

"Good," he said. "The day after tomorrow then, magistrates' court, public entrance, be there at nine-thirty. Wear a nice suit."

The way things were going, if I'd been offered the choice, at this precise moment I'd have taken Ecias over Earth.

CHAPTER THIRTY TWO

ECIAS

TWO POLICEMEN CAME into my cell. This time, the door stayed open. I could see Anna standing behind them.

"Mr Dan Waldon," the one with the most braid spoke. "I'm Detective Conner. We were called to Ecias by Mr Strand. He told us that there had been a murder, and that you were the only suspect."

"Yes," I said. "And I'm..."

He held up his hand. "Not so fast, I said that you *were* the only suspect. Now we've arrived there seems to be a lot more going on. We've learned that there's been a kidnapping and strangely, or significantly, it involves your wife."

Anna came in. "They know who I am, Dan. I've given them all the evidence that you told me about, showed them your notes. Their expert has examined the crime scene. Between us, we've had a good look around. We found the tree with the bullet in it. It's been recovered and is being compared with all the others, compared with the pistol that Ove found by your trailer."

The policeman waved at her to be quiet. "Thank you, Ms Durban. You're private security, we're the law. We're still investigating but on the face of it, you're no longer a suspect. There is a bigger problem; it seems from what this lady has told us that this planet is under some sort of attack. The death of Mr Kendall, your involvement, your wife's disappearance, everything that's going on, it's all connected."

At last, someone had put all the pieces together and could see the bigger picture. That still left the most important thing to me. "Never mind that, have you found Vanessa?"

Anna shook her head. "Not yet. The police are flying over to the plant hunters' camp later today."

"Do you think that's where she'll be?" I asked. "For various reasons, I think that they're a lot closer. Even if they were taking her to the Canal, she can't be there yet." He gave me a quizzical look. "The plant hunters don't have aircraft," I explained. "It's at least four days drive from here."

"I understand but we have to start somewhere. We'll follow the road," the policeman said. "See if we can spot them. If they're en route we can attempt a rescue."

"Please be careful, I know you have a bigger problem but she's still my wife. Don't let her be collateral damage."

Conner nodded. "We won't put her in more danger, or attempt to rescue her if we're not sure we can do it. Ms Durban tells me that these three so-called plant hunters have been very clever, casting suspicion on you and threatening your wife. The evidence from Mr Kendall's video that I've seen backs it all up. On video, several times, he says that you both have been nothing but helpful."

That was good to hear. All the messages that Vince had been sending had shown our real relationship.

"There was no trouble here until the plant hunters turned up," I said. "If they really are plant hunters."

Conner looked at me. "We can find little about Kalesh Pharmaceuticals," he said. "They seem to be a company owned by Tontranix, although that information is well hidden."

I looked at Anna. "I told you they were wearing Tontranix boiler suits," I said and she nodded.

"I passed your notes over," she said. "All the evidence that we have from Mr Strand showed that they had been moving around the vicinity of their camp since they got to it. Their EPIRBs have never come this far."

"Did you see the film that Vince shot? They were in their vehicle; we saw them on the road."

Conner interrupted us. "That and the other film he shot is what's convinced me that you're right. Then there was the camp we found in the trees outside town. It was exactly where your notes said it would be. As far as the police are concerned, you're free to go."

That was a relief, I was out and now I could start to do what I should have been able to do from the start. "I want to help you find Vanessa."

"One thing at a time, let's get you out and into the sunshine, you can help us organise our next move. The word is, you know the forest better than most."

"Thank you," I said as they led me out of the building and I tasted the fresh air. "How long have I been locked in there? I've lost track of the time."

* * *

"Will you make an official statement?" asked the policeman, Conner. Anna and I were sat in Whistles, it was still inside but at least it had proper windows and no lock on the door. There were three other policemen with him, two men in combat gear and a woman, dressed in a flight suit. As I'd left the farm compound and walked across the settlement to get here, I'd got a couple of strange looks from people, but no one was outwardly hostile. Perhaps recent events had changed their minds, they had another suspect now.

"Won't my notes be sufficient?" I was itching to get involved in the search for Vanessa. But Conner seemed to be wasting his time on paperwork. I tried not to show my frustration, it wouldn't help to upset him, he was my best chance of getting Vanessa back.

"Yes, I guess they will be, if we get them typed up and you sign them, in view of the situation we'll do it later. They're very comprehensive; we have managed to verify most of what you said. As you were told, we found the tree and its bullet. We found the campsite the people were using. Our forensics expert is checking the bullets and the gun now."

"Like I said before, I don't think they can be based at the Canal," I said. "Their camp can't be that far away from Richavon. They wouldn't want to do all that travelling; it would be a waste of their time. They must be somewhere closer, to keep an eye on the settlement."

"That's a good point; they are all shown at the camp down by the feature you call the Canal or at least in the vicinity, all the time. But the evidence that we have from you shows that's not always the case."

"That's enough to get them thrown off planet," said Anna. "They all signed up to carry EPIRBs at all times."

The policeman nodded. "We're getting organised to visit their camp at the Canal. We'll see what they're up to over there. As for another camp, where do we start to look? I only have the cruiser and a small team. I want to keep a couple of them here, so I can spare three. We can't search the planet, not even the area around Richavon properly."

"How about scanning for them from the ship?" I asked. "Surely you can spot a group of four people in a vehicle?"

"It's not that simple," he said. "Maybe we could find them, but that's only the first part. Even if we did, our engine noise would alert them. By the time we found a place to land and get to them, they'd be long gone. We haven't got all the assault gear, we're just a patrol. I can see that you want us to do something, but trust me, this is safer. Vanessa has no value to them dead, they will have to come to us. When they do, we can act in Vanessa's best interests."

I digested that; I could understand why Conner didn't want to find the bad guys. They would know we were onto them, have a chance to run, to kill Vanessa. I wasn't as sure as he was that keeping Vanessa alive was worth their time, she might have already served her purpose. Like it or not, I would have to be patient.

"Now that you're here, we can have a proper briefing," Conner said. "I've told Ove to come over as well." He looked frustrated, unaccustomed to being kept waiting. "We can't wait for him all day, he'll have to catch up. Dan, can you start by explaining the physical situation at the Canal. I understand that you've been on the ground over there." I noticed that he said told, not asked, he must still be unsure if Ove was part of the problem.

I got up and went to the map of the area from Richavon to the Canal. It was up on the big screen that was normally used to show the video films and sports that we got with the supplies. The three police sat up and started to take notice as Anna passed me a tablet. "It's paired with that," she said. I looked down, both screens showed the same picture.

"Who's this guy, boss?" asked the lady in the flight suit.

"This is Dan," said Conner. "He's the local expert and so you know, we're pretty sure that the bad guys have his wife."

"I'm sorry to hear that, Dan," she said. "Tell me where I need to go."

"I'll do my best, what can I call you?" I asked.

"I'm Dyce," she said. I must have given her a strange look. "It's my call sign, not my name," she added, "it'll do for now."

"I'm Jack, and this is Kento," said one of the uniformed officers. "That's our real names, we don't get call signs, we're just the muscle." The two high-fived.

Dyce looked pained. "You see what they give me to work with?"

"Saved your ass," one of them said. They high-fived again. "Sure did," said the other.

"Can it, people. Listen to the man," said Conner. They all mumbled 'sir' and shut up. I had no idea if they were any good at what they did, they seemed frighteningly gung-ho to me.

I pinched and zoomed the map to show the road between Richavon and the Canal. On the big screen the image swirled and moved in synch. "This is the road they will have taken," I said, "if they're heading away from town."

"Can't they have gone any other way?"

"No, the road only goes down to the harbour. And short of walking cross country, there's no other way to get to the Canal."

Dyce nodded. "OK, so what's it like at this Canal place then?"

I swiped the display and got to the coast. "It's around eighteen-hundred kilometres from Richavon, the road's not brilliant so it's four days' good driving. If that's where they were going, they must be nearly there." The map showed a wide, sandy beach with low rocky dunes, a huge grassy area between the sand and the forest. "There's plenty of room for you to set down." I pointed to a red dot flashing in the middle of the grass.

"That's their EPIRBs," said Anna. "There're pictures of the area loaded as well, click on the icon, Dan, bottom left."

I saw it and clicked. There was a short slideshow of the area. The beach with its low line of rocks and the grass. It looked like about two hundred metres to the trees, plenty of room for their ship.

Dyce nodded. "Easy enough to set down," she said. "We'll take the long way around, over the land at low level and come in out of the sun."

Anna spoke up, "Do you want to see the video that Vince shot?" She turned to me. "Remember when he left you, he was going to take a look."

I remembered the panic we had felt when he had gone missing, the inhospitable conditions and the march to try and find him.

195

And his story that he had got lost, when he had been the one to leave. "Was all that slogging around we did a set-up then, a faked survey expedition to get him close to the plant hunters without attracting suspicion?"

"Only in part," she said. "Burgstrom did want the survey data from those locations, it all fitted together. There was some suspicion of the motives of the Kalesh team, at a higher level. We thought, Harald and I, that a 'chance' meeting would be a good way to see what was going on."

"So we were decoys?" She had the grace to look embarrassed. "Let's not get involved in that now, we did what we did. Watch the video, it won't take long, I'll just show you the important bits."

The picture on the big screen changed to Vince's face, with a background of the inside of his tent. "Day twenty-one," he said. "I'm waiting for Dan and Vanessa to settle, then I'm pulling camp and heading towards the target."

There was a jumble of pictures for a few seconds, then a point of view shot of a speeded-up walk through a forest. When the picture settled I recognised the place, it was where we had found Vince's gear. "I'm now five k from the beach," Vince whispered. "Time to travel light."

"This is it," said Anna as Vince set off, the picture showed a view of dappled shade, of tall trees and large shrubs. He walked in silence for a while, then the palette changed as Vince put a filter in. Everything was now blue, except for a sudden blaze of red and yellow. "That one," he whispered, "that plant is hotter than the rest." The picture dropped to just above ground level. Vince was crawling across the ground, using the undergrowth as cover.

When he reached the plant, it was obviously a fake, a metal frame with a camouflaged tent over it. Inside it, there were banks of screens, behind it, a path leading away towards the beach.

Vince put his camera down on the desk, we could see his hands on the keyboard as he scrolled through the screens. "They have remote cameras, showing the area around this location," he said, "and there's a lot more. It looks like a database…"

Off camera, there was a noise. "Someone's coming," said Vince, the camera moved as he got up. Now it pointed at the entrance to the hide; Vince slipped through.

We could see parts of the struggle that followed. As the two men wrestled, they popped in and out of view. We could hear grunts of pain and hear the snap of branches breaking, overlaid with rapid breathing.

Finally, Vince reappeared, he was covered in earth, there were twigs in his hair and blood on his shirt. He was breathing heavily. "I've killed a man," he said. "He went for me with a knife and I managed to turn it back on him." He picked up the camera and went outside. There was a body in a dark boiler suit. He was lying on his back in a pool of blood. The one thing I did notice as the camera panned over him was the lack of a beard. "I have to get away," Vince panted, "before he's found. There's no time to download any of the data, I need to give myself a chance to get back to Dan." The camera went blank.

Conner looked at Anna. "When did you see this?" he asked.

"Last night," she replied. "He hadn't sent this footage back, I guess he was keeping it until I got here, for security. I found this memory card in Dan's pack, he must have hidden it there. You would have found it if you hadn't had to run."

The picture came back. "I've hidden the body as best as I can and covered the blood with earth and leaves. It's not perfect but I can't waste any more time here. I'm heading back to my camp, hopefully Dan will have found it by now, if not I'll keep going till we meet up."

The pilot, Dyce, spoke up. "Seems like there's more than just a camp for three people?" The other two nodded and grinned. "I hope so," one said. "I didn't come here to stroll around the woods and go home."

"Gimmee some action," said the other and they high-fived

again. This seemed like strange behaviour for trained professionals, they acted like they were wound up and itching to shoot something. Not that that particularly bothered me, I couldn't do what they did. As long as they were careful around Vanessa, they could shoot the plant hunters or anyone else they found as much as they liked.

"Go and have a look," Conner said. "Find out exactly what's going on. But take it careful, no crazy heroics. And don't follow the road, it's too risky. You're right, Dyce, there appears to be a lot more going on than we thought. Don't take chances, get as much information as you can and get out. Keep your cameras on."

The three nodded and got up. As they filed out Dyce looked at me. "Relax, Dan. We'll get her back for you," she winked as she passed me.

The other two grinned. "Action at last," one said.

"Don't worry about them," said Conner as we heard the police ship's engines start. "They talk a lot, it's their way of dealing with the tension of combat. When it comes to it, they're solid men."

We sat and waited, drinking coffee. I was pleased just to be out of the cell, but still concerned about Vanessa. The police had a remote feed from the ship on the office computer screen, we watched as they took off and swung out over the sea. "Where are they going?" I asked Conner.

"The long way around," he replied. "Heading away from the Canal then swinging over the country before heading inland. They'll go on until they're out of sight of the road, then drop down behind the hills and head towards the Canal." That made sense, if Vanessa was on the road, the ship wouldn't spook them. If it flew over the sea, they might spot it.

I had made the journey overland; on the ground it was hard. From the air, you could see the beauty of Ecias. Seen from above, the scenery was so much more impressive, the view from the ship's camera was panoramic. There were unbroken ranks of trees in deep valleys, rocky hilltops and in the distance, the flickering blue ocean. In no time, they passed our cabin. It was off to one side of the road, up a narrow track, it looked deserted. I longed to be there now with Vanessa, just the two of us, away from all this madness. The scanners recorded no sign of humanity, no infrared or any EPIRB signals. Where had they vanished to? Then the ship dropped down and followed the treetops, keeping out of sight.

After another few moments, the ship arrived at the Canal and swung around to land at the camp. There were three tents and a small hut on the edge of the trees, the hut must have been the mobile laboratory that had been packed on the ship. We had helped unload it, it had caused so much grief, shuttling stores around when they had been incorrectly loaded, or so we thought at the time. The ground around the tents was churned by what looked like multiple tyre tracks, a wide ramp had been cut in the bank to allow vehicles to get onto the beach. There had been a lot of activity here, far more than three men would have been responsible for. They had done more to the area than they could have with what they had brought on the ship. Building the ramp would have needed a lot of work from an earth mover. As far as we knew, they didn't have one. They were supposed to be plant hunters, it looked like they were building a base, a beachhead. Yet there was no sign of any of the equipment, just the tents and the hut.

"Mr Strand should have been over there to check the site," said Conner. "I don't like the look of what I'm seeing. Where is he?" He picked up a radio. "Lewis, where is Mr Strand? Get him over here now." There was a crackling answer. "Mr Strand said he was busy, I asked him ages ago. Has he not arrived yet? I've been helping the forensic technician."

"Understood," replied Conner. "Stop being polite. I need to see him now, find him and escort him over." The policeman acknowledged.

We looked back at the screen, the camp was deserted, nobody came from the tents or the hut at the sound of the ship's arrival.

"The EPIRBs are showing as being in the tents," said one of

the police on the ship. "It's strange that they haven't come out to see who we are."

"What's that, over there?" said Dyce, the picture swung. We took our eyes off the feed as Ove came in, with a policeman. It was clear from his expression that he was not a happy man.

"What do you want now?" he asked, he sounded exasperated. "I'm very busy, can't you investigate anything without me being here?" He looked the screen. "What *is* that?" he repeated the pilot's words. He saw me. "What's he doing out?"

Conner ignored him and we all looked at the screen. Over to one side of the clearing was a strange looking patch of undergrowth, about fifty metres wide, it stretched from the ground up into the trees. Close up it didn't look right, didn't fit in with the rest of the foliage. The pilot had noticed it and moved across the clearing. As they got closer, it fluttered.

"What have you found, Dyce?" said Conner.

"Looks like camouflage netting, sir," the pilot said. "We're landing to take a look."

"Roger," said Conner. "Exercise caution and keep your helmet cams on. Stay in the ship, Dyce. Keep the engine running, in case you need to get out quickly."

Conner turned to Ove. "Mr Strand, what do you make of this? When was the last time you inspected this camp?"

Ove shook his head. "I've never been over. I was going to go, then we had the killing and I got distracted."

I nudged Anna. "That was part of their plan."

"I agree," Anna said. "The fact that Vince was working for us may have been random. He never reported all his findings, and he never got caught over at the Canal. I think that they were killing anyone in Whistles that day, to put you off the scent. They wanted to get everyone in the settlement taking sides and ignoring them, giving them a chance to get organised."

"I've messed up," said Ove. "I can see it now." He turned to me. "I'm sorry, Dan. I should have believed you. I'll do what I can to get Vanessa back, to get things under control again."

Conner was still watching the screen. "It may be beyond you now. Look at this."

CHAPTER THIRTY THREE

THE SCREEN WAS SPLIT SHOWING both helmet cameras, as the policemen searched the camp. One went to the netting; it was strung out between the trees and anchored to the ground with metal pegs. "Can you see this?" he called. "There's something behind all this netting." Conner focused on the image, cutting the other out. Close up, we could see fine netting, with plastic foliage attached by metal clips.

While we concentrated on that, the other man was walking towards the tents, we heard his voice but couldn't see him. "Before we go over there, we should check the tents and that hut."

Conner switched cameras, we saw inside one of the tents. "There are three EPIRBs in here," the policeman said. He picked one up, the green light was on. We saw the serial number. Ove looked at his paperwork.

"That number matches one of those issued to the plant hunters."

Another part of my story, that they were moving about undetected, was right.

Next, the policemen went to the hut, it was full of scientific equipment, but it was unused, it was stacked with the wooden crates I remembered sitting on. Some were closed, some were empty. The things that had been taken out of them were still wrapped in anti-static plastic sheets.

"All the stuff here is new, it's not been touched," said the policeman. "I reckon it's a front, to put off anyone who turns up. They certainly don't do any science in here. Wait a moment, there's a box I don't recognise." The camera moved onto a grey box, tossed in the corner. It had two mounting holes and two cable clips, a thin covering of splattered mud. I recognised it immediately.

"That's the inverter, from our buggy." So they had taken it.

The policeman nodded. "Anna told us about that. Wasn't it when Vince shot the film of them in their vehicle? When they were supposed to be at the camp?"

"That's it." I was triumphant. "We only saw two of them, the third must have been around here, waiting for us to get back." Waiting for someone to shoot. Vince had been looking for the stuff he had forgotten, in the wrong place at the wrong time.

"We're going into the trees," the policeman said, as they crossed back to the camouflage netting.

"Tell them to be careful." It seemed unlikely that Vanessa was already here, but then, the rest of what they had found so far was unlikely too.

The two policemen moved around the sides of the netting, our screen was split again, with each camera showing. I found it very disorientating. There was a cleared space behind the net, trees had been felled and, in the gap, sat a small shuttle lifter. Seating six, it was used for atmospheric flight and ferrying supplies, there was a flat load area on the rear. It was a bit like a flying pickup truck. We had two of them ourselves, only ours were larger. This one was painted grey, ours were blue.

"Where did that come from?" asked Ove. "There are no shuttles on Ecias apart from ours. That never came on any of the supply ships."

The policeman sat back. "They must have been supplied

under your noses. Look at the tracks and what's been done on the beach. Ships could arrive on the other side of the planet every night and unload, you'd never know unless you went over to check regularly. It seems that your planet is under attack. There's plenty of evidence in what I've seen so far. I'll give my boys a little longer to look around then call them back." He reached for the radio. "Dyce, get on the secure radio to Ventius, tell them to send a full squad, as soon as possible."

The pilot acknowledged. We turned our attention back to the video feed; the view had changed to one camera, the two men were creeping down a narrow path. The lead policeman kept up a running commentary as they moved away from the clearing, his voice a whisper.

"I've immobilised the lifter, if they want to use it, they'll be disappointed. There's a trail; it must have seen lots of use, the ground is well worn. Maybe it heads to a latrine pit."

The picture bobbed up and down as the policeman moved along the trail, now they had gone into single file, the other one was no longer visible. Then they stopped, there was something moving between the trees off to one side. We saw it in the edge of the picture, then the camera turned and we could see it more clearly.

"Hang on, there're cabins here, rows and rows of cabins. And all sorts of machinery. They're all scattered around in the gaps between the trees. There are people, there must be thirty of them, moving about, sitting around a table, eating."

Conner zoomed the picture, we could see faces. They were all dressed in black boiler suits, the word Tontranix was on the backs of the ones facing away from us. Behind them was a row of vehicles.

"Can you see the lady?" Conner asked.

"I can't," replied the policeman. "Shall we move closer?"

"Negative; get back here. Dyce, prepare for take-off."

There was the sound of rapid gunfire, the camera we were

watching suddenly jerked backwards and pointed at the sky. Then it went dead. Conner tried the other, with the same result.

"What happened?"

"I think they were discovered and shot. There's a lot more there than just three plant hunters, they must be the advance party from Tontranix."

"What do we do now?"

"It looks more and more like you were right, Anna," said the policeman, switching to the camera on the ship. "There's an invasion in progress. Dyce, get back here now. Have you called Ventius?"

"Yes, sir," said the pilot. "What about the others?"

"They've gone," said Conner.

"Roger, I'm taking off now." Her voice was emotionless, as if the two men she had been talking to five minutes ago had never existed.

We could see the ground drop away as the ship rose into the air. There was a clunk as the stern ramp closed. The view swung, clouds chased across the screen as it lined up on a course to return. Suddenly there was an alarm. "Missile launch," the pilot called. "I'm taking evasive..."

The picture flickered out. It was so sudden that it was almost unbelievable. Conner called but there was no reply. Outside the office, there was a faint rumble, like distant thunder.

"How many of you are left here?" I asked, in the silence that followed.

It looked like we had just watched three policemen and their ship brutally disposed of; the casual nature of it shocked me. If that was a taste of what was to come when they got to Richavon, we needed help, and fast. We were ordinary people; we had a few rifles and some other weapons, but only for hunting game. I for one had never shot at a person. On the other hand, if that person was hurting Vanessa, I reckoned that I could overcome my hesitation.

"Just four of us," Conner replied. "Myself, two officers, the CSI, some of our equipment. You heard Dyce, reinforcements are on the way."

Anna spoke up. "There are security coming from Burgstrom as well. I don't know how long they'll be."

"Well they've been discovered now," said Conner. "I would expect that an attack is imminent. Don't forget, they might have more men coming in as well."

It looked like we had a choice. We could run and hide. Or we could surrender and see what happened when everyone else turned up. Either option was risky. If they wanted to kill us all, hiding would only delay things, it could make them angrier. If we stayed here, perhaps we would be spared. By the way they had dealt with the police, that looked unlikely.

The other option was a mixture, evacuate some of us, the rest could stay and mount a rear-guard action, making life as difficult as possible for them until help arrived.

"We need to get everyone together, decide what we're going to do."

CHAPTER THIRTY FOUR

EARTH

WHAT WAS HAPPENING on Ecias had shocked me. Why was I creating a dream that had started out so happy and gone so wrong? Perhaps it was my subconscious finding a way to end it.

Dr Borth called me in; he had my results. I was sitting at home. I wasn't used to not having a job to go to. It had only been a few days since I had done any work but already I was contemplating some decorating, a job that I normally hated, just for something to do. I had the court to look forward to tomorrow, if that was the right word.

After that, I didn't know what would be happening. I suppose that it all depended on Cath's plea, and any sentence she got. I researched the court procedure online, if she pleaded not guilty, there was a chance of a crown court trial. Guilty and it all depended on the severity; there was a limit to the penalty the magistrates could impose. They could fine her or send her to prison for up to six months. Surely she would just admit it and accept a fine or whatever? Simon had said that all the evidence was against her. I hoped that she didn't call me as a witness; that would do neither of us any good. There was also the question about what this would do to her job, would the hospital still want to employ a nurse who had been in court on assault charges?

It was a relief to be called in by Borth for my results, but I was still apprehensive as I walked into his office.

We sat in his armchairs again. "Here are your scans and the radiologist's notes," he said, holding a slim folder in his arthritic hands.

"Is it what you expected?" I had been wondering what the scan would show, I had no reference point to look for on the internet, searching for brain scan and insomnia gave results that seemed incompatible with my other symptoms.

"First, let me tell you, the scan was to determine if you had a PCS."

"I'm sorry, Dr Borth, you've lost me there, what's a PCS?"

"It's the paracingulate sulcus; it's a fold in your prefrontal cortex. Evidence suggests that people without it can't distinguish between dreams and reality. And about a quarter of the population either don't have it or don't have a complete one."

To me, it sounded absurd. "Are you telling me that one in four people can't always tell the difference? That they can't always tell if their dreams are real or not? Anyway, there's a flaw there. How can I not tell the difference? It's obvious which is real. My dreams are on another planet; I'm living there with someone else."

He sighed, the reaction of an expert when faced with someone who doesn't understand. "It's not that it's reality," he said, "it's that when you're there, you can't tell that it's not reality. It means that while you're dreaming, you don't know that you are."

I guess that I had to accept that he knew what he was talking about, it sounded dubious to me, almost as if he entertained the possibility that Ecias was real in some way.

"I wanted to see if your PCS was present, it would help me to diagnose you. If you didn't have the PCS, then it's possible that you may be suffering from schizophrenia."

The word had so many associations that it was hard to know where to begin, my mind spun, it was as bad as when I had discovered the pinches, or the particles under my skin. "So do I have one?"

He smiled at me. "Your brain is normal," he said. "The scan showed nothing of note; the PCS was well formed, a little smaller on one side but nothing unusual. It means that you may be susceptible to vivid dreams but you're not schizophrenic, at least not by that measure."

It was a relief in a way, but it still left the bigger question. "Then why is it happening?"

"Ah..." He sat still for a moment. "The brain is an amazing thing, we have no idea about a lot of what it does, we can only guess. There's the relationship between lack of sleep and dreams, for example. And the effect that some drugs have on individual brain chemistry. What affects you may not affect someone else, brains appear to be more different than we might expect. I think it's a combination of things, lack of sleep, the drugs and stress. Look at how different people react to stress for example, some keep calm, some get agitated. By your own admission, you've been working hard, your mind has been filled with images of places that you will never get to.

"So, is that why my dream life getting worse?" I asked.

"In what way is it getting worse?"

I told him everything that had happened since we had last met. All about Vanessa's kidnap, the deaths of the policemen and the imminent attack on Richavon, in which we might all die. About how, on Earth, Cath was due in court.

"Well," he said, "consider your life here. Events are all coming to a head. Cath is in court and you're getting these results. There's a direct link between the rising stress you feel and the worsening situation on Ecias."

"Do you mean that when Cath's court case is resolved, things on Ecias will settle down?"

"You're talking of Ecias as if it were real... but yes. Your mind has constructed Ecias as a way to deal with your life. Cases like yours can help us understand how the mind works, if you would be willing to help."

"Doctor, at the moment all I want is my wife back. An explanation of why this is happening is less important than convincing her that I'm not having an affair."

"I understand, but it's something to bear in mind, we could do more tests, maybe a twenty-four-hour trace of your brain waves, or some controlled sleep. There are so many things we could look at. Anyway, that's for the future. I will send all this to Colin, then it's up to all of you to get around the table and decide what to do."

CHAPTER THIRTY FIVE

I ARRIVED AT THE MAGISTRATES' court and found my way to the waiting room. At the door was a sign for the public gallery, I wondered if I would watch Cath from it? Did I want to see what it did to her? The whole place was very sombre, large oil paintings of judges looking severe, lots of dark woodwork and a general air of sober legality.

Colin greeted me with a smile. "Hi, Rick. Your wife is next up. I've spoken to Simon. He's still not sure if they might want you as a witness. You'll have to wait in here, in case you're called."

He seemed on edge. "Simon is in a quandary. He still wants her to plead guilty. He has advised her against using you as a witness, in case you make things worse. After all, questions about your wife's motives might start an argument; the bench would take a dim view. But she's adamant." He shook his head. "Why can't people leave it to the experts? Everyone has seen some movie where the little guy triumphs in court, outwits the other side. They all want to be that guy, it very rarely happens in real life."

"So do I have to wait out here?"

"I'm afraid so. If they want to call you, you can't go into the public gallery. Once you're inside then you can't be called as a witness."

"This way I won't know what's going on," I said.

"Yes, but I will. I'm not involved; I can go and sit in the public gallery. Stay here; if you're required then they'll call you." He left and followed the signs I'd seen, the route I thought I would be taking to the gallery.

I sat alone in the room for a few minutes. I still couldn't understand why Cath had suddenly rushed off to confront Esther Phay. Was it just because of what Tina had told her? I could see how knowing that might have made her react, surely she had been told to keep a low profile? And I wondered why she was so set on fighting the accusations. She was guilty; why make it worse?

I heard a door open, and joyful shouts, the case before Cath's must have finished. By the sound of the shouting, someone had been found not guilty of some motoring offence. The sounds of celebration receded, then I heard a voice say, "Catherine Wilson." That was her, now we would see what was going to happen.

I was ready; I knew that I would say nothing to make matters worse. I wanted her free, whatever the cost. If it meant admitting that I was a delusional madman in the eyes of the magistrates, then I would be one. I imagined Cath walking into the court, with her solicitor.

Twenty minutes later, I was still waiting. Colin came back.

"You won't be called," he announced. "She pleaded guilty. Simon must have persuaded her at the last minute."

"What happens now?"

"They're just sentencing. Like I said, it's relatively minor and she said sorry. It'll only be a fine, maybe a conditional discharge. They'll be out in a moment. Simon knows I'm here. I suspect he'll come in and say hello, try to arrange a meeting. I'll tell you all about what happened when they've gone."

I heard the door open again and heard a man's voice. "I'm going to see him, wait here, please."

Shortly after that, a tall man in a dark pin-striped suit came in.

"Hello, Colin," said the wearer; he held out his hand to me. "Pleased to meet you, Mr Wilson. I'm Simon Walsh, representing your wife."

"Hello," I said, shaking the offered hand, I turned to Colin. "Is it OK for me to talk to him?"

"Yes," he laughed. "He wouldn't be here unless your wife knew and that means that it's OK."

"It's been a learning experience for your wife today," Simon continued. "I think she's realised just how stupid all this was getting."

Cath came into the room, Simon shot her a look. "I asked you not to come in here," he said.

She ignored him. "Hello, Rick," she said. "Can we stop all this nonsense now and talk?"

I was shocked at the change in her, she had lots of make-up on, much more than usual. It didn't fully hide the tiredness and stress on her face when you got close. She looked like she had lost weight as well. The suit she saved for special occasions hung on her.

"It's not up to me," I said, determined not to be led into an argument about who started it. "I never wanted any of this. I'm not having an affair; I can see why you think I am but I'm not. I don't want to talk about it here and now but I'm willing to sit down and go through it all sensibly. What I don't understand is why the change in your attitude? Last time we met, you wanted to take all my money and make me suffer."

She looked about to cry. "You know, Rick, when I was stood there, in front of the magistrates, I realised that it was all stupid. I had no proof, and believe me, I had looked. I came to your office because I felt wronged, frustrated that I couldn't prove that you were seeing Esther Phay. When she wouldn't admit it I should have felt pleased but instead I felt cheated. I said some nasty things to people who didn't deserve it. And I hurt Esther Phay.

You told me it wasn't true and that should have been enough. I wish I could go back and say that I believed you." Just then some people came into the waiting room, they must have been connected with the next case.

"Let's meet and discuss it properly," suggested Simon. "Come along, Mrs Wilson." He took her arm.

"We'll be in touch," said Colin. Cath smiled weakly.

"See you soon, Rick," she said as they left.

"Well that was a surprise," I said to Colin after they had gone. "Cath doesn't just give up and change like that, what happened in the court?"

"Come outside," he said, "and I'll tell you."

We sat in his car. "Nothing special happened. She was asked to confirm her name and address; she gave your marital home as her address. When she said it, her shoulders slumped and I thought that she would cry."

Had that changed her mind, the reminder that as far as the system was concerned, she was still thought of as living with me, at our house?

"She was charged with common assault on the person of Esther Phay and damage to office equipment, and asked how she would plead."

I had expected her to say not guilty, try and argue it out, blame me, blame Esther, all sorts of things, but she hadn't.

"She said guilty, straight away," Colin said. "Which surprised me, it wasn't what was expected. Simon looked surprised. He must have got through to her, explaining the ramifications, that there were witnesses and that she *was* guilty. It would be better for her to admit it, show contrition. You get credit for that."

"Then what happened?" I had looked online at the procedure, but only for a not guilty plea.

"The magistrate asked for evidence of any injuries to Ms Phay, minor bruising and emotional trauma was the answer. Simon was then asked for any mitigation."

"And did he have any?"

"Oh yes, he pointed out that, apparently, Ms Phay did not bring these charges, there was a letter from her asking for leniency. He read it out. Your wife also read a statement."

"What did she say?"

"That she was sorry for her actions, which were inappropriate and in the heat of the moment. That she had apologised to Ms Phay. Then she went on about 'personal issues in her life which she had allowed to influence her actions'. It was obviously written by Simon but it sounded good. She said that she was a nurse and understood that she should not have acted as she did."

It sounded like a plea for mercy. Would she still be a nurse once the news got out? Was that part of the reason for the change of heart? Was she frightened of losing her job, did she know that I had?

"I've seen it so many times," said Simon. "Law-abiding people end up in front of magistrates and it gets to them, scares them. Career criminals see the law as a hazard of the job, they take little notice of it."

I could see what he meant. I was only in the waiting room, yet I felt nervous and even guilty. And I wasn't on trial. It must have been the building; you could feel the weight of the law in it.

"What did they say to that?"

"They've heard it all before, but they do recognise someone who's been affected by their first brush with the law. And they have a sixth sense for remorse. They fined her two hundred pounds and gave her a six months' conditional discharge."

"Set up a meeting," I suggested, "whenever you want. I'm only painting the bathroom." I explained about my change of circumstances.

"That's unfortunate, but now that we can get this sorted, perhaps you can go back to work."

Perhaps I could, but I thought that Hughie had been too quick to dump me; maybe this was the spur I needed to do something

215

different. Maybe we both ought to. As I got back in my car I realised that I hadn't told him that Borth had seen me again, that his report would be on the way.

CHAPTER THIRTY SIX

A WEEK LATER, I was in Colin's office, waiting for Cath to arrive. I hadn't been to Ecias since the night before I had seen Dr Borth. I had painted the bathroom ceiling, wallpapered the stairs and watched a lot of daytime TV.

Strangely, I didn't really miss Ecias, it had retreated in my mind, it was now more like a fondly remembered holiday than an alternative life. Dr Borth's report had given me an explanation and I had accepted it. As he suggested, my dreams had stopped with the decrease of stress in my life. I no longer cared about what happened to Vanessa, or to the settlement. My sleep was back to being dreamless and reviving. Ecias had gone, that was another new start.

I had decided, when I had Cath back, we would go somewhere new, begin again, I didn't care what, run a pub, do B & B, whatever. Just the two of us and we would be happy. And we would never mention Esther Phay or Ecias again.

Cath and Simon Walsh came into the room and sat. Coffee was served and biscuits were passed around. We talked about the weather and Christmas, now only a few weeks away. With everything else that had been going on, I had completely forgotten about the season of goodwill.

"Perhaps we should get onto the subject," said Cath, "after all we're paying." She might have changed in some ways but she hadn't lost her blunt approach.

"Very well." Simon held up a thin folder that I recognised. "This is Dr Borth's report. Thank you for sending a copy over."

Colin nodded. "I think that the conclusions are... interesting."

Simon flicked through the pages, more for effect than anything else. I had seen Colin's copy before they had arrived. I couldn't understand more than one or two words per line. The conclusion was the only thing I was interested in anyway, and I already knew that was good, Borth had said so himself.

"I haven't seen this, can you just summarise it for me?" asked Cath, she leant forward in her chair.

"Certainly." Simon read the last paragraphs. "In conversation, this patient has a vivid recollection of his dream state, which I initially diagnosed as Lucid Dreams. However, the patient reports that in the dream, he is not aware that he is dreaming. Furthermore, he claims to be able to exert some degree of control over the dream characters, narrative, and environment. The patient shows no signs of schizophrenia; under MRI scanning, his PCS is within the normal range. Other brain physiology appears normal. He is on a clinical trial of a new drug which I have not been able to obtain information about. I am forced to conclude that he is suffering from enhanced dreams brought on by sleep deprivation, augmented by a dopaminergic reaction to an experimental soporific."

"That's what I thought." Cath sounded triumphant, being a nurse, she had an opinion on everything medical. The annoying thing was that she was usually right. "I'd like to see the full report though." Simon passed it to her.

"Do you believe me now?" I asked. She nodded.

"Why the change of heart?"

"Tina," she said. "I found out that Tina was a stirrer, someone else told me that she had broken up their marriage with

218

malicious gossip. Looking back, I could see how pleased she seemed to be, when she thought that she had convinced me. Not only that, Simon has done some investigating for me. He could find no link between you and Esther Phay before she came to Creative for the job. I've had time to think about it. What really made me change my mind was the letter that Esther Phay sent, saying that she didn't want to press charges. She professed her innocence in writing, expressed sympathy for me. If she was after you, if she was guilty, she wouldn't have done that, she wouldn't want anything on paper that could come back and haunt her."

"Fair enough," I said. I was relieved and decided not to push the fact that she had believed Esther and not me. "Will you be coming home?"

"Let's take one thing at a time, Rick. If I do, there are going to be some changes."

"That's fine, whatever it takes. I want some changes too."

She gave me a strange look, as if it wasn't up to me to demand things. "I've been speaking to Simon and there's something else that I'd like you to do before we get to decide when I'm coming home. Call it closure if you want."

Simon turned to me. "Cath would like you to undergo hypnosis," he said. "Professionally. Under strict conditions, all recorded."

"What's the purpose of that?"

"She thinks that once she sees you talking about living on Ecias under hypnosis, when you can't lie, she'll be convinced. Then, when you see the recording later, you'll see that it's just a dream. It'll help you to come to terms with it."

"So you want to film me to prove to me that Ecias is no more than a dream." In a way I could see that it would be a good thing.

"Please, Rick, do it for me, we can put this behind us and move on."

"If I do this, Cath, will that be the end of it?"

She nodded. "It will, do this for us, it will be the last time I ever mention it."

"Fair enough, we'll investigate some possibles and arrange an appointment." There was just one more thing I had to know. "Cath, why did you make me think that you were calling me as a witness in the magistrates' court? I was waiting, expecting to be questioned. I thought that you were intending to make me look stupid."

She smiled. "That was pride, and embarrassment. I couldn't let you see me in court. I'd already decided that Tina had wound me up; I felt awful. Simon had tried to persuade me to plead guilty; he said that I might have a chance of keeping my job if I did. It would have been awful for me to know that you were watching. I was guilty; there was no sense in denying it. I looked it up, if I told Simon that I wanted you as a witness, you couldn't come in."

"See what I mean," Colin said, "everyone's an expert."

CHAPTER THIRTY SEVEN

MY DOORBELL RANG, I was about to go to sleep. It had been a boring day and although I hadn't done much, I was tired. I guess that the lack of activity was getting to me. I had a meeting with Cath and the solicitors in the morning, we were sorting through prospective hypnotists and I wanted an early night.

I opened the door. Hughie was stood there, with a grin and a bottle.

"Hello," he said, he was swaying gently from side to side, already slightly drunk. "I need to talk to you, can I come in?"

I looked along the road. "Did you drive, Hughie?" I asked, hoping that the answer was no.

He shook his head. "Not me, Ricky boy, I got the *bus!*" the last word was spoken in triumph, as if he had mastered a new skill.

He pushed past me and weaved his way into my front room, using the walls to keep him pointing in the right direction. "Get some glasses," he said as he collapsed onto the sofa with a sigh.

I returned with them, he managed to pour two full tumblers of neat whisky. "Cheers," he said as he handed me one of them, a few drops spilled as he passed it over.

I took a sip; he gulped a quarter of his down. I wasn't a big fan of whisky, unless there was at least a little water in it. I preferred beer; it was all I normally drank. I could still remember the whisky I had drunk when Cath left, how I had felt when I awoke. I needed to get rid of him before he led me astray. I wanted to have a clear head in the morning.

"So," he said. "Where was I? Oh yes, I've come to apologise."

"Apologise, whatever for?" I was confused, maybe not as much as he was in his present condition but confused all the same.

"My behaviour, I acted badly." He paused, then nodded furiously. "Yes I did. I told you to go away. I dumped you when you needed me, after Cath came around. I'm sorry."

He gulped more whisky, put the glass down with exaggerated care on the table and refilled it. He waved the bottle at me. "Top-up?"

"No thanks, Hughie, I'm fine."

"Suit yourself, more for me." He belched, covering his mouth with his hand. "Manners, pardon. Yes, I should have said, 'come on, Ricky, Cath might have found out but us blokes must stick together. Don't you worry, I'll look after you'." He peered around. "She's not here is she?"

"No, she's not." I was relieved that she wasn't. She had seen Hughie drunk before, after Claire had died. She had been sympathetic, until he had been sick on the carpet. She had told him to sort himself out and shut him in the porch, calling a cab to take him away.

"Cath hasn't found me out, Hughie, I haven't done anything."

He took another gulp of whisky and tapped his nose. "Mum's the word, Ricky, my old friend. You stick to your story if you want but it's me you're talking to, I can keep a secret." He started mumbling to himself.

It was hopeless; Hughie was getting more incoherent as he slurped the neat spirit.

"I mean," he said, "why did you invent all that stuff. All that sci-fi, why go to all the effort? Is she a fan, what's her name? Is it her fantasy too? You tell me your secret and I'll tell you mine."

"Hughie, you're drunk, you don't know what you're saying. I'll get you a cab."

"I don't need to go." He suddenly shouted, "Don't throw me out like Cath did. Molly knows all about it, you know Molly, she's dependable, she loves me. Let me tell you my secret."

"I don't want to know, Hughie," I said. I doubted if he would take any notice of me, he was too drunk for reason to have much effect. I had a feeling that he was going to tell me about him and Molly. I really didn't want to know. I might have to face Molly one day, knowing for sure what I already suspected, what Deanne and Cath had both hinted at.

"She's gone," he suddenly said, I wondered if he meant that Molly had left him after what Cath had said, in front of all those people. But he didn't mean that at all.

"Claire's gone," his voice was sad, despite the slurring speech, it was full of sorrow. "I was happy with Claire, until I found out what was going on. She introduced me to Molly, it was all her idea. That's what people don't know, it's my secret. Me and Claire and Molly. That's my secret. Nobody knows. Claire called me to tell me it was all over. I was at Randalls when she called. She said that it was time to go. She wanted me to be happy. Did you know that I was talking to her when her car left the road?" He started to sob, his hand shook and whisky spilt.

I didn't know what to do, what he had said made little sense to me. Did he mean that Claire had been leaving him? Why was Molly a secret? I debated calling Molly, it might not do any good if I did. Perhaps it would be better to let him get it all out; the amount he had drunk, surely he would go to sleep soon? In the morning he wouldn't remember what he had said.

He sobbed for a minute, then he slumped sideways and started to snore.

I tried to move him, but he was heavy and uncooperative. In the end I just removed the empty bottle and his glass, put them in the kitchen. I lifted his feet onto the sofa; made sure he was on his side and removed his tie. The remains of the whisky went down the sink and I went to bed.

Hughie woke me up at six a.m. He was blundering around, shouting that he couldn't find the bathroom. I went downstairs and helped him to the cloakroom by the front door.

"Thanks," he muttered, when he came out. "My head hurts."

I got him a glass of water. "Drink this, it'll rehydrate you. I'll get some coffee on."

"You're a real friend," he said. "Did I say anything stupid?"

"You said you were wrong to tell me I wasn't wanted at work." I couldn't ask him what he had meant about his 'secret'. Partly because I didn't really understand what he had said, mostly because it might not have been true. He had been so far gone last night that it might have all just been his conscience talking.

"Can I use your phone, call Molly to come and get me?" he asked. "Mine's dead."

"Of course you can." I handed it to him, he dialled. I waited to see if he would say anything about work.

"We all miss you, you can come back when you want," he said.

It was awkward until Molly arrived. I made more coffee and some toast, which we sat and ate. He seemed embarrassed, as if he could remember being obnoxious but was frightened to find out what he had said.

"You said a few strange things last night," I said, trying to get him to open up.

"I was out of it, I don't remember. I had a few drinks, I was on my way over to ask you to come back but I met an old mate of ours in the pub. He was a friend when it was me and Claire. We got talking and it turned into a session."

So that explained his maudlin behaviour, he had got stirred up with old memories. The drink had made it worse.

"What did I say?" he asked.

"You were talking about Claire, and a secret, it didn't make sense."

He was about to answer me when the doorbell rang.

"That'll be Molly," he said. He looked me straight in the eye. "Not a word about secrets, I'll tell you one day."

Molly came in, she was worried and annoyed. "I was getting frantic," she said. "Why didn't you call me, Rick? I've been up all night, his phone was dead. I didn't know what to do."

"Sorry," I mumbled. "I never realised."

"Not his fault." Hughie put his arm around her. "I came to offer him his job back and it all got out of hand."

"Come back, Rick," said Molly. "Please." It was great to feel wanted.

"I will, just as soon as I've finished decorating."

CHAPTER THIRTY EIGHT

CATH and I were sat around a table, in Simon's office this time. Colin was absent; I had taken the chance, I thought that we had progressed to the point where I didn't need him. Hopefully this would be our last meeting with solicitors. This was the second meeting I had been to. At the first, with Colin, we had started discussing possible hypnotists for me. That had gone well, Cath was conciliatory, hence I had agreed to come back alone this time.

As I had said, if I was going to let someone take over my mind, I wanted someone that was a bit more than the sort you see on talent shows. Cath had not disagreed, we had left things with both of us searching and finding out as much as we could.

Now we had reconvened, I was explaining that, and my other conditions, to Cath and Simon.

"I don't want some weird woman from the back of an alternative living magazine," I said. "I want a proper, medically registered one, even if it's a bit more expensive. I don't want to end up a casualty of someone who doesn't know what they're doing."

Between the two meetings, Cath had left me to scour the internet for hypnotists. I had found plenty, but most of them I discarded as they only seemed to offer 'psychic connections' or 'past life regressions'. Cath had indicated that she was happy to let me find one that I was willing to work with, she had changed a lot since her court appearance. The hospital had interviewed her, they said that they would consider her request to keep her job; she was on tenterhooks waiting to hear. I hoped they showed a bit of common sense and let her stay on.

We discovered a lot about the qualifications and experience needed to be a proper medical hypnotist. There were several societies and colleges representing hypnotists. And I read up about the correct way to put someone into a trance, so that either of us could bail out if we weren't happy with the way things were progressing.

I gave her my list; there were only three names on it. The three of us now looked in more depth at them, read reviews and investigated their work. In the end, we all agreed on a man who was fairly local to us, Trevor Ingram.

It was hard to get an appointment with him. He was booked up for several weeks and the time passed slowly. I still hadn't returned to Ecias, neither had Cath returned to me. I had run out of decorating to do.

The best thing was that I had started back at Creative Concepts; it was a relief to get back to work. When I got there, we had new contracts. Phay was just a memory, in fact we saw their campaign, it had been done by another firm, the adverts were good, the message the adverts conveyed was completely different to mine. Plant hunters were not mentioned.

Nothing else was ever said about what Hughie had told me; he and Molly carried on as they were. Deanne had a new boyfriend and was in that first-love euphoric phase, arriving at work every day looking like she had been up all night, yawning and generally acting smug.

At last the day came around; Trevor Ingram's consulting room was in an old house, behind a thick hedge. The house was at the end of a long curving gravel drive, out at the other end of town.

We got out of our cars, we were still travelling separately.

Hopefully after today our relationship could move forward. Maybe only in small steps but perhaps we could start to get back to where we were. It was early afternoon as we walked up a flight of steps to the front door, despite the cold breeze, the sun felt warm on our backs. Pushing through the swing doors we walked down a brightly lit tiled corridor and into a reception room decorated in wood panelling and gleaming brass. The whole place was more like a hotel than a consulting room. On the wall were framed pictures of celebrities with Trevor Ingram. He was tall and thin, with a beard and designer glasses, the pictures were all fake smiles and handshakes. It felt like the kind of place that I had not wanted to end up in, but according to our research, his practice was the best choice.

The receptionist would have graced a magazine cover. She introduced herself as Olivia and asked us to wait and brought us coffee.

After a few moments, Trevor welcomed us from the waiting room. "Come in both of you," he said leading us to his room. We sat next to each other at one side of his desk.

"Now," he said, sitting opposite us and rummaging in a drawer. "I understand that you," he indicated me, "have had vivid dreams that you wish to re-visit."

"Not exactly," Cath spoke up, once again taking the lead in matters medical. "My husband has been suffering from lucid dreams that he wishes to erase from his subconscious."

Hang on a minute, that wasn't what I thought we were here for. "Cath," I said, "I don't want to erase them, I just want to prove to you that I'm having them."

She shook her head. "No, the deal is that you forget all about Ecias, or I'm out of the door and away."

So that was her plan, if I wanted her back, I had to have my memories wiped. "Can you even do that?" I asked.

Trevor nodded. "If you want; I can suggest to your subconscious that all the memories associated with your dreams can be forgotten. But I must stress, I can't do that without your written permission. It would be unethical and unprofessional."

Cath looked shocked. "But we talked on the phone..." she said. So her change of heart had only been for show, she was talking about me behind my back. Was she jealous of Vanessa, the woman in my dreams? Or just making sure I forgot that she looked like Esther Phay?

"Are you telling me that you discussed this behind my back?" I blurted out. I could see Trevor's face, he was puzzled.

"Have you both talked about what you hope to achieve here?" he asked. "Are you both in agreement?"

Cath spoke before I had the chance. "Of course we have. Darling, it's what we both want, isn't it?" Cath gave me a look. I could tell that I had been backed into a corner, agree to Cath's demands or lose her forever. What choice did I have? I hadn't been to Ecias for ages, even if I had, the situation there was hardly the idyll it had been. Did I really want a fight to the death with invading mercenaries more than I wanted her?

"You're right," I said. "Let's forget it all. You have my permission."

"Thank you," he said. "Will you sign this release form?" He handed me a sheet of paper, on it were a list of conditions: that I would not hold him responsible for anything I said while I was in a trance, that Cath would not try to interfere with the procedure, that his methods were confidential, there was to be no recording of sound or video. There was a long list of things, including calling the police if he thought that I had committed a crime. It all seemed designed to cover his arse, in case of any litigation.

I had no choice, although I wasn't happy about the way it had been done, it was probably for the best. I signed, then Cath did.

"Right," he said, putting the papers in a folder. "Now that's out of the way, can you sit in the chair behind you please, Rick." I looked around. There was a chair behind the door. I hadn't noticed it on the way in. I got up and went over to it.

"Mrs Wilson, can I ask that you refrain from talking until your husband is awake again, unless I specifically ask you to say something."

Cath nodded. I sat in the chair. It was identical to a dentist's chair without the drill. Trevor pushed a button on his desk and the curtains closed. He came and stood in front of me.

"Try to relax. So that you know," he said, "this session is being recorded, for my personal use as an aid to training and in case you require verification of what you say in in future. This is what I will do. First, I'm going to formally ask you for permission. He paused for a second. "Mr Rick Wilson, can I hypnotize you?"

"Yes, you can," I replied. I could just see Cath smile as I said it.

"Good, please sit in a comfortable, upright position. I will shortly tip the chair back, so that you are nearly horizontal. Now can you confirm your name and the place where you are living, not your real address, the one in these dreams?"

"It's Dan, Dan Waldon, I live in a settlement called Richavon. It's on the planet Ecias, orbiting the star we know as 61 Virginis." That probably made him understand why Cath wanted my memory erased.

Trevor picked up a marker pen and drew a small cross under his right eye.

"Now I'd like you to focus on the cross I've just marked underneath my right eye. Clear your mind of all thoughts. Keep our eye on it and don't look away from it as I'm speaking to you."

He stared at me, unblinking behind the glasses, the lens made his eyes seem distorted. I pulled my gaze back to the cross. "Five, Four, Three, Two, One," he said in a soothing, low voice. "Your eyelids are becoming heavier and heavier." I felt wide awake. He said it again.

"Your eyelids are growing heavy, as if heavy weights are pulling them down. Five, Four, Three, Two, One." The voice seemed to change to a monotone, and this time, I felt totally relaxed. I could hardly believe that it was working. I watched the cross, listened to the voice.

"Soon, your eyelids will be so heavy they will close. Five, Four, Three, Two, One. The more you try to open your eyes, the heavier they are becoming, the more stuck shut they will be."

He was right; I could feel myself drifting off. The monotone was like an anaesthetic, my eyes closed.

CHAPTER THIRTY NINE

TREVOR TURNED AWAY from Rick's prone body. He moved to stand next to Cath, speaking quietly.

"Mrs Wilson, please don't talk, just nod if you understand. Your husband is now in a hypnotic trance. I'll talk you through what I'm doing as I prepare his subconscious, don't be alarmed. I'm shortly going to touch Rick's shoulder and then he will go limp. It's important that I tell him what is going to happen before I touch them. This will set his mind up to understand that I'm going to give him commands. Don't be alarmed if he slumps over or leans back in the chair. This is a sign that he is completely relaxed and that he's under hypnosis. When he goes limp, I'll tip the chair back."

Cath nodded, she was fascinated to see how this worked.

"Now, Rick," said Trevor in the monotone, "when I touch your shoulder, you are going to become loose, limp, and heavy. Ready?"

Without waiting for an answer, Trevor touched Rick's shoulder, immediately he slumped in the chair. Trevor pressed a control in the back, the chair rotated backwards, until Rick's knees were above his head.

"Thank you, Rick. You are now under hypnosis, do you understand?"

"Yes," said Rick, in a voice that was devoid of any emotion.

"You're safe, Rick, trust me and listen to my voice. Your right arm should now be loose and heavy. It feels limp and relaxed."

Trevor lifted Rick's arm, he pulled it one way and the other. Cath could see that it was floppy and loose. He gently placed it back down on the armrest.

"This confirms that you are now in a deep trance. You will listen to my voice and my commands. Now if I want you to wake up, I will say 'Come back'. The next time you hear these words you will wake up immediately, do you understand?"

"I understand."

"Good. Now, I want you to take me to Ecias. You are Dan Waldon and you're in Richavon. Tell me what's happening, right now."

CHAPTER FORTY

ECIAS

OVE HAD TRIED to gather everyone together so they all knew what was about to happen.

There were about fifty of us, we had all congregated in Whistles. There were people that I didn't know, people that I hadn't seen for months. Some new arrivals who must have been wondering what they had got themselves into.

Apart from the crews of two fishing boats out at sea and a couple of technicians from the farm who had important work, everyone that was supposed to be on the planet was here. If only they would all stop trying to talk at once. There were a lot of worried faces.

"So you're trying to tell us that there's an army over at the Canal," shouted one of the farmers, "and they're going to attack us at any minute."

"That's right," said Conner. "They just killed three of my men and destroyed my ship."

Everyone was shouting at once, I had to raise my voice to be heard. "We have to decide how we're going to protect ourselves and defend the settlement."

"Why are you free?" another person shouted. "Wasn't it you who killed Vince?"

"No," said Anna, "it wasn't. Vince was killed because he had discovered the plot that we're telling you about now. That was all a plan to distract us, so was kidnapping Vanessa. We've wasted time while they have been preparing."

"But why do they want Ecias, there are plenty of planets?"

Ove spoke up. "We've discovered a lot of valuable things here, and somehow, the wrong people have found out about it. They've decided that taking over here is cheaper than going out and finding their own stuff. Now be quiet all of you, let Detective Conner and Anna tell you the whole story. Then we can decide what to do."

There was silence, at last. Conner stood in front of everyone, flanked by his two officers and the civilian technician.

"Thank you," he said. "I'm Detective Conner, and these are my officers. We're from the police on Ventius. I was called here to investigate a murder, but it seems that there's more to it than that, much more."

He pointed to Anna. "This is Anna Durban, she's from Burgstrom's security; she has a much better idea of the whole story. I suggest that you listen to what she has to say."

Anna moved to stand beside him. There was a ripple of muttering, which stopped as she spoke.

"Thank you. Vince and I were sent by Burgstrom to investigate a rumour that a company called Tontranix intended to take over control of Ecias."

There were gasps at this. "Is Dan one of them?" shouted someone from the back. "If he didn't kill Vince, then who did?" called another. "I've heard of Tontranix, they're a lousy company," Ollie added.

"Dan is not involved." Conner continued, "It's the three plant hunters, the ones who arrived with Vince, who are our main subject of interest. They claimed to work for a company called Kalesh Pharmaceuticals; they actually work for Tontranix. As some of you know, Tontranix are competitors of Burgstrom. Vince was using Dan and Vanessa as cover to try and see what presence they had on Ecias, how advanced their plans were."

It explained all the things that I had thought about while I was locked up. Vince's absence, which he had put down to a secret job and asked us not to mention. I knew now that he was off scouting the trees for evidence of a camp, of extra people. His habit of filming everything. Keeping apart from us in camp, while he reported. We had been close to the area where they were, I had thought we were being followed, we must have been. We had seen them on the road. Hell, they had even sabotaged our buggy.

"As we now know," Conner continued, "as well as killing Vince, Vanessa has been abducted by these people. We're pretty sure that it was another thing designed to distract us from seeing what they were up to. We came to investigate Vince's death. We went to see the plant hunters in their camp and were attacked. We found the camp that Vince didn't, my men were ambushed. They were killed, their ship was destroyed. The video I've seen suggests that there are at least thirty armed men over there, ready to attack and take over the settlement."

There was uproar. "We have you police here, what are you going to do?" one of the farmers shouted. "You have to protect us."

Conner shrugged. "We are the law but there are only four of us left. After what they did to my ship, I'm guessing that a polite request that they pack up and go home won't be very effective. We've called for reinforcements, just like Burgstrom has. It's certain that Tontranix will have some on the way as well. It just depends who gets here first. Meantime, we have to deal with the present threat." Once again everyone started shouting.

"You have to keep us safe, till they turn up," Marcus said, repeating what I could hear everyone else saying. "You're the police, it's what you do."

The policeman gave him a despairing look. "As I've just said, there're only four of us. Our ship, with all its equipment and three other officers, is gone. I suppose we'll do what we can. The first thing is to decide where would be the safest place for you all to be."

There was more muttering, a few voices suggested splitting up and hiding in the woods, others were all for doing nothing, carrying on as normal, waiting to see what happened.

The farmers said that we could all go and stay behind their safety fence. If anyone wanted to take their chances in the woods they were welcome to try.

The fishermen suggested that we all go and camp out on one of the islands up the coast, in the opposite direction to the Canal.

That was all well and good, the trouble was, all those options only gave us something else to argue about. What we needed was a decision.

Nobody suggested that we do anything about Vanessa. That was the only thing on my mind. They had said they would hurt her. I was more worried that they had already killed her. Whatever else happened, I wanted a chance to make them pay for taking her.

"Why shouldn't we just let them take over?" Abel, one of the men who had guarded me, asked. "I don't care who I work for, as long as they pay me."

There were mutterings; the suggestion was having a seductive effect on the waverers.

"It's true," said one. "What's so bad about a change of management, they'll still need us."

Anna tried to dissuade the talk. "Don't forget," she said, "they haven't done this peacefully. You know what happened, do you think they'll let you go and tell anyone? Vince is dead and three policemen. Why didn't they negotiate, buy Burgstrom out, they wouldn't need a secret army, or an invasion?"

"There was no trouble till they turned up," I reminded everyone. "We were all happy working for Burgstrom, why change, just because they have guns."

"I suggest evacuation, get everyone out, just leave me and the police here," said Ove. "Maybe I can stall them until help comes."

"Where can we go?"

Lance, a fisherman, spoke up. "We can take you to the islands, along the coast, there's drinking water there and a camp that we use. It's the best bet, they would have to search all the islands, there're camps on all of the big ones."

The farmers were determined to stay behind the fence. "The livestock needs us," Jarvik, the farm manager said. "We can shut and block the gates, turn the electric fence on. They'll have to blow it to get in."

I remembered the lifter we had seen at their camp. It might have been immobilised but was it their only one? If they had another, it could just fly over the fence and drop men inside. I didn't bother mentioning it.

In the end we decided that a few of us would stay. I was one, in case I was needed to negotiate Vanessa's release. Ove would stay because he was in charge, and Anna, as a Burgstrom representative. The policemen said they would do what they could to ensure our safety. They went off to scout sniper positions on top of the hostel, the tallest building in the settlement. Ollie revealed that she had army training and offered to take a rifle and join them. From there they would have a commanding field of fire over the whole town. She was given a radio and told to await orders. The senior man, Conner, stayed with us.

We all helped get everyone and some stores down to the harbour and the boats put out to sea.

Once they had all gone, we got all the vehicles and set about making roadblocks on the main route into Richavon, we couldn't block the approach through the trees but we could stop vehicles from getting into town the easy way. Whistles was the logical place for us to make a stand, it had several exits and was close to the trees, we could get out of the back quickly and be safe in seconds. We barricaded the windows and barred the doors. The farmers departed to the relative safety of their compound.

Ove opened the stores and gave out guns and ammunition. It was all very well shooting animals for food, would we be able to shoot at people? I reckoned that I would if they were shooting at me. And if I had found out that Vanessa was harmed, I would be able to kill anyone who had hurt her.

Anna was in touch with the Burgstrom office. She updated them on what was going on, they told her that she was doing the right things. They had tried to tell Tontranix that their plan was known, but they had been ignored. The extra security guards were on the way but would still be at least a day. They wished her good luck.

The policeman then used our communications set-up, repeating his call to his superiors. They told him that they had been speaking to Tontranix, who were denying any involvement. More police were also on the way, they had left when he had reported the shooting of the officers at the camp. Their arrival was also imminent.

The question was, would Tontranix attack us before any of the other groups got here?

Now that they knew we were onto them and had discovered that there were more of them than there should be, it was very likely. "Perhaps they aren't ready yet," suggested Anna. "They might not have got everything they need for an assault."

We had done all we could. The fishermen radioed to say that they were all safe on the island. The farmers were barricaded in and watching the road from the harbour from the top of their building. We all spent a sleepless night, jumping at every noise but in the end, nothing happened.

Next morning, we opened the front door and walked out to see what was happening. It was another beautiful day; the sky was deepest blue, with a few small clouds. With the absence of human activity, there was birdsong. A small herd of Sawgrass had come into town and were foraging in the weeds at the side of the hostel. It all seemed so tranquil; it was hard to imagine that we could soon be fighting for our lives.

There was faint noise in the air, like bees swarming. It got louder, Conner called up to his snipers for information.

They reported back that it was all quiet on the roads. The noise grew louder and we realised that all the effort we had put in was a waste of time. They weren't coming by road, Tontranix had arrived by sea. We called the farmers, who had a better view of the harbour. They told us that they could see five landing craft, with guns on the hull and vehicles inside them. They had rounded the cliffs and were headed for the harbour entrance. Tontranix must have been bringing equipment in over the last few months, a ship here and there would not have been noticed, as long as it kept out of sight of the settlement. They had probably built a forward base on the coast, ready for a waterborne attack. No wonder they didn't want our supply ship to land out there, it might have disturbed their operation.

The farmers gave us a running commentary; they said that the fishermen must have laid nets across the entrance to the harbour when they had left. The first of the craft got its propeller caught in them. There was a plume of black smoke that we could see, its engine died and it drifted, blocking the entrance. The others altered course and ran up the beach.

"Let's get back inside," suggested Conner. "They'll be here any moment." He called up to the snipers, his men said they were ready, a second later Ollie confirmed that she was in position. She had chosen to make her hide on the flat roof of Whistles. We all headed inside and barred the door. We hadn't blockaded the road up from the harbour, there was nothing to stop them.

The men at the farm called out the numbers as the invaders came up the road. They said that the vehicles all turned off towards the farm gates. They must have decided that it was the place we would all take refuge. The lead vehicle didn't slow down for the gates, it increased speed as it approached and rammed them. There was a flash of electrical sparking as the metal frames touched each other. Flames started coming from the cab. The men inside must have been fried, one of the gates was bent, but nobody could get in past the flames or without touching the wrecks. Jarvik kept up a commentary on the radio, it looked like they were safe inside for the time, the farm was secure. One vehicle dropped off some men near the fence, then the remaining three turned around and came up to the settlement.

Peering through a space we had left in the corner of the window, we saw them arrive. They stopped in a line in the square and unloaded about twenty armed men, well equipped with body armour and full gear. They held assault rifles easily, relaxed. They had the air of conquerors, we were the helpless population. They formed a curved skirmish line, facing the buildings. Two of the three plant hunters were in the lead. I realised that I still didn't know any of their names. They stood, tall and bearded, wearing Tontranix boiler suits with bare heads and assault rifles.

"Ove Strand, where are you?" shouted one of them.

"Hold your fire," said Conner into his throat mic. "That's Dermott talking; his mate is called Sanko. Morgan, the other one, isn't there." It was the first time I had heard any of the names of the three of them. In a way it made it more personal.

"Dan Waldon," Dermott shouted, "if you can hear me, my friend Morgan has your lady, we were going to bring her in to see you, but she's stuck outside town, thanks to your roadblock. It's Morgan's turn with her today. I'm afraid that she's a little the worse for wear, sorry about that. She's a feisty one, she should learn to enjoy it and not fight back so much."

At that moment, I wanted to get outside and kill him, Anna held me back. "Leave it," she said. "It might not be true, he's just trying to get you wound up, distract you so you make a mistake."

"She'll heal," he continued. "She might get the chance, as long as you're all sensible. This isn't your fight; it's a business matter,

Tontranix and Burgstrom. We have no quarrel with you. If you all come out now and accept that we're in control, we'll hand the woman over and you can go. Or you can stay if you want. Tontranix is a fair employer. This isn't your fight; we only want to run the place, like Burgstrom did. You can carry on doing what you did; it'll just be for us. The only ones we're interested in are Ove Strand and the policeman. Oh, and that bitch Anna. Just those, send them out and this is over. Think about it, but don't take too long."

"Before anyone asks," said Conner, "we don't do what they say. I can't let any of you be taken by them. I'll go out and try to talk to him."

"Don't be ridiculous," I said. "Do you think you can talk him out of killing us all? If you go out there, you would just be the first."

"They're going to kill us all anyway," said Anna. "Why make it easy by going out? Make them work for it."

I wondered what would happen when we didn't go outside, if they were going to kill us all, then Vanessa's fate was as certain as ours. Would it be quick or slow?

"Is Vanessa here yet?" I wondered out loud. Maybe Morgan had got through the roadblock. I desperately wanted to see her one more time.

"I'll ask my boys on the roof." Conner spoke into his microphone. "Can you see the hostage?"

"One, negative," was the first reply. "Two, nor me," said the other man. "But I can see a black vehicle behind the roadblock we left on the Canal road." Ollie was silent.

"Hurry up," shouted Dermott. "My boys won't wait all day."

We all stood and contemplated his words.

"I'll go," said Ove. "It's my settlement, my error that let them get this far. If I go and try to negotiate, at the least it'll buy us some time. Help is on the way, perhaps I can stall them, get them to give us time to leave. It might stop any more bloodshed."

CHAPTER FORTY ONE

EARTH

"THIS IS INCREDIBLE," Trevor Ingram said quietly, shaking his head. He moved to stand closer to Cath. "I've never heard such a detailed dream. You can answer me, Mrs Wilson, if you speak softly. Is this the same sort of thing that Rick's been telling you?"

"I've never really listened," Cath admitted in a whisper. "It all sounded like a load of old rubbish to me, like an episode of *Star Trek* or something like that. I was sure that Rick was just making it all up, using it as an excuse to hide his affair with the person he calls Vanessa."

"But surely you must have noticed whether the story was the same every time. From what I'm hearing, nobody could make this much information up and remember it. And there doesn't seem to be any sexual element to it. As far as I can tell, the woman Vanessa is absent."

"I don't know," replied Cath, she could see now how this had been a good idea. No wonder Rick had been under so much strain, he needed to be rid of all this, only then could he get back to living a normal life.

She had been as surprised as Trevor at the depth of Rick's dream, all the details he had revealed in the new voice, that was his yet somehow wasn't. How did his mind keep track of all the things that were happening, all the people and places in the world of his imagination? She even felt sorrow when he described how Vanessa was being held. Rick had been active in the chair, moving about, thrashing his arms and legs, as if he was working and living in the world he described. He was only quiet when he had slept in his dream, but that had been over in a flash.

"What can we do?" Cath asked. "I'm worried that he'll hurt himself."

"At this stage, we have very little control," Trevor answered. "I can't just wake him; the shock would be too great. All we can do is let the dream play out, after all, he's safe enough here. You have to remember, it's only a dream; he can't be hurt by anything that happens. If he gets too distressed I'll try to bring him out of it gently. I'll use the control words."

"Shouldn't we restrain him?" Cath pointed to the webbing loops on the chair, by wrist and ankle.

"No, the constriction will affect his state, we have to leave things natural; he'll be fine."

"When can you tell him to forget everything?"

"Not yet, he needs to reach the conclusion of his dream, whatever it is, then I can tell him. If I do it too early, fragments will remain. They could pop up in his mind at any time and confuse him."

Rick started talking again. "We have to give them an answer," he said.

They both waited to hear what would happen next.

CHAPTER FORTY TWO

ECIAS

"WE HAVE TO GIVE THEM AN ANSWER."

I had a vision, a memory, something from an old film I had seen years ago when I was a child. The outlaws were trapped. They decided to come out, all guns blazing, thinking they had only a couple of enemies to deal with. Not knowing that an army was outside, waiting for them. We were in the same sort of situation now, except that we knew what was outside. It would be a stupid, futile gesture, yet in a way it felt almost better to die doing something, instead of sitting here, knowing that it was going to happen anyway.

"Time's up," shouted Dermott. "We're coming in to get you."

Ove removed the wooden pole that barred the door. He opened it, stepped onto the veranda. "Wait," he shouted. "I'm coming out to talk."

"Hands where I can see them," said Dermott.

Ove walked out into the sunshine, his arms outstretched. We shut the door behind him. He was clear of the veranda, time seemed to slow down as he walked towards the group. "OK, let's talk," he said.

As if in answer, the man to Dermott's left raised a pistol and shot Ove, the sounds blurring with a barrage of automatic fire from the troops. They poured bullets into the buildings, the hostel and workshops, everywhere but Whistles.

As the firing started, we scrambled for safety behind the rough barricades we had made from tables turned on end, boxes of provisions, anything solid that we could hide behind. There was a pause, perhaps they were reloading. Then they turned their attention to us, the air was filled with flying glass as the windows and front wall of the building disintegrated before our eyes.

"Take them out," shouted Conner into his microphone and there was the sound of single, spaced shots as our three snipers fired from the rooftops. The invaders hadn't been expecting that, the automatics fell silent, there were screams of pain. Then training took over and the Tontranix men scrambled for cover. We peered cautiously over our shelter. As well as Ove, several bodies lay in the dust, most were still, one or two moved weakly. Dermott and Sanko were not among them, they seemed to have survived.

There were sporadic shots as the situation outside changed to one of intermittent shooting, from both sides. Our snipers were changing position on the roofs, moving around and firing at any Tontranix soldiers they could see. Fire was returned, the game of attrition, of cat and mouse, was on. We only had three snipers but they were up high and mobile. The Tontranix soldiers were sitting ducks unless they kept well out of sight.

In the confusion, there was a noise at the front of our ruined shelter. Someone had reached the entrance of Whistles. When they had got under the veranda, they were hidden from us and safe. They couldn't get into the back of the building, we had barred all the doors. They didn't need to, there was little to stop them at the front. The windows were gone and the door was filled with holes. Anna and I fired our rifles at the wall and the door. After one shot we heard a grunt of pain and a thud, one of us had hit someone. I expected to feel some emotion, sadness maybe, but I only felt elated, that was one less of Vanessa's captors.

Two small canisters came through the shattered windows, landing on the wooden floor with a clunk and a hiss.

"Gas! Come on!" shouted Conner and we retreated to the storeroom, shutting and barring the door as we went. In the rush to get away from the gas, I had left my rifle behind, now I only had a pistol.

We assessed our situation.

"Poor Ove," said Anna. "They didn't give him a chance."

Conner was talking on his radio. "My boys and your girl have them pinned down," he said. "Apart from whoever threw the gas, they're all in a group over by the hostel. They can't get across to us."

"We need to make a break for it then, out of the back while they're occupied at the front," Anna said. "They won't come in for us now until they think that the gas has worked. If we can get out and make it to the trees we can head up country."

"What about Vanessa? I'm not leaving Richavon without her."

"You can't do anything for her if you're dead," Conner said. "We can't help her from here. She's probably not in town anyway. Dermott said she was at the roadblock with Morgan, we can head there and try to rescue her."

The shooting had almost stopped; surely Burgstrom or the police would be here soon?

"Sounds like a good plan to me," said Anna. "If we can take Morgan out, we can use his vehicle to escape."

"Our cabin's in the woods a day away, we can rest up there," I added.

"Agreed," said Conner, pointing at the door. Yellow mist was creeping under it. "We really have to go."

We left by the door in the side of the storeroom, hoping that no-one was standing guard. In a rough line we sprinted for the safety of the trees.

It was only twenty metres. We ran, expecting all the time to hear shots, feel the bullets hit us. I remembered the last time I had gone through that door. Then I was running from a man with a gun, that time Vince was dead. I wondered if this time I was running away from Vanessa's killers.

Nobody shot at us; they had more important things on their minds. As we ran under the shade of the trees, we heard the sound of a ship approaching. That was good, provided they were friendly. The ship could belong to one of three groups; two of them were on our side so the odds were in our favour that it would be help. We reached the trees. "Who's arriving," Conner called on the radio.

"Grey hull," one of the police on the roof replied, our hearts sank. The Tontranix lifter the police had found had a grey hull; all Burgstrom ships were light blue.

We watched from the edge of the trees as the grey ship passed low over our heads, it hovered, preparing to land. The blast from its engines blew dust and branches into a whirlwind that obscured our view. It looked like it was a lot bigger than our supply ship; or the police cruiser, it seemed to fill the sky. While it was still fifty meters off the ground, its ramp opened to reveal a line of vehicles and armed men, ready to disembark. They started firing; they must be aiming at our snipers. They were exposed on the roofs and vulnerable.

There were cheers from the attackers and more shots. Our snipers must have reached cover, they returned fire, we saw bullets ricochet off its hull, one man fell, spinning in a tangle of limbs before his body hit the ground. The ship headed away to find a quieter place to set down. It looked like it was going for our landing field, just outside of town. As it disappeared behind the buildings, there was a shout over the radio. "I'm hit!" It was Ollie, before Conner had the chance to reply, things went crazy.

"Blue ship, blue ship," one of the policemen called on the radio.

The grey Tontranix ship suddenly reappeared, filling the sky as it lifted sharply. Turning away from us, it rose back up at a sharp angle. Its stern ramp was closing, but not quickly enough, we saw objects, men and vehicles fall from it. It picked up speed as another ship flashed past us, chasing after it.

"That was a Burgstrom ship," said Anna. "It's one of ours." We ran to the side of Whistles to get a better view, feeling safer now. Rescue had arrived, was it in time?

The blue ship launched a missile at the fleeing Tontranix craft. They were escaping over the sea, towards Claudius, hanging in the sky. I wondered if the missile would reach them when there was a tremendous flash of light. It covered the moon and half the sky. It looked for a few seconds as if the grey ship had gone. Then I realised that it had merely fired up its trans-light engine in atmosphere. That was crazy; the engines weren't designed to work in anything but vacuum. They couldn't go trans-light here to escape.

"They're trying to confuse the missile," shouted Conner. It was a risky manoeuvre, a last-ditch attempt to evade the warhead.

The idea seemed to have worked; the fleeing ship was still there, just a dot on the horizon. It was still being followed by our rescuers. The sound faded, replaced by the noise of another ship arriving. Whose was this one? We looked up, the ship was black with yellow flashes down the side. The words VENTIUS COLO-NIAL POLICE were clear on it.

"I'm glad to see that one," called one of the policemen. As it hovered, a swarm of men slid down ropes.

The surviving Tontranix soldiers had ceased fire while all the ships were moving around; they had seen one of theirs and had assumed victory. Our snipers had also held their fire once they had seen the police cruiser arrive; now the Tontranix men were firing at the descending policemen. The men fired back as they slid, our snipers joined in. Several fell from the ropes but the majority landed and moved towards their quarry. After a brief exchange of fire, it all went quiet.

We could hear barked orders, "Lay down your weapons,

hands up." It looked like it was over, the Tontranix men were all rushing to surrender. Conner had already gone to meet the arriving commander and explain the situation.

"Let's get to the front, see what's happening," I said. Anna and I moved around the side of the building.

We saw a line of black clad police, guarding a line of kneeling men. Their hands were over their heads. Bodies were scattered around; it looked like there were a lot of them. Medics moved between them. Conner was in discussion with the leader of the new arrivals. The Burgstrom ship had returned and was landing beside the police cruiser. As we watched a stream of vehicles poured from it and headed our way. The two police snipers came down from the roofs. Where was Ollie? She had shouted that she was hit. She must still be on the roof of Whistles.

"Where's Ollie? She said that she was injured, come on." Anna and I grabbed one of the medics and pulled him with us. "Where are we going?" he asked, his satchel swinging by his side.

"Our friend, she's on the roof." I panted as we ran for the stairs at the side of Whistles.

We reached the roof. There was a trail of blood leading into the corner. We followed it and found Ollie. She was unconscious; her leg was a red mess. The medic reached into his bag. He pulled out a tourniquet, which he applied quickly around her thigh. He felt for her pulse. "She's lost a lot of blood, her pulse is weak but it's there, if we can get her onto our ship, our doctor can take a look. What's been happening here?"

"You wouldn't believe it," we both said together.

He looked over the settlement. "It's such a beautiful place. Isn't that a pig?"

The remark was out of place, we followed his gaze. The burnt-out vehicle had been dragged clear of the farm gates, it smouldered by the side of the road. The gates now hung open. It looked like the farmers had had some excitement. There were bodies on the ground, they had put up a fight like we had. As we watched, another two pigs came through the gap and disappeared into the trees. That was the end of us keeping our livestock separate from the native species.

We left the medic putting a line into Ollie's arm and went back to the ground. The Burgstrom vehicles had stopped next to the Tontranix, the square was now crowded, there were more vehicles on the planet than there had ever been. The door of one opened and a tall, middle-aged man stepped out. Harald Burgstrom had come to see us, flanked by soldiers in light blue armour. We went over to him.

"Hello, Anna," he said. "What's been happening on my planet? I understand from my officers that Ove is dead."

"I'm afraid that's correct, sir," she replied. "I'm sorry but you were right."

"So I can see. A pity but we do seem to have won the day."

"We weren't quick enough," she said. "Things escalated so quickly."

"They tend to." He looked around at the destruction, the bodies, the shattered buildings. "It's all so unfortunate." He looked close to tears. Then his gaze rested on me. "And who are you?"

"Dan Waldon," I answered. "I don't think that we've ever met."

He shook my hand. "We haven't but I owe you a lot, I believe it was you who found the Praseodymium."

I nodded. "That's right, and seeing what's happened because of it, I wonder if it was worth the cost."

"Oh yes," he said. "It was. People like Tontranix can't be allowed to get away with what they've done. You and everyone here, you've all done so much for Burgstrom. I want to know all about it, and your suggestions for the future of this place. Vince told me you want horses, for some reason. Perhaps you and your wife can tell me all about it. Where is your wife by the way?"

How had I forgotten about Vanessa? In panic I ran over to Conner. I grabbed him. "Has anyone seen Vanessa?" He looked blank. "The hostage."

Anna pulled me away. "Calm down, Dan. We'll find her."

Conner straightened his uniform. The other officer looked like he wanted to shoot me for interrupting him.

"I'm sorry, Mr Waldon," he said. "I understand your concern. At this moment, we have not located her. The police are about to take off again for the Canal, mop up any of the Tontranix men that are left. Do you want to go with them?"

I was going to say yes, then I thought about it. Vanessa wasn't at the camp. Dermott had said that she was with Morgan, in the vehicle on the Canal road, stuck behind our abandoned bulldozer.

I left him and went across to where Dermott was being held; Anna followed me. A policeman blocked me. Anna showed him her identity card. "He's with me," she said and we were allowed through.

Dermott was sitting, his ankles zip-tied together, hands behind his back. His capture had not been without incident, his nose was bleeding, yet he still looked defiant.

"Where's your mate?" I asked.

He said nothing. "Where's Morgan and Vanessa." I grabbed him and shook him, his expression changed to one of amusement. A policeman dragged us apart.

"Oh her, the fit thing," he said. "We had some fun, I can tell you. Morgan was sorry to miss all the excitement. He was on his way to join in, bringing her to watch, then he got stuck behind the bulldozer; he'll be on his way back to the camp. Our ship will pick him up." He looked triumphant. "He's probably shot her by now though, she'll only slow him down."

What could I do? Then I had an idea. "Anna, are you with me?"

"Of course," she said.

252

"Come on then, we're going to get Vanessa back." I ran off, hoping that she would follow.

The two lifters stood in the shed, just like usual. I hadn't flown one for a while, but I reckoned that I could manage it. Anna and I strapped in and I started it up, ignoring all the pre-flight checks. We hovered a foot off the ground and I backed out of the shed. As I got clear I was just about to accelerate when I saw Conner. He ran to stop me, waving his arms.

"Where are you going?"

"Vanessa is on the road; Morgan's heading back to the camp."

"Stay here." His tone left no doubt, he was ordering me not to try and save my wife.

"You'll have to shoot me to stop me," I said.

"And me," added Anna.

"Don't be crazy, you're not cut out for this, our ship's on the way. We'll divert and pick them up."

"No, that's not good enough. Dermott told me that Morgan's going to kill her, I have to go."

He shrugged. "OK but you're on your own. Just be careful." Anything else he said was lost as I hauled the lifter into the sky.

I followed the road, straight up the hillside and along the crest. I flashed past the lookout and raced towards the Canal, skimming the treetops. "Watch the road," I said to Anna as I put as much speed on as I dared.

We caught up with Morgan; I saw the black vehicle ahead, bouncing along the road. I pulled away and cut across country, racing to get ahead of him before he knew that I was there. The road was passing between tall trees; it was unlikely that he had seen or heard us. I was well past him, now I spun the lifter around, looking for a place to land.

I settled the lifter in the road, blocking it. We were on a short straight, just past a corner that was sharp enough to make him slow right down to take it safely. Anna had her rifle; a pistol was jammed into her belt. I had a pistol and my rage.

We got out and hid in the trees.

"I'll take a tyre out when it passes," said Anna. "That'll make them stop, then we'll play it by ear. If we split up we can outflank him."

"Don't try anything heroic. I can't risk her getting hurt."

"Don't worry," she said. "I'm a very good shot."

CHAPTER FORTY THREE

IT WAS ONLY a minute or so until we heard the sound of a vehicle approaching. Sure enough, it slowed for the curve, but not as much as I had expected it to. As it went past us, I could see that Morgan was driving. There was no other face, the tinted glass hid any other occupants. I had a sudden panic, what if Morgan wasn't alone with Vanessa? He could have two or three more armed men with him.

There was a single shot as Anna put a bullet into one of the rear tyres; the vehicle skidded, hit a log at the side of the road and rolled over. It slid along the road on its side and stopped just before it collided with our lifter. As we watched, we saw Morgan climbing out of the back. He dragged someone out of the wreck. I could see that it was Vanessa. She looked dazed, swaying as he held her in front of his body. He looked at the tyre, then at the lifter blocking his way.

"Come out, whoever you are," he shouted. "Come out or the lady gets it."

I looked around, Anna had vanished. Play it by ear she had said, she must be trying to get around behind him. It was time for someone to distract him while she got into position.

I stepped out from behind the trees. "I'm here, Morgan. You

lost, just let her go." It looked like she had her hands tied behind her back. He must have been holding her with one hand, in the other was a pistol.

"Well done, Dan," Morgan said. "It seems you've found me. I would say that we are at an impasse."

I raised my pistol, aimed it at him, my hand was steady. He moved behind Vanessa, her head shielding his. When he spoke it almost looked like she was talking.

"Put down your gun," he said. "I don't doubt your seriousness, Dan, but is it worth the risk? Are you such a good shot? You might hit the lovely Vanessa."

He was right, there was no way I could risk it. I lowered my arm.

"Sensible man, now drop it."

I let the pistol fall to the ground. Anna would soon be ready. All I had to do was keep him occupied and give her a clear shot. Before Morgan got fed up with talking and shot me.

"The lady is here to make sure that I can go on a little trip, we just need to get to our ship, then we'll be on our way." He backed off, until he was shielded by the side of the lifter, I realised that he was on the other side of it to Anna, she would have to cross the road behind him. I had to keep him focused on me.

"You can't get away, Morgan," I said.

He laughed. "Yes I can. Nobody is going to risk hurting Vanessa to stop me. I'm off to where I left our shuttle. I can use this lifter, since you've wrecked my vehicle. I can catch up with my friends in orbit. I'm afraid that you have to die before I go, or shall I kill her first, make you watch?" He raised the pistol.

Vanessa gasped. "NO!" she shouted. I tensed, ready to leap.

"Don't try it," he snarled, as the pistol held steady.

Out of the corner of my eye, I saw Anna, she was twenty yards behind him. She kept low, shielded from his sight by the hull of the lifter. I had to keep him talking for a few seconds more. Even though I knew, I was just about to ask him why, then Vanessa took matters into her own hands.

She suddenly went limp, Morgan must have been holding her by the cord tying her wrists, the movement jerked him forward. He staggered back, into the hull of the lifter as he pulled her upright. "Now's not the time for silly games, bitch," he warned. I saw Anna run across the road, she was now behind him.

Vanessa's move had unbalanced him, now she used the wrestling skills that I knew so well. She shifted her weight onto her left leg as she straightened, then hooked her right leg around his. In one fluid move she flicked her right leg straight, bent her left knee and pushed back. As it did with me, every time, he went over backwards. She landed on top of him. He grunted as her weight knocked the air from his lungs.

He must have let go of her as he fell because she stood upright and ran towards me. I lost sight of Anna. I didn't care what she was doing. I ran towards her. I just wanted Vanessa in my arms again.

As she reached me, I could see Morgan lift his head, the pistol swung up. I grabbed her and pulled her sideways, shouting her name. I heard two shots before I hit the ground.

CHAPTER FORTY FOUR

EARTH

CATH WAS GROWING MORE concerned the longer Rick carried on with the story. As he described his confrontation with Morgan he was getting more and more agitated. He suddenly shouted 'Vanessa' and lunged forward. His body jerked out of the chair and he sprawled on the floor.

Cath and Trevor were stunned; they had been so engrossed in the story that they had almost forgotten that it was reality for Rick. Rick got to his feet but it was clear that he was totally disorientated. "Vanessa?" he shouted, grabbing Cath, pushing his face into hers. She tried to pull away as he started kissing her but his grip was too strong. "Vanessa, are you alright. I love you, have they hurt you, darling?" He covered her face with kisses, she tried to push him away.

He suddenly stopped and shook her. "You're not Vanessa! What have you done with Vanessa?"

Cath managed to pull herself free. "There's no such person as Vanessa," she screamed in panic. "It's only a dream."

Trevor had been watching, a disbelieving look on his face. Suddenly he realised that this was serious. "Get him back into the chair," he said. "I can wake him gently." He spoke the words that he had told Rick meant wake up. "Come back."

Nothing happened. Cath tried to move Rick towards the chair but he resisted. "Vanessa, Vanessa." He kept repeating the name.

Trevor tried again, "Rick, come back." Once more, there was no response. He said it a third time. "Dan, come back," his voice pleading. Rick stood still looking around, eyes wide open, gaze vacant.

"Your fancy words aren't working," said Cath. "Let's try this my way." Raising her right arm, she slapped Rick, just as the door opened.

"Is everything alright, Trevor?" asked the secretary. "I heard shouting."

Rick turned his head towards the voice, saw the open door. "Vanessa?" he said and pushed Cath aside. He ran to the door, barged past the secretary, who fell. He went down the hall, his feet clattering on the tiles.

"Stop him," shouted Trevor. "Liv, go and lock the doors."

Cath and Trevor chased after Rick as he approached the front door. By the time they got there, he had pushed through it and was running down the steps to the drive. As the door closed behind him, it locked with a clunk.

CHAPTER FORTY FIVE

WHERE THE HELL WAS I? I had grabbed Vanessa and pulled her to the ground. There had been shots. Now I was awake and instead of the forest floor of Ecias, I was in some sort of building. Had I saved Vanessa? I was still holding her. I kissed her, told her it was alright. Then I saw that it wasn't her. There was a strange woman in my arms, shorter than Vanessa, her hair darker. She was shaking me. Then she pushed me away, slapped my face. It wasn't Vanessa, it wasn't Anna. It should have been one of them; only Anna, Morgan and Vanessa had been with me a moment ago.

I had to find a way out, I had to get back and make sure that she was alright. Desperately I looked around, there was another person in the room, another stranger. He had a thin face and glasses. That wasn't Morgan, or the policeman, Conner. Why had my reality been replaced by this?

I heard a door open. "Is everything alright, Trevor? I heard shouting," a woman's voice said. No it bloody wasn't alright! Was everyone else outside? Who was Trevor? I stepped past the dark-haired woman and ran to the door, pushed through it.

A long white tiled corridor was in front of me, there was a bright light at the end of it. I must have been injured when I dragged Vanessa to one side. No, that didn't make sense, I must be dead. A wave of sadness swept over me. I had tried to save Vanessa and failed, there was nobody to stop Morgan now. He could kill both women and get away. He must have shot me, the bright light that people were supposed to see was in front of me. I had to run towards it.

CHAPTER FORTY SIX

EARTH

"UNLOCK THE DOOR, LIV," Trevor shouted as Rick disappeared around the curve in the drive.

Rick had a good start on his pursuers when the door opened. Ahead of him was the main road.

As Cath and Trevor ran towards it, there was the blare of a horn, a screech of brakes and a thump.

Cath ran faster than Trevor, she got to the end of the drive just in time to see Rick fly through the air and over the cab of the van that had hit him. He landed on the pavement in a lifeless jumble of limbs. Traffic screeched to a halt around them as they ran across the road.

Cath went to Rick; he was motionless on the ground. There was blood seeping from his ears and nose. The driver of the van had got out, he was distraught, his body shook. "He just ran straight in front of me," he said.

"I've called an ambulance," said a pedestrian, as a small crowd gathered. "I saw it all. What made him run out like that? It looked like you were chasing him. I've never seen such a frightened face. And he was shouting a woman's name. Are you Vanessa?"

"He was under hypnosis and he just flipped," panted Cath. "I tried to wake him and he ran out."

"You really shouldn't have done that." Trevor had arrived. "The shock of coming out of the trance disoriented him, it's rare but can happen."

"Don't blame me," Cath said. A woman brought a blanket which they used to cover Rick's body. "You should have restrained him, kept the door locked."

"How was I to know that he was some sort of action hero in his dreams?" he replied. "You told me nothing about him, just what you wanted me to do. Most people respond well to hypnotherapy. It's rare to see confusion like that."

"It's no good hiding behind theory, this is the real world," Cath snapped back at him. "Rick, stay with us."

The sound of sirens grew louder. An ambulance arrived, followed by a police car. The paramedics pushed Cath out of the way. "I'm his wife, and a nurse," she said.

"I'm sure you are, but leave him with us," one said. A policeman took her and led her away.

She sat with Trevor in the back of the police car. Rick had been immobilised, his neck supported. He was loaded onto a stretcher and placed in the ambulance. The police had taken their details while they watched. Cath felt numb. Was this all her fault? She had got angry when Rick had started shouting for Vanessa.

Maybe she shouldn't have slapped him, once he had grabbed her and kissed her she had forgotten for a moment that he was still in a trance; the fact that he had called her Vanessa had made her angry. With a wail of sirens, the ambulance moved off.

"I'll follow them, drop you off," said the officer. "My mate will stay here. We're going to need to speak to everyone, try and work out what's been going on."

The ride to the hospital was silent. Cath didn't want to talk; Trevor sensed that he should keep quiet.

"We're going to need to talk to you both again," the officer said as he dropped them behind the ambulance. Rick disappeared into the hospital and they followed.

CHAPTER FORTY SEVEN

ECIAS

THE SUN WAS SHINING BRIGHTLY as I opened my eyes and stretched. It was just another day in paradise.

I was free; Vanessa was returned to me, she was bruised and battered, there were visible signs of her ordeal but the doctor who had arrived from Ventius had told me that those injuries would heal quickly. I would love her and hold her and tell her everything was alright, in time she would forget the physical pain.

Of more concern was her mental state. After her ordeal at the hands of the plant hunters she had initially been withdrawn and flinched from my touch. I hoped that, as the days passed, she would start to think less about what had happened while she was a prisoner, with love and patience the memories would fade. I made sure that I gave her time and understanding, trying my hardest to provide the supportive environment she needed. The doctor told me that I should let her deal with things in her own time and way. He said that the most important thing I could do was just to be there for her. I told him that I felt guilty; as far as I was concerned, I hadn't protected her when she had needed me the most. He said it was typical behaviour, the term he used was 'survivor guilt'. It was natural and a part of the healing process. He assured me that Vanessa would feel the same.

After about a week, Vanessa said that she wanted to tell me what had happened while she had been captive. Even though I knew it would distress me, I understood that she needed to, to get it out of her system. She told me that after I'd heard, if I didn't want her, she would understand. I listened as it all came out, she felt guilt that she hadn't believed me, and in a way, that she had let me down by being captured. I held her tight and told her that it didn't matter, that we were together, alive and that was all that was important. We both cried copious tears, hers were a release, mine were from relief. As the days went by, the old Vanessa slowly reappeared. I think we both knew that things would never be the same, that wasn't as important to me as just having her alive and safe. We could always begin again, on her terms.

We had been debriefed by Anna, then by Conner. Anna had got up close behind Morgan and shot him, just as he fired at us; my grabbing Vanessa had pulled her out of the way. I had hit my head as we landed and was out of it, so I didn't see the end, the final surrender of the Tontranix men at the Canal. Anna said that Burgstrom and the police would have been there sooner, when they arrived in orbit they had found another Tontranix ship; presumably they were the second wave. They had chased it away before landing.

Harald had addressed us all; he praised us for our work and thanked us for our loyalty. We had a short moment of silence for the people who had died in the fight, for Ove, for two of the farmers who had been killed and for Ollie, who had never regained consciousness.

The police had left, taking their casualties and the surviving Tontranix men with them, all secured and under guard. Burgstrom had survived the attempt to kick them off Ecias, largely thanks to the information that Vince and Anna had sent back, and a lot of luck. The camp that the police had found, the one Vince had been looking for, was huge. It had space for far more men than it housed, with stores and equipment that must have been amassed over months of supply. There was some state-of-the art gear there, everything needed to run a prison colony, which is what Ecias would have been if their plan had succeeded.

All that gear belonged to us now. Tontranix could never ask for it back, without admitting their part. Burgstrom also left a squad of their security guards on Ecias, to ensure that nobody else tried to take us over. They used the camp at the Canal and kept their presence low key. Burgstrom said that they had no intention of letting Ecias become a military stronghold. Mostly the men trained and helped us in heavy lifting and labour-intensive projects.

We buried the bodies on the cliffs, with a view of the bay, Burgstrom and Tontranix together. Ove, Ollie and all the others who had died in the fight would guard this place forever. And it would be Burgstrom's place.

The nightmare was over. When we were ready, we could get back to doing what we loved, in the place that we loved. I had discovered enough Praseodymium to keep Burgstrom happy for a very long time. While they made plans to mine it, there was so much of the planet for us still to survey. Who knew, we might find something even better next time out. Along with our latest instructions had been a message, 'prepare for the horses', it said. Harald had remembered, we had better get a paddock and stables sorted. That was a job for the troops over the next few weeks.

I looked across at Vanessa, she was asleep, her forehead smooth. As I watched, her eyelids fluttered and she awoke. She saw me and smiled. She reached out for me.

"Dan," Vanessa said. "Are you OK? Earlier, you were muttering something in your sleep."

"It must have been a dream," I replied, trying to remember what had been happening in my head. It was almost gone, like most dreams, cancelled by the new day.

"But you don't dream," she said. "You told me that you never remember your dreams."

That had been true once; recently I had been getting vague memories of my dreams, just snatches of conversations and places. There was never quite enough detail to tell if they were good or bad. When things started to go wrong, I'd had nightmares but then, who wouldn't have?

The details that I could recall of this one were oppressive and painful. Like the last few weeks had been. First, Vince had been shot, I had run. There was the possibility of a murder conviction hanging over me. Followed by the shock of Vanessa being kidnapped by Morgan. Then there was the invasion. And the rescue. No wonder I had had some bad dreams.

I tried to make a joke out of it. "Probably because of all that time I spent in the lock up, and everything else that happened."

She nodded, her face colouring as she looked at me. I wished we hadn't started this conversation. "That was more of a nightmare than a dream," she said. "But you came through for me. When the chips were down, you saved me."

I kissed her, she was slowly becoming more relaxed when I held her or kissed her. I smiled. "That's what we do. I'm fine; what do we have planned for today?"

"Burgstrom has sent us new maps; they still believe in us, let's get back to work."

"OK." I got out of bed and walked towards the bathroom. "First breakfast, then we'll get the drone set up and ready to fly."

"Bacon sandwich?" Vanessa had got up and was stood behind me; she put her arms around my waist.

"That'll be great, but there's a change of plan." I felt her tense.

"What's that then?"

"This time, I'm driving."

I felt her body sag, her usual wrestling feint. I sensed an argument coming on. Here we go again, I thought, as her leg flicked out. The room spun.

It was good to be getting back to normal.

CHAPTER FORTY EIGHT

EARTH

SITTING BY THE HOSPITAL BED, Cath held Rick's hand. On the other side of the bed, his ventilator clicked. Like a metronome. As well as its click, there was the constant bleep from his monitor, lines crawled across the screen. Cath knew the meaning in the lines, had seen them so many times. Rick's hand was warm, the flesh pink and healthy. He was relaxed, the face unlined, so much better than he had looked when he was in the trance. She had managed to get him a side-room in the intensive care unit, a bit of privacy, mainly so the staff couldn't see her crying. It had been a week since the accident and she had hardly left his bedside.

He had been stabilised at the scene, a badly broken leg and crushed ribs were his most visible injuries, he had probably struck his head on landing, the doctors had said. They had operated to remove a blood clot that was compressing his brain, set his fractured bones. Now they were just waiting for him to wake up.

The police had questioned her and Trevor. Trevor had pointed to the paper that Cath and Rick had signed and claimed patient confidentiality. Cath had complained about the lack of security at the building and Trevor had passed all the blame for the unlocked door onto his secretary. Sick of the buck passing,

Cath had passed everything over to Simon Walsh and left it to him sort out. At the moment, she had no stomach for a fight with any of them.

They had all left her in peace. "Our enquiries are ongoing," the detective had said. It was more than Cath could take in. The one thing she had noticed was that Trevor Ingram had not come to the hospital, after his initial visit and attempt to shift the blame to anyone but himself.

Hughie came in to the room, he stood beside Cath. He had visited every day, as had Molly and Deanne. They seemed to be taking it in turns to keep her company. Nothing much was ever said about the past, often they just sat in silence. She didn't need to talk, didn't want to have any opportunity to relive her guilt. She was just grateful for the company.

"Any change?" Hughie asked.

Cath shook her head. "No, he's just the same as yesterday and the day before that. They did another brain scan this morning. Dr Malhotra told me that he would give me the results when he came around this afternoon."

Hughie pulled a chair up and sat beside Cath. "How are you keeping?" he asked.

Cath shuddered, he asked that every day. Normally she just said 'fine' but today for some reason, she felt that she had to say more.

"Hughie, I feel awful..." she stared to cry.

Hughie put his arm around her shoulders; she buried her head in his chest and sobbed. "I feel like it's all my fault," she said, the words muffled.

"Stop," he said. "You must never think that."

"But if I had believed that it was all a dream, right from the start. If only I had listened to him. I shouldn't have been so keen to believe everyone else." She was shaking and Hughie held her, not really knowing what else to do.

"You can't torture yourself, Cath," he whispered. "We all do what we think is right, and it is; because it's based on the information we have at the time. And I should know that more than most."

"Can I ask you a question?" she said.

"Yes, of course you can."

"Even if it's about Claire and Molly?"

Hughie sighed. "I'll tell you, Cath, but only to show you that it's not the same thing as you and Rick. If you're looking for comparisons you're wasting your time."

He paused, took a deep breath. "I've never told anyone this before, I've put up with all the sly looks and unspoken judgement. Claire and I were so very happy. Molly was a friend at first. She was Claire's friend then she became ours. I mean that literally. What I've never told anyone else is that Claire chose Molly for me, she encouraged us to become more than friends."

Cath looked up. This wasn't what she had expected to hear.

"Claire had cancer, it was incurable. We never told anyone, she found out when she went for tests to find out why she couldn't get pregnant. She chose Molly, to be my second chance when she'd gone. She called me that morning, from her car. She called to say goodbye, she knew it was close and she wanted to go on her own terms. She wished us luck and happiness together."

Cath was trying to absorb that when Dr Malhotra came into the room.

"Mrs Wilson, good afternoon," he said.

"Hello, Doctor. This is Rick's boss, Hughie," she said. The two shook hands.

"Now, Mrs Wilson," the doctor said, looking at the papers in his hand. "We have the results of the latest brain scan. It's good news. Since we relieved the pressure the brain has regained its normal shape. Blood flow, measured by the dye we injected before the scan, seems normal too."

"That's great," she said, relieved that his brain was functioning normally.

"When do you think he will wake?" asked Hughie.

The doctor's face had a puzzled expression. "We can't say. We find it strange that he isn't awake. We don't understand why he's in a vegetative state. We can't call it persistent until it has gone on for several weeks. As you're a nurse, Mrs Wilson, I expect that you know that. There's every sign of normal brain wave activity. It's almost as if he was alive and functioning. His scan is the same as it would be if he were moving, talking, eating and sleeping. The only thing that's missing is consciousness."

"Then where is he, where does he think he exists?"

"Ah... now that's the big question. Most likely he's dreaming. We don't know if he will ever wake up, but as long as he's showing brain wave activity, we'll keep him ventilated."

"And I'll be here with him, every day," she said, as she sat by the bed, holding his hand firmly.

I hope that he's happy on Ecias, Cath thought. Vanessa had better be looking after him.

AFTERWORD

I hope that you have enjoyed this book

I hope you've enjoyed reading these stories. As an independently published author, I have no huge marketing machine, no bottomless budget. I rely on my readers to help me gain attention for my work. And next to the readers who love my work; reviews, either by word of mouth or online remain one of my most important assets.

Talking about my books, telling your friends and family and reviews on websites help bring them to the attention of other readers. If you've enjoyed reading this book, please would you consider leaving a review, even if it's only a few words, it will be appreciated and might just help someone else discover their next great read!

Find out more about me and my worlds at richarddeescifi.co.uk. where you can see details of my other novels and short story collections.

Thank you very much.
Richard Dee.

WHAT'S NEXT

To find out what happens next, watch out for the sequel. Wake me Up.

Here's a brief glimpse:

When I woke up, I could tell that I was inside. My situation made no sense to me. As far as I was concerned, the last thing that I remembered was being in the open, in bright sunshine.

Wherever I was, it was quiet, except for a regular clicking from something by my side. I couldn't turn my head to see what it was, in fact I couldn't move at all. I tried to move my hands, then my legs but there was nothing. It didn't feel like I was restrained, it wasn't like they started to move and couldn't.

Panic rose in me, I must be suffering from some sort of paralysis. Perhaps that was why I was inside. I tried to move my fingers; my toes, I was telling them to work, they ignored my commands. All I could do was look straight at the ceiling, white tiles and a fluorescent light fitting were my world. The light hurt my eyes. I tried unsuccessfully to close them. Why was I here? What had happened? I must have been in some sort of accident, been knocked unconscious for a while. But I couldn't remember. At least I was still alive, if slightly the worse for wear.

My ears were working, as well as the click, I realised that there was a conversation going on out of my view, it must have been about me, even though the name I heard was unfamiliar. Panic shot through me, was that my name? I didn't know my own name!

"Is there any change, Doctor?" a woman said. She had used the word Doctor, so I was injured, I must be in a hospital. Once I could talk, I'd be out of here and back to... I couldn't remember, what did I do?

"I'm afraid not," replied a deep voiced male. "The brain waves indicate normality, he might even be able to hear us but there is no sign that he can move or speak. As I said before, it's similar to a cataleptic trance."

The doctor was right, I couldn't move, I tried to shout, to prove him wrong. 'I can hear you, I'm here and I'm alive.' My mind sent the words, but my mouth wouldn't utter them.

"It's been three months," said the woman, "surely he'll wake up soon."

"We have to consider the long-term implications," the doctor said, "and we're no nearer to determining the cause. He was like this when we got to him. Apart from the obvious causes, it may be due to a number of other things, schizophrenia or epilepsy, hysteria or cerebellar disorders; it could have been induced by hypnosis. We need to find the cause before we can progress. I'm getting questions about the long-term prognosis from the hospital management."

What did he mean? I was alive, just paralysed somehow. None of the things he described meant anything to me, schizophrenia or all the other stuff. All I needed was time to recover. Three months? I couldn't have been asleep for three months.

"We have to keep him alive," the woman said, I could hear pain in her voice. "That's my husband, you can't just turn him off."

Turn me off, what was happening? And I had a wife? Why couldn't I remember?

A face came into my view, brown hair framed sharp features,

lined with worry and exhaustion. She was pretty but could have been anyone as far as I was concerned. Maybe she was a nurse, then I saw the collar of a boiler suit and a white T-shirt at the edge of my vision. "He's awake," she said, "his eyes are open." Her face moved from side to side, I realised that she must have been shaking my shoulders, I was moving, not her.

"Dan," she said. "Dan, it's Vanessa, can you hear me?"

It all came flooding back to me, I was Dan Walden, and Vanessa was my wife. I knew the reason I was here. In a flash the last few minutes of memory poured into my consciousness. I had been riding my horse through the forests of Ecias. She had been spooked by something, reared up and deposited me on the ground. As I flew through the air, I saw what had frightened her, and it had frightened me.

"His pupils have dilated," the woman shouted. "His eyes are moving, jerking all over the place."

Her face was replaced by the doctor's. I could barely make it out through the images of the last things I'd seen. I knew that I had found what everyone on Ecias had been looking for, the thing that made it complete. It was out there; we were starting to understand why we hadn't encountered it before. Seeing me and the horse, neither of us native species, must have been a shock to it. Soon, it would overcome any fear it might have of us. I had to find a way of telling everyone what was coming.

RICHARD DEE

Richard Dee is from Brixham in Devon. Leaving school at 16 he briefly worked in a supermarket, then he went to sea and travelled the world in the Merchant Navy, qualifying as a Master Mariner in 1986.

He has also worked as an Insurance Surveyor, Lockmaster, Harbourmaster and Ships Pilot, taking over 3,500 vessels up and down the Thames, passing through the estuary, the Thames Barrier and Tower Bridge.

Since the publication of his first Science Fiction novel, *Freefall*, in 2013, Richard has written another twelve novels, a textbook and a selection of short stories. He has been featured in several anthologies, including *1066 Turned Upside Down* and *Tales from Deepest Darkest Devon*.

He writes Science Fiction and Steampunk adventures and also chronicles the exploits of reluctant amateur detective Andorra Pett.

Richard is married with three adult children and three grandchildren.

He can be found at https://richarddeescifi.co.uk
    and contacted at richarddeescifi@gmail.com

Printed in Great Britain
by Amazon